Cargo's Flower Universal Laws and Sins

Taz Will

ISBN:1939764041
ISBN-13:978-1-939764-04-1

Keep It Funky Publishing LLC
4579 Laclede Ave #349
St. Louis, MO 63108
keepitfunkypublishing@yahoo.com
kifpstl.com

DEDICATION

I would like to take this time to dedicate this book and all the others to the readers. If someone would've told me back in 2005 that I would one day write a book or even would've suggested that I write, I would've told them their insane. I can't lie and say I've always been an avid reader but I've done more reading than most people I know.

With life being so full of ups and downs I know it takes time out of your life to read something that someone has taken the time to write down. So for that I thank any and everyone that has ever read anything I've written. No matter if they thought it was good, bad, or just plain ugly. Either way, I've always encouraged the readers to let me know what they think. For those of you who've left your comments, suggestions or complaints, thanks for keeping it funky!

I'd also like to take the time to dedicate this to any and everyone that I've ever come into contact with in my life. Without you, I sure wouldn't have much of anything to write about. So thank you and I hope you all take the time to read my work.

CONTENTS

Cargo's Flower
Universal Laws and Sins

1 AVARICE

"Why da fuck do I have to take her?"

"You're listed as the child's grandmother Ms. Jennings. If you don't take her she'll go to the state."

"I can barely afford myself! Why the hell you think I can take carrre of this child?"

"Ms. Jennings, the child will receive a monthly check and you'll be able to apply for benefits as well."

"Say word! Bitch, give me my damn granbaby!"

"Now Jasmine, you'll be living with your grandmother and you'll be safe with her." I nod my head as the woman referred to as my grandmother pulls me away.

It feels like we've been walking forever, I watch the cars speed past. My grandmother drags me into the streets without looking or caring about my safety. Cole Street, I read on the sign and I can see big buildings that can reach all the way into the sky. My grandmother turns and heads towards them.

Turning left on Ninth Street she pulls me walking faster like we're about

1

to miss something. She stops at the stop sign across from a church and tells me to sit and wait. I do as I'm told and sit there where my grandmother told me. I watch my grandmother walk up a parking lot towards one of the smaller buildings.

I count the cars as they go pass, once I hit one hundred the sun slips away. I stay and wait for her to come back. People try and talk to me but I turn away. I remember my mother told me to never talk to strangers so I hide behind the tire of a car parked next to me.

I can hear loud music for a couple hours but the laughing of the other kids has stopped. I sit and wait. Suddenly I hear loud pops, screaming and someone coming towards me fast. The car that I was hiding behind comes to life and speeds away almost taking me with it. I ball up on the side of the big brick wall with the circle in the middle and the iron fence.

When I open my eyes the sun is shining bright. I have to pee but I don't want to leave and miss my grandmother. I squat behind one of the cars and go back to the tall brick and wait. I count the cars again and hide once more, then one pulls up closer to where I am. Closing my eyes I wait for my grandmother to come right back like she said she would.

"Get yo' stupid ass up! Where da hell you been all damn night?" I open my eyes and it's my grandmother. I try to stand but she hits me across the face knocking me back down. I cry and my grandmother pulls me by my hair and I stand.

"Come on herrre so I can teach yo' lazy ass 'bout staying out all damn night!" She pulls me down the street and we walk into a big building that is smaller than the others. Once inside the smell makes my stomach hurt and I cry more when I realize how hungry I am. She heads down the hall still pulling me and opens the door to the apartment. Inside she tosses me to the floor, I land in a wet spot and slide into the wall.

"I'm finna beat yo' lazy ass," she says as she walks around to the other side of the room. When she comes back she has a belt wrapped around her fist and starts hitting me. I cry for my mother and father knowing they won't come save me.

"Please Grandma, I won't do it again. Please," I beg, she ignores my cries and continues until she's breathing heavy and bent over.

"Bitch don't chu eva' in yo' life call me dat shit! I'm Queen Ruby! You herrre me? Queen mother fucking Ruby! Dis my muthafuckin' house and my muthafuckin rules." She sits on a small square with holes all around it and lights something and smoke comes out the end.

"Clean nis' muthafuckin house ho!" I try to stand, my legs hurt, my body hurts, I slip on the wet stuff and crash back down. She gets up and hits me more, then pulls me down the hall and tosses me into a room.

"Since yo' dumb ass wanna be lazy, you can sit in herrre! Clean nis' bitch up while you in herrre too. If I catch you sleepin', I'ma put my foot in yo' lazy good fa nothin' ass!" She slams the door and I hear her cursing me as she leaves me alone. I cry hard begging for God to not let this be happening to me. I don't know what I did to be treated like this. I'm only six years old, what could I have possibly done to deserve this?

I look around the small room, it's about the size of my closet at home. It's covered in trash, clothes, and I can see mice shooting across the floor. I don't have anything to put the trash in or anywhere to put it. I knock on the door to ask Queen Ruby and she storms in a couple minutes later.

"Herrre bitch! Take dis shit down na' hall and dump it. Hurry da fuck up!" She kicks the can into me sending me tumbling to the ground. It's already filled with trash so I go down the hall in search of a place to put it. Once I make it back to where the elevator is a girl points to a door, I go over and open it. The smell is horrible, it's already three bags sitting in the closet. I open the door in the wall and a stronger smell comes blasting me in the face. I toss the bags already in there into the hole in the wall, I try to lift the can but it's too heavy, I take small clumps of the trash out by hand. I try again and it's still too heavy for me to lift.

"Hold up, let me help you." I look back and it's a young boy, not that much older than me. I move back and he lifts the can careful not to spill anything on his nice clothes. I move forward to help him and he shakes his head and hands me a backpack and nudges me out the door. Once the door opens he smiles and I give him his bag back.

"What's yo' name, I'm Tr——" I don't answer, I grab the can and take off running back down the hall. I can hear him laugh as I go back inside. I clean the room taking smaller piles out to the door in the closet so I can lift it. Once I finish I tell Queen Ruby and she whoops me again and tells me I'm not finished until she says I am. I spend the rest of the day all the way until the sun comes back up cleaning the house. I take my shirt and shorts into the bathroom and wash them in the water. Queen Ruby made me use them to wash the floor so I tried my best to clean them back up.

I come out the bathroom, Queen Ruby is not here, I look around and I don't see her. I go back into the room and I try my best to not fall asleep so

Queen Ruby won't whoop me again. I practice my karate, read the newspaper clippings taped to the walls and dump the mouse traps when one is caught. My stomach is screaming at me, I peek out the door.

When I can't find Queen Ruby, I look around for something to eat. I see some pickles and grab a couple out the jar and eat them. The water in the jug looks yellow at the bottom so I climb on the sink and drink from the faucet. The room in the hall has a can of beans and two cans of some meat looking stuff. I open the can of beans and eat them from the can.

I run as fast as I can down to the door in the closet, toss the can in, and run back in Queen Ruby house. I go into the room and pull a sheet from the pile I picked up. I climb on top of the deep freezer and wait for Queen Ruby. I open my eyes, it's dark and Queen Ruby is still not back, I grab a couple pickles and look out the door to the balcony.

I don't open it, I watch as all the kids start coming outside and play on the playground. I hear someone knock on the door so I run back into the room and peek out. Then the door opens and some lady comes inside. I hide in the closet and pray that she doesn't come in looking for me.

The door closes and I can't hear anyone so I go look. I can smell some food so I look in the refrigerator. The plate is filled with food, I take a little of everything and eat it. I go back in the room and get on the big freezer and wait.

To keep busy I spend the day practicing, reading, and nibbling off the plate of food. When I wake up, still no Queen Ruby so I do it all again, three days I count go by, no Queen Ruby. The plate of food is gone and I don't know what she'll do when she gets back. I hear a knock at the door so I hide again, just like last time the door closes and I go into the kitchen. I find the plate of food and eat some and go back in the room. Seven days more I sleep on the freezer.

Suddenly I wake up because I feel my body falling to the ground. When I open my eyes, Queen Ruby has the belt and starts hitting me over and over until I can't keep my eyes open. When I open my eyes back up, I'm on the floor and I feel stuff crawling on me. I look down and I'm almost covered by roaches, I jump up and try to shake them off. The door crashes open and Queen Ruby walks inside, she starts to laugh at me.

"Bring yo' ass out herrre bitch!" I follow behind still knocking off the roaches from inside my panties.

"What da fuck you doing herrre? Where da fuck is Shawana?"

"Queen Ruby you told me to stay here. My mother died." I cry at the thought of my mother.

"That's right! Where dat rich ass lawyer she fuck wit', ain't dat nigga yo' daddy? Where da fuck he at? Why da fuck didn't he take yo' ugly ass in?"

"My daddy died with my mommy Queen Ruby." I cry harder and fall to my knees with pain.

"See dat stupid? See dat right der is gon' get yo' head knocked off ya fuckin' shoulders. Shut da fuck up. I'm da one dat should be cryin'. Now I'm stuck wit' yo' simple ass!" She stands and kicks me out of her way and walks to the back room. When she comes back someone knocks on the door and she steps outside with them. When she comes back in she spits on me and paces the floor.

"All my fuckin' boys! All my muthafuckin' boys locked up now, ain't dis a bitch. All because of stupid ass Shawana. I should've aborted dat bitch. Dat's what I should've done! What da fuck am I gon' do now? Damn, now I'm stuck wit' yo' slow ass an—fuck dat, I'm beaten' yo' ass!" She storms away to the back, I ball up in the corner. When she comes in, she has three long cords, she tells me to hold one end of the three cords and braids them together. Then she folds it in half and twists them into a rope wrapping it in her fist.

"See dis speaker wire gon' teach yo' ass." She starts swinging it and I feel my skin rip open with every lash she lands on me. When she's finished I'm bloody and can barely keep my eyes open. I feel her pull me down the hall and push me in the room. I cry hard and fall back. All I dream about is not waking up, the pain is too much to bare.

I spend the entire summer getting hit, left alone and hungry. I cry everyday for my mother and father until it turns to anger. My father promised me we would spend this summer at Disney Land because we spent last summer at Disney World. My mother never told me about my grandmother. She never once told me how evil she is.

I miss my room, our yard, my toys, clothes and my parents the most. I miss everything that I once knew and hate everything that I know now. I cry myself asleep and awake. One morning Queen Ruby stormed in the room and threw a paper bag at me.

"Get yo' dumb ass to school befo' dem people come back lookin' fo' you!" I don't care where I go as long as I can get out of here. I put on the too little pants and long sleeve shirt with holes in it. I put on my sandals and walkout ready to go. Queen Ruby looks at me and hits me in the back of the head.

She throws some white shoes at me and tells me to put them on. I do as I'm told even though they flop off my feet.

"The school across da street dummy! Get da fuck out." I open the door and shuffle out the building. I can see the school and all the kids as they walk towards it. As I make it to the parking lot a group of kids stop and laugh at me. I keep going until a girl comes and stops me.

"Look at dis bum ya'll," she says as they all come around me laughing and pointing at me. The girl pulls my hair as a boy kicks me in the back of the leg. I push the girl off and they all start hitting me. I hear a boy telling them to stop and they all run off leaving me on the ground. I reach for the too big shoe and the boy reaches down and gets it for me. I grab it and pull off the other shoe.

"What's yo' name, I'm Tri—" I don't respond, I take off running towards the school. When I get inside I can smell the food so I get in the line with the rest of the kids. The lady behind the counter looks at me and comes around leading me behind the food counter and into a back room.

"Baby what's your name?" I start to cry.

"I'm Ms. Wilson, what happened to you baby?" I shrug my shoulders and she tells me to not be impolite.

"Nothing that God didn't want to happen to me Ms. Wilson." I clean my face and focus in on the words that I know are true.

"Ain't dat da truf baby. I'm gon' get chu some clothes and shoes dat fit. I'll be back wit' dat an somefin' fo' you to eat chil'." She walks away, I wipe my face, fix my pony tails, and wait for her to return. When she comes back I change into the clothes and put on the shoes. I eat and she walks me to the office, the lady behind the counter takes me to class.

I stay out of sight for the day, the work in class is way easier than what I'm used to so it's easy for me to keep up. By the end of the day we're walked downstairs and let out the side door. I walk fast to get back even though I don't want to go. Once I reach the light the same group from this morning but larger comes from nowhere.

"I should beat yo' ass fo' dis morning bitch!" the boy who kicked me says. I run across the street and they follow, before I can make it to the parking lot they jump on me again. This time they don't stop until they get tired. I get to my feet and head into the building. Once inside the girl pushes me into the elevator.

"You keep coming outside lookin' like a bum we gon' whoop yo' ass like you a bum bitch!" I pull open the door and go up the steps, she follows me. On the second floor she pushes me into the door. I had enough, I hit her back and continued to hit her until she cried and screamed for help. I didn't stop, I kept at it.

"What ya'll doin'?" I hear so I stop and try to run up the steps but I see three people coming down the steps towards me.

"Ahh, I see you getting' yo' payback huh? What's yo' name I'm Tris—"

I push past them and run up the steps, then realize I passed the floor. I didn't want to go back that way so I hid in the trash closet until I thought they all were gone. I ran back down and knocked on the door so Queen Ruby could let me in. I waited and no answer, I heard the kids from earlier on the steps so I ran back down the hall into the trash closet and waited. It was dark so I tried again at the door still no answer, I sat there and cried until I couldn't anymore. The door opened suddenly and a man stepped out, I crawled in and went in the room.

The school year came and went, it was hot outside and everyone was talking about some center they would go to. I wanted to find out what the 'Center' was so one day I followed them. When I went in, a lady stopped me and asked me if I was there for skating or boxing, I told her boxing. She pointed me upstairs and I walked in with all the other kids waiting in the line. From that day on I stayed over there doing everything that I could. I stayed out of the way and made sure I didn't mess with anyone.

2 CONSCIOUS DETACHMENT

The years passed, things weren't getting any better. I was still getting beat on every chance Queen Ruby found the time. Only thing that was different is she has a full time boyfriend. His name is Melvin, everyone calls him Worm. Even at eight years old I can see why they call him that. He's rotten to the core and she loves him just the way he is.

Some nights he comes in my room and opens the freezer just to smash me in between the door and the wall. Then he laughs and walks out slamming the door behind him. Sometimes I slept in the window sill to stop him from crushing me. By the time I was twelve, his nightly visits were so routine I would sleep with one eye open.

"Wake up bitch!" I open my eyes and see Queen Ruby coming in the door, behind her is Melvin.

"Go 'head nigga! Beat her dumb ass den let me get dat good from ya'." They both laugh, I start to cry.

Melvin walks over and pulls me off the freezer sending me across the room into the wall. He kneels down and starts punching me in my side, I ball up and he continues while Queen Ruby laughs. He pulls me up by my hair and hits me in the face holding me steady while he continues. When my eyes open I feel something against my side, I struggle to get free. Queen Ruby screams at me to keep still, Worm is humping and grinding into my side.

"Oh shit, I'm comin' baby! I'm comin'...come herrre." He pulls out his penis and Queen Ruby puts it in her mouth. Something white explodes out of him, I throw up and look away. Queen Ruby laughs and Melvin smacks her and tells her to shut up and bend over. Queen Ruby screams at me to look, when I don't Melvin punches me hard in the back. I look as he pumps into Queen Ruby, she laughs and screams with excitement. When they're finished, Queen Ruby kicks me into the vomit and tells me to clean it up. I do as I'm told and cry until the sun comes up.

During my eighth grade year, a month before school was out I was called to the principal office. Mr. Knight, the principal, and Mrs. Smith, the counselor, were waiting on me and told me to take a seat. They explained to me that they had been trying for months to get Queen Ruby to come in and meet with them. When I asked why, they both heard the concern in my voice.

"It's nothing bad Jasmine. We need to get an answer on if you will attend private school next year. We sent several letters home and have not heard anything back. You've received a scholarship to attend and will only be required to pay a minimal amount to cover the balance," Mrs. Smith says.

"All we need is your guardian's signature and you will be able to attend next school year." Before I knew it, I jumped up out the seat thanking God and the two of them. I laughed then started to cry like a baby. I was over whelmed with joy hearing what they had to say. They gave me the papers and I flew back to Queen Ruby house for once begging that she's home. It was just my luck she was, I walked in and gave her the papers.

"What da fuck is dis bitch?"

"Queen Ruby, these are the papers that you have to sign so the check will keep coming. It's for the school saying I attend, if they're not signed they won't send the check." She hurried up and signed everywhere I pointed. I was so happy I ran out Queen Ruby house back to the school. Mr. Knight was talking with the secretary when I came storming in the room. I gave him the papers and was on cloud nine the entire day. I headed back to the building and went on the roof until the sun came up the next morning.

Like clockwork though, my life spins out of control with the beatings, drugs and sex taking place. I hide out as much as possible in the shadows at the Center or school. I find peace when I'm alone playing basketball, studying and practicing my fighting. Whenever I don't sneak around I get jumped on and it's too many to fight off by myself. I take the beating because I'm actually getting used to it.

I also find alternate routes, even if it means going in the incinerator room to get in the building. I don't care how I get to and from. I found a hoodie in the trash that I keep pulled over my head no matter how hot it gets. Whenever I'm out I hide and move in the shadows.

At fourteen I realize that I've spent more time living in Hell than I did happy with my parents. I've become accustomed to my surroundings and the place I call home. Whenever I feel like I can't go on, I think back at the time I spent with my parents. When times really get hard, I remember what my mother told me, 'God won't put anything on you, you can't handle.' And it pulls me through.

Every day that I'm at the Center and everyone is leaving out I grab a bag to pick up the trash under the bleachers. I truly do it because I can usually find money or something to eat. I go to every place in the building that I think I'll find something and clean it.

"Here baby, let me help you with that bag." I look back and it's the lady Mrs. Terry, she helps me load the bag onto the cart.

"What's yo' name baby?"

"Jasmine."

"Jasmine, I been watching you for months clean this damn building. Here, from now on when you work you get paid." She hands me one hundred dollars, I give it back.

"I can't take that. I found enough see." I pull out the thirteen dollars and sixty eight cent I found today. She laughs and tries to hand me the money again and I refuse.

"What building you live in baby?" I don't answer, she asks again so I take off running down the steps leaving the building. I let a couple weeks go by before I go back to the Center just in case she's looking for me. I stay low key and out of sight the entire day.

Once I see her leave, I start cleaning then I shoot the ball until I hear the older men start to come in and play their games. I watch under the bleachers most games and listen to them talk drugs, money and sex. These seem to be the best times to clean the bleachers and locker room. They drop five and twenty dollar bills and don't even bother looking for them.

Most nights they leave and the last person locks the gym so I spend hours in the dark alone. I skate, jump rope, play kickball and whatever else I feel the need to do. I spend weeks and weeks saving money and hiding what I find in the broken panel in the locker room. I head out for the night once I think Queen Ruby is asleep or too high to get up.

"What you doing here baby?" I see Mrs. Terry standing in the doorway of the locker room.

"I, I, was about to leave out." She looks around, I tell her I didn't steal anything and she starts to laugh.

"I know chil'! Come with me. And don't run off or I won't let yo' little butt back in here anymore." I follow behind her into the office, she gives me some paperwork for a savings account.

"Take this to your mother and have her sign it so you can get a savings account. I have all the money you've made and will give it to you to deposit since you say you can't take it from me."

"You don't understand Mrs. Terry. I can't take it because Queen Ruby will spend it. I mean, she won't sign anything like this. I'm sorry but I can't." She shakes her head and pulls the papers out of my hands. She asks if I want her to open the account for me, I tell her yes, she says to come back tomorrow. I go back the next day and she gives me a receipt and tells me where the bank is and tries to explain to me how the account works. I let her try but I clearly know more about how a checking and savings account work. I don't tell her that, I let her think she's talking to a dummy.

I grab the money that I hid in the locker room and run straight down Cass to Broadway, up Washington to Seventh Street and don't stop until I reach Mercantile Bank. I go in and deposit the six hundred dollars I collected over the years into the account. I decided to get another account number just in case Mrs. Terry had a copy of the one she opened in my name.

By the time I leave out of there I'm so happy I go to the McDonalds boat and eat until I'm stuffed. I sit there with my chocolate shake and I'm all smiles the entire time. I feel someone staring at me and when I look over it's a group of boys a couple years older than me. I turn away and mind my business.

"Hey! I know you from somewhere don't I? What's your name? I'm Trist—" I get up and walk around the table, he blocks my path and smiles at me.

"Don't I know you from somewhere? What's yo' name Ma'?" I still don't respond but push past as he chuckles, I walk the riverfront.

I head back to Queen Ruby house and fall asleep because she's not home. I don't sleep long before I hear her and Melvin come stumbling into my room. After the beating and humping Queen Ruby pulls on my jogging pants and stumbles out the room. Two days later they both come back in my room. This time Queen Ruby has the speaker wire wrapped around her fist screaming at me.

"You lil bitch you. You out dere ho'n and not givin' me my cut? I'm beatin' yo' ass." Before I can respond she's coming forward swinging like crazy, I dance around the room out the way. I try and make it out the door and Melvin back hands me to the floor. I ball up as they both beat on me, they begin to slow and I feel Melvin start to hump into the back of my knee.

Once they're spent, Queen Ruby pushes me into the freezer.

"Let me find out you ho'n and not givin' me my money! Dat ten dollars dat nigga gave yo' stupid ass gon'. You can have dese back, dey too little anyway." She tosses my jogging pants to the side and walks out the room naked. I cry and want to kick my own tail for leaving the change from my McDonalds in my jogging pants in the first place. I get up and put them on and sneak out Queen Ruby house and run to the Center.

I make my way to the locker room and bawl causing the mice to all run for cover. I climb onto the tiled divider and watch as the mice play until I fall asleep. Once I get up it's still early, I check the clock in the office, it's a little after five in the morning. I grab a ball and play a full court game like it's nine other people out there and the buildings packed. I head out and go back to the riverfront laying out eating what I want with no care in the world.

I make it back to Queen Ruby house a little after midnight. As I open the door and look in, no one is in sight, I step inside. When the door closes I turn and see Queen Ruby flat on her back on the floor and Worm pumping into her. There's a man on the side of her face, another man on her right side, she's holding his penis while another man has his penis resting on her forehead and another man's is in her mouth. She looks at me and my body is rigid.

"GET OUT BITCH!" is all she screamed, she didn't have to tell me twice, I snatched the door back open and ran back to the Center. Once inside I found my spot in the locker room, watched the mice and fell asleep.

"You headed to the Center?"

"Yeah Bobo man, 'bout to get a quick workout and open up for Terry. She called me earlier to see if I could do it for her so if you need me that's where I'll be." I get to the Center and head upstairs to turn on the ovens so they're good and ready when my aunt Terry comes in. I run in the locker room to change so I can get a workout on the court before she gets in.

Damn, who is that? I go over closer, I see a chick straight knocked out on the top of the wall separating the showers. I go over and check her out, I'm surprised she hasn't fallen and busted her damn head on that thin ass wall. I back out the room trying not to wake her or scare her for that matter. I go in the office and wait just to see how long she stays in there. After about a hour I hear the toilet and water go for a minute. Couple minutes later I see her walk past the office into the gym.

From the office I can see her and hear her having a good old time running a game full court. I can't take it any longer so I get up and creep over to watch what she up too. This chick is the truth! About five five, one thirty, all I can see is titties, hips and ass moving up and down the court. I walk in to get a better look. On her way back down she sees me and stops, I don't move; I'm already by the door. She moves closer to me as she nervously licks her lips looking up and down from the floor. This girl is beautiful, green eyes, honey smooth complexion, plate sized dimples in both cheeks and full lips. I feel like my mouth wide open just looking at this girl up close.

"Don't let me stop you. I'm Cargo, what's your name shorty?" Why in the heck does everyone want to know my name. I drop the ball and take off running out the gym. I don't go back to Queen Ruby house, I go back to the riverfront and bask in the sun.

"Morning Auntie!" Terry walks over and I give her a hug and unload the food she has onto the cart. Once we get it off the elevator I help her unload the stuff into the kitchen.

"How long you been herrre Tristan?"

"Since the time you told me to be herrre! Not a minute late either." She laughs as I sit up on the counter watching her work.

"Check though Auntie. When I came in it was this chick sleeping in the locker room." She nods her head like she knows who I'm talking about.

"She always sleeps herrre or what?" She starts to giggle.

"Naw, only on goodnights she sleeps herrre. You found her in the locker room? Did she have a blanket or anything?" I can't believe my auntie talking like shorty a puppy or something.

"What's up Auntie, why dat girl sleeping herrre in the first place? What does it matter if she had a blanket when she sleepin' in a locker room at the neighborhood recreation center?" That got her attention, she put down the bag and looked over at me.

"Look Tristan, leave that girl alone. Like I said, only on goodnights she sleeps herrre. I'm gon' make sure I leave a cot and some blankets for her from now on."

"You keep saying only on 'goodnights' she sleep herrre. Where the hell she sleeps on a bad night?" She picks up a big ass can of corn and throws it at me, I catch it and laugh. I put it back down as she tells me to watch my mouth, I tell her to answer my question.

"That girl is going thru hell where she at so if she does come herrre to rest, then this is the place she needs to be! I been watchin' that chil' for a minute clean this place. I caught her in the locker room one night and told her I would pay her to clean. You know what the chil' told me?" I shook my head no.

"She pulled out a hand full of change and told me she found enough money for the work she did. I opened up a savings account for her and put all the money she earned in it. I don't know too much about her, I think she related to somebody down herrre, I just don't know who. She did mention a Reba or Robin but I'm too old to remember all these new faces down herrre." She walks out and comes back in. I jump down so I can head out.

"Hold up Tristan! Whatever you up too, leave that baby be! You hear me boy? Leave that chil' alone and don't make her feel like she can't come herrre if she need to." I kiss her on the temple and assure her that I won't and leave out.

"Back already Cargo? Man, when do you sleep?" I laugh at Tiny as Bobo walks up.

"You can sleep when you dead nigga! Look herrre Bobo, you know a shorty wit' green eyes be over at the Center?" He looks in the air tryin' to place a face with the description I gave him.

"Can't call no name off hand. Why? Need me to find her or what?" I laugh at his old private investigator face ass.

"Yeah man, she supposed to be related to a Reba or a Robin down herrre. Let me know what you find out. I'm out, holla at me if you need something."

3 LUST

"**D**amn Bobo, it's been damn near two months and still no word on ol' girl you said you could find." This nigga start laughing.

"Check Cargo man. I don't know who the hell you was talkn' 'bout, I checked around, even been up at the Center. I ain't seen no chick in dat bitch come in wit' no damn green eyes but two. I'm sure you know Melanie and Kionna, who the hell don't know dem ho's. You sure dey not contacts or some shit?"

"I don't know nigga, I figured if you saw her you would know she was the one I asked about. Fuck dat, don't trip, if you see her you do, if not it's all good. Any luck on her people though?"

"Cargo man, I know six Reba's and 'bout ten Robins down herrre, all of them you know. So naw man! Check dou', I know it's my turn to go on a run by now right?" I laugh at his ass and walk off.

I don't know why all these nigga's down here be frontin' like they can handle anything outside the hood. How the fuck you gon' do dirt if you got a gang of nigga's with you? Shit, you gone do some shit, you do it alone, that way you don't have to worry about a codefendant. I learned that shit way back.

It ain't failed me yet so fuck what that nigga talking about. I wouldn't take my right hand nigga wit' me on a mission. That shit can get me life if the nigga flip. Again, fuck dat shit! If it ain't Ghost, then I'm going solo, even then it's on some separate shit. I jump in a rental and head for Dallas to hit up the clubs.

"Esta! Esta get in herrre!" I go in to see what Queen Ruby wants with me. She throws her hand at the pile of trash surrounding her so I clean it up being careful not to stick myself with the needles on the floor. Once I finish she's out cold, Melvin walks in and pushes me out his way as he joins her. I leave out before they decide it's time to hit on me. I take the bus like I'm going to school, I get off and walk around for hours. Then I find a mixed martial arts studio, I go in to see what's going on inside.

"Hello, are you coming to sign up?" A tall white guy asks me once he sees me watching what's going on in the ring.

"How much does it cost?" He smiles and heads behind the counter, I follow and wait. He passes me a flyer, one month free is in bold yellow letters across the top.

"Right now we're running a special for newcomers, one month free with six month sign up. It's twenty dollars a month." I run out the door and come back, I find him on the other side of the ring.

"Here, sign me up!" I give him one hundred dollars, he walks back over to the register and tells me to fill out the paperwork. When I'm done I give it back to him, he looks at it and says I need my parents' permission. I take the form and tell him to keep the money and I'll be back in the morning. I head back trying to make it before the sun goes down.

"Mrs. Terry, it's for MMA training by my school; it won't interfere with my work, I can do it before or after school, please." I hand her the form as she laughs.

"Sure baby. I know you won't let anything come before your school work. What happened to your books too? I saw it under the table all ripped and taped together."

"They tore it up to clean up beer that was spilled on the floor. I tried to dry the pages and put them back in, I try to hide my books but they keep disappearing." She stands up and pulls her purse from out the desk behind her.

"Herrre baby! Go get you some more books, if you want you can keep them herrre and not have to worry about hiding them."

"No thanks Mrs. Terry, I can buy the books myself. I can't keep them herrre because I leave for school at five in the morning. The Center won't be open."

"Chil' please, that ain't ever stopped you in the past!" I giggle and tell her I'll think about it.

*   *   *

"What's good man? You from 'round here?" I look across the crap table and see a black nigga lookin' over at me.

"Not these dice! Shit, I'm from a few places why you ask?" I throw off my accent as much as I can trying not to say anything that is so fucking St. Louis.

"I hear you man. I'm Dirty Red. They hostin' a party for me around the way, if you want to get a Dallas welcome come thru." I spit with the nigga for a minute, jump in the Tahitian black candy coated Seventy Seven Impala, sittin' on way too fucking much wit' the black and white guts.

Just lookin' at da bitch make me shake my fuckin' head. Can't believe nigga's get a lil bit of money and waste the shit on this type of bullshit. But what can I say? Nigga's see this type of shit and do whateva to get down wit' you, I follow him over to the club. The club is poppin', these bitches thick as fuck down here.

"Damn daddy, you new here huh?" I watch as she walks over, I pull her into my arms and hand her my drink.

"Here, finish this so I can use both hands to work this ass of yours." Her dumb ass laugh, toss the shit back and start twerkin'. I bend her ass over and let her work me over song after song.

"Where you from Daddy?"

"Philly, now stop all the yappin' and get that ass back clappin'!" She go into over time, I laugh at her silly ass. I catch the eye of a light skinned skinny chick with big tits and a round ass lookin' on.

"Aye, what you say yo' name was?" She lean in and kiss up my neck.

"Jackie! Why don't you come thru tonight after the club so I can finish what I started." I put her number in my phone and watch as she disappeared into the crowd. Light skin makes her way over after I get another drink at the bar.

"I see you ready for the truth now huh?" I look past her as a thick ass heavy hitter walks behind light skin. I can see baby girl fat ass from behind light skin, she looks over at me. Dark skin, pretty girl with way too much ass on her wink, I smile back.

"What's yo' name Ma'?" I ask light skin moving her in closer.

"I'm Chantae, where you from?"

"I'm from Detroit, now you wanna dance or talk?" She pulls me out onto the floor and starts to move.

I feel her up and pop her ass err chance I get. I see a chick on the side of me about five eight, one sixty, got a nice ass, small waist but huge tits. I walk Chante off the floor and get her a drink, she give me the number and tell me to call. The dark skinned heavy hitter comes up as I head to the bathroom and start rappin' with me. I run the same lines all night long. By the time the club close, I have eighteen bitches all thinking I'm from different spots. Don't none of these ho's even know my fuckin name.

Before I leave I'm stopped by Dirty Red in the parking lot. He tells me he got the weed I was looking for. I get in and tell him to pull up to my car. We chill and wait for the parking lot to empty out, once everyone is gone he get out and pop the trunk. I get out and take a look at what he got for me. I look the shit over, he offers me a blunt. I turn him down and get the bag out my car and get back in his car with him.

"All of it's here?" I look over at him and laugh.

"Yeah Dirty Red, here, you can count it." I pass him the bag he says he trust me and toss it in the back.

"So when will you have some more? This shit here will be gone in about a week so I'll need to reup." He starts to laugh and say he can get some before next week.

"On the real this smell like some of that shit I picked up when I stopped thru St. Louis a couple months back." The nigga laugh hard at something he was thinking about.

"Yeah nigga, it's that loud from St. Louis, I got a little connect up there that break me off right."

"I knew that shit smelled familiar. I been trying to get my hands on some of that shit for months now. I just don't know none of them hot heads up there. I heard they go crazy." We both laugh at the thought.

"Yeah my cousin Sherm, he good people. He looks out for a nigga and shit. I can set you up with him for fifty thousand and you can get a connect up there." I look over at the nigga. I hold my hand out to shake his hand, he puts his hand up and with one move I take the nigga hand off. He starts screaming like a bitch fumblin' for his piece on the side of the door. I stab that nigga in the chest so many times I lose count.

I put the nigga hand in the bag of paper I gave him. I don't bother to wipe down the car, nigga didn't even ask why I had on gloves. It's hot as a bitch down here! I jump in the whip and send two rounds into the gas tank. I laugh as the whole car jump into the air and come crashin' back down. I pulled up behind a vacant building I peeped earlier, burn the Impala, and get in the Ford pickup I rented in Louisiana and rolled out.

I call up Tiffany, the dark skinned heavy hitter. She thinks my name is Lamont, I'm twenty seven and from Edison, New Jersey. I send a cab to bring her to the hotel I'm at, when the cab pulls up I take her straight to the room. I bang this chick all around the room with no words spoken between the two of us except hi.

I wake her ass up at nine in the morning give her three hundred dollars for the cab and send her on her way. I spend the rest of the week hittin' the clubs running the same lines with different info. At the end of the week, I stayed in six different hotels and fucked over twenty bitches. All these ho's in Dallas think I'm from different places and none of them know my fuckin name. I laugh my ass all the way back to the Lou thinking about the shit.

*   *   *

"Excuse me Miss, you can't sleep here." I look up and see the park ranger standing over the bench I'm stretched out on.

"I'm not sleeping here Sir. I must have dozed off in the middle of studying." I pull up my book and show him then raise up my notes that I've taken. He apologizes then walks off. I struggle to sit up, pack up my bag and leave the riverfront before anyone else stops me. Lately I've been finding myself sleeping anywhere I can, I don't even care as long as it's not with Queen Ruby. I've been sleeping on that deep freezer for nine years, I don't even remember what a real bed feels like.

Tomorrow is my fifteenth birthday and I plan on celebrating six years of happiness the best way I know how. I hang out at the Center until it closes and clean to find any and all that I can. I don't leave for Queen Ruby's house until three in the morning, when I make it in, the house is empty. I rest my eyes just until the sun comes up and make my way back out the door. I stop a white lady standing under the bridge downtown and pay her to get me a room at the hotel.

She comes out with the keys, I give her twenty dollars and go to the mall. I pick up two pair of jogging pants and two black shirts. I get under clothes and personal items from the store and go back to the hotel. I head straight to the tub and fill it up to the top, I sit for hours sleeping in the water. By the time I wake up its dark and the water is cold. I clean up and plop on the bed and watch TV until I fall back to sleep, I order room service and stay in the room for three days.

When I leave the hotel I head straight to the Center. I hide out and watch as the older men play their games. I listen in on their conversations, collect money and anything I can find after they leave. By the time I make it to Queen Ruby house, they're still not there. It's hard for me to sleep on that freezer after spending so much time in a real bed. I do my best to adjust and fall asleep.

Luck must have been on my side because Queen Ruby and Melvin spent less time around. That was fine with me because I didn't get beat as much. I think they were hiding out from the police. Plus, the last beating they gave me I went to school and my teacher sent me to see the counselor. She asked me what happened, I told her some girls jumped on me.

She didn't believe me and they wouldn't let me leave. The police showed up and took me to Queen Ruby house. They waited with me for hours, Queen Ruby finally showed up around ten at night. She wasn't high but she was drunk, she told them that I was always starting stuff with the neighborhood girls. They finally jumped on me and that's what I get for *running my mouth off.*

The counselor warned her that if I came to school beat up I would be taken away. Queen Ruby was livid when they left. She told me as soon as winter break came around she was going to teach me to keep my mouth shut. She didn't wait that long though, they did minimum damage to my face but worked my body over good.

By the time school let out, seemed like Queen Ruby was determined to teach me a lesson on closing my mouth. Almost every day I was getting hit in my mouth by the two of them. They didn't show any mercy unless a social worker was coming by to check on me. Queen Ruby hated me more because she felt the worker was trying to be in her business.

At times she wouldn't let the worker in and they would threaten to take me and stop the checks from coming. She would reconsider and let the worker in and watch as I spoke with them. As soon as they pulled out the parking lot she would come in and beat me with the speaker wire.

"What's hood Cargo man? Where you duck off too? I ain't seen you in about two months cuz," I hear Mike say as I head into the gym to join in on the pickup game. I was still coming down from my high of offin' the nigga's for the past couple months.

"Nigga Please! Yo' ass sho' didn't come lookin' fo' a nigga! What's good wit' ya'll? Ya'll nigga's playin' or what?" We all laugh and run three games back to back. It's five in the morning, music blasting throughout the place and we kickin' it. Lil young nigga, Poncho come in and holla at Bobo for a minute then dip out.

"Aye Cargo man, that nigga Poncho say some nigga's rolled thru on some drive by shit." We all look at the nigga like he silly.

"And? So what nigga! You act like that shit something new." He starts to laugh and say he need to holla at me.

"Only reason I said something Cargo is because they hit up Fourteen Fifteen building, he said they carried some chick out of there, he didn't know who she was."

"You think it's the shorty?"

"I don't know if it is or not, hell, I ain't eva' seen who the hell you talkin' 'bout all this time. I damn sho' don't know what building she be in."

"A'ight see what you can find out." I see Terry come in and we call it a night.

4 MANIFESTATION

After leaving Forest Park for the day I head back to Queen Ruby house right as the last bus takes off. I start walking down Tenth Street past all the construction and homeless hangouts with a purpose. I never walk under the metal scaffolding because once inside someone can easily block you in with nowhere to run. Over the years I've taught myself to be ready for anything and always have a way out.

Before I cross over Cole Street I hear all types of noise, I take a seat on the bus stop and wait. Seems like the warmer it gets, the more shootings. I know it'll be well over an hour before the police come so I sit and wait. Two hours pass and I see the first police car come speeding past. I follow behind making sure to keep out of sight and make it to Queen Ruby house without being stopped.

School is the only thing I look forward to, the longer I spend in class, the longer I'm away from the madness. Queen Ruby is always on my case about needing to have sex so she can get her money. She even went as far as taking me with her on Broadway where she says all the good money is at. It's sickening to see Queen Ruby sucking and screwing any man that pulls up.

They don't even try and go somewhere private. After each 'job' as she calls it, Queen Ruby doesn't even clean herself. Some of the men wear condoms, but most don't and Queen Ruby doesn't care one way or the other.

Ms. Terry was persistent on trying to get me away from them. She was even nice enough to suggest I live with her. My mother's words came to mind, something about the grass being greener. I don't remember exactly why she told me that but I take heed to any memory I can from her.

The more I think about my mother, the more I want to find out exactly where they're buried. I don't want to ask Queen Ruby because I know she won't tell me anything. If anything she'll beat me for bringing them up.

Searching the internet gives me no leads to their whereabouts and leaves me down and out. By the time summer hit I gave up on finding them figuring it's for the best that I don't right now. Ms. Terry stopped me late one night as I finished up cleaning the building.

"Hey baby. So what did you decided about working for SLATE?"

"That's not a good idea for me Ms. Terry. I'm trying to stay away from all the craziness that goes on down here. Besides, if someone saw me working then I wouldn't get the money anyway."

"I understand but you can work away from here. Go into another neighborhood and work and you won't have to worry about anyone seeing you." After Ms. Terry told me that I was all game. It would give me even more time away and I can use the money to take care of myself.

"What's good Cargo boy?"

"What ain't Pandillero? What's good witchu?" Pandillero sits down on the stool at the bar.

"I'm chillin' just wanted to know if you were tired yet." I take a seat knowing this about to be another lecture.

"I just made it to eighteen so how can I be tired?" Pandillero chuckle.

"That's why I asked. Seeing eighteen is something most nigga's from the hood haven't and won't see. So with all that being said I have an idea for you." He look over at me, all I can do is drop my head because I know where this is going.

"Please enlighten me." He's laughing like the shit funny.

"Check, T wanted me to holla at you about running a few clubs in the Lou. She can set all the shit up to make it legit but they all yours so some shit go down, naturally, it'll fall on you."

"I hope not this hole in the wall joint you called me in. This place has seen better days man." We both laugh at the site of the old head club from back in the day. It's musty as hell with a bar and seating for maybe twelve people. The faded out occupancy sign says fifty on it and there's not even a dance floor.

"Believe it or not yeah! This place can be cleaned up and turned around. Your best customers will be over fifty because they not into fighting, shooting or slanging drugs out of here. T even suggested you get some booze cruises lined up when you get up and running." We both turn as the door to the club is shimmed open, I figure Pandillero knows who's coming in because he doesn't reach for his trick.

"Damn it stink in nis' bitch. What's hood Cargo?" Bateador says as he comes over to where we are.

"It's all good man."

"So what you think youngin'?" Bateador says so I know he's in on this little intervention.

"I'm cool with it but ya'll know I have my pops shit to run so this herrre would have to be sort of a hobby." They both laugh.

"Yeah we know but if you want to see twenty outside of those two boxes you need to make it more than a hobby," Pandillero says.

"What will it take for you to walk away from yo' pops shit? We all know five years is the max on street life. With the way you operate, you been granted a little more time. But no one is guaranteed shit," Pandillero say as they both stare at me.

"Shit, I can't call it. I'm straight cheddar wise, don't get me wrong, you can never have enough but it ain't that. I mean on the real, that's all I been doing since I can remember so what else is there?"

"Look, you young with a good head on yo' shoulders and can make more money legit than you could ever imagine. If you know better youngin', you do better. So take it from me, find that girl you been looking for and take a minute to get to know her. If she has her head on her shoulders then yo' pops shit will be the last thing you want," Pandillero says and looks at me waiting on me to doubt him.

"Man you crazy if you think a chick, that I don't even know, can make a nigga walk out on some shit I been doing forever. I know you wife'd up and shit but I don't see that in my future. I'm into variety and how the hell you know I'm looking for someone anyway?" We all laugh.

"Why didn't you ask us to help you find her? You know that young ass Bobo don't know shit. I know you not schoolin' that nigga on shit you doing either right?" Bateador says.

"It's not a priority, I just wanted to know a little something about her. And hell naw I ain't schoolin' shit! None of them nigga's can be trusted. Ghost has more heart and sense then all them nigga's put together so no." We all laugh again.

"Cool, but if you find the right one Cargo, I'm telling you the shit will change not only your life but she'll make you want to change the world. It ain't shit like your own family."

"If that's the case Pandillero, then why would my pops want me to take over his spot on the team? So what you trying to say, my mom's wasn't the right one?"

"No disrespect but, did you ever ask yo' pops why he didn't marry yo' moms?" I tell him no.

"Like I said, it's all about finding the right one. Maybe your moms wasn't the one for your pops and he knew it enough not to wife her." I take that in for a second.

"Take it from a nigga who met his when he was fifteen, two years later he figures out she the one. Man, I thought I'd never hear the end of T this and T that. This nigga herrre!" We all have a good laugh at Bateador rippin' Pandillero.

"Hell yeah nigga. I been knowing my wife since she was eleven, I was fourteen and so the fuck what! Nineteen years youngin' I been with my wife and it took a minute to finally have her. I'm trying to save you from all the bullshit that I went thru to make sure she was mine. Know better do better! The sooner you find her, the sooner you can start to really live your life. But enough of all this shit, we outta herrre," Pandillero says as he stands up, we all walk out the deserted club.

"You sure lil nigga, you don't want to know about the shorty you looking for?" Bateador says with a big ass grin on his face.

"Nope, I'll find her. Ain't that what you nigga's were just saying? *I* need to find the right one?" We all laugh.

"Nigga don't get it twisted, this nigga had more than enough nigga's tracking Treasure," Bateador said.

"Ain't that the truth. Finding her wasn't the real problem, it was keeping up with her ass that was," Pandillero said as they walked off.

"How's it going Jasmine?"

"Fine Ms. Terry, they have me working over in Tower Grove mostly, I get to clean up around the park. When I get off I can hang around and I'm thinking about teaching a class over there after I'm off. I need to get it all put together but other than that, I can't say anything bad about it."

"That's good to hear. How about at home? How are things going over there? You know you never told me anything about who you're staying with or in what building."

"I have to get out of here Ms. Terry, I need to get back before it gets too late."

"There you go again Jasmine. Every time I bring it up you run out of here not wanting to tell me anything. Why won't you let me help you? If you don't want to tell me who it is that's beating on you at least come stay with me."

"I can't Ms. Terry. I'll see you later." I walk out before she continues to probe me for answers. When I make it to Queen Ruby house it's jammed packed with nothing but dope feigns. I back out the door and head for the roof, no need in drawing unwanted attention. All night it sounds like a war is going on down there, I'll never understand why blacks act the way they do.

My father, Dante Vanaria came over from Enna, which is in the center of Sicily; when he was sixteen. I don't remember if he told me why but I do remember him saying he didn't have any family there. My mother Shawna Vanaria called my father Romeo. I remember her saying he was a ladies' man and swept her off her feet.

Back then I didn't understand what the heck a ladies' man was but now I giggle at the thought of my father being one. It's been so long since I last saw them that the images that I have of them have become fuzzy. Queen Ruby doesn't even have any pictures of my mother or my uncles. I wish I had a picture of my parents to remember how they looked.

Every chance Queen Ruby gets she brags about how her sons doing time for being real G's. When she gets low on drugs and starts to detox, she really talks about 'the good old days'. From what she says it was only good because she had a steady flow of drugs. To her they all were just a means for her to get high without paying. Those are the best times for me because she leaves out for days at a time trying to get a fix. Either way I'm just happy that my mother wasn't like her.

"Hold the fuck up lil nigga." Before they walk over to me Big Hen walks out the club, we look at each other then at the two nigga's coming up. The one with the mouth is about six one, one sixty with long dreads tied back.

He rocking red and white down to the J's on his feet. His badge is hanging from a platinum chain in the middle of his chest. His partner has a matching chain, short cut, with a Cardinals hat on. He about six even, one eighty, with a too little True Religion t-shirt on. He still rocking the tag on his Red Monkey jeans with Tims on his feet.

"What the fuck you two nigga's doing comin' out this spot herrre?" The dread head says as they take up positions around us. We both look at the nigga like he crazy and wait on what the fuck they want.

"I see you two nigga's can't herrre Officer Brown huh?" Cardinals hat says moving in closer holding on to his piece on his hip.

"Eske nou kwe nou anba arestasyon?" They both look at me like they didn't know I knew how to talk. I know it's because I asked them in Haitian Creole, are we under arrest?

"So now you don't know how to speak English huh lil nigga," Cardinals hat says as they both laugh.

"What's you and yo' man's name big boy?" Cardinals hat asks Big Hen.

"My name is Brandon Hen, I'm a bondsman and work as personal security for this gentleman herrre. The only name I know for him is Maynard Thomas, that's his attorneys name just so we're clear gentlemen." They both laugh harder.

"You hear this shit Brown man? This nigga claim he don't know the man name but work for him," Cardinals hat says.

"Naw Franklin, did you hear how this nigga den lawyere'd up on our asses on some slick shit," Pig Brown says as they continue to laugh.

"If you two can excuse us we have another appointment we need to be making our way to. That's if we're not under arrest," Big Hen says.

"Nigga you can leave when I say yo' fat ass can fucking leave. Bondsman or not, nigga we run this shit, you shut the fuck up and fall back until we say different," Pig Brown says.

"You two nigga's not going anywhere until this nigga herrre quit with the no English shit," Pig Franklin says. I look at Big Hen and hold my pinky and thumb to the side of my face like a phone. He nods his head and looks back at the two pigs.

"My man herrre wants to make a call. I need to get my phone out my pocket so he can do that." Pig Brown moves back unclipping his pistol.

"Go 'head you fat, black neck, greasy lip having bastard. Make a move so I can give you heart burn." Big Hen looks at me and we both burst into laughter.

"So yo' ass do understand English huh? Quit fucking around lil nigga wastin' our fucking time. I don't wanna take you two mufuckas downtown but I will if you don't come off a name other than your lawyers." I cross my arms out in front of me and wait for the cuffs to go on. They both chuckle.

Both Pig Brown and Pig Franklin look at each other and pull out their phones that we didn't hear ring. They both look serious for whoever is speaking on the other end. It must have been a three way call because they both hung up at the same time. Pig Brown looks like he about to explode and Pig Franklin is laughing.

"Damn lil nigga, I don't know who the fuck you are but I'm damn sure gon' find out. Come on Brown man so we can get the fuck back before Chief Jeffery has a fucking heart attack." I get in the passenger seat and Big Hen gets in pulling away.

"Damn, you nigga's never cease to amaze me with the connections ya'll have. The fucking Police Chief nigga? Where dey do dat at?" Big Hen says as we laugh our asses away.

"Man fuck dem nigga's! Drop me off in na hood."

"Esta! Esta, I know you hear me." I try and walk off but Melvin comes behind me and pulls me around to face him.

"What da' fuck you doing all da' way over herrre in na park?" I try and pull away but he digs his nails into my arm. My supervisor, Ms. Simpson, comes over and asks what's going on; Melvin let's me go when she says she's calling the police.

"Esta, you out herrre working? I can't wait to get back." Melvin turns and leaves. I can't believe I'm busted and didn't see his sleazy tail coming. By the time I get back, Queen Ruby is standing in the hall waiting on me. I already know I'm about to get it because she has the speaker wire ready in her hand. Before I can make it in the door she starts in on me swinging the wire hitting me all over with no remorse. When she's good and tired I can feel the blood swelling under my skin.

"Bitch, first thing tomorrow you betta bring me my money. I don't know where da fuck you hid it but I want my mufuckin' money. From herrre on out, you better be on time wit' my check, try da shit again and I'll kill yo' worthless ass." I stammer to my feet as she sits on the crate reaching for her crack pipe. When I make it in the room I see what little stuff I have has been tossed on the floor. It's not much so I pick it up and climb on the deep freezer to sooth the pain over my body.

"What's good Cargo man? Just the person I wanted to holla at." I dab Lil C off as we take a seat at the table.

"I can't call it. What brings you to my lil juke joint anyway?" We both laugh.

"Shit, I wanted to holla wit' you about Tanielle." I look at the nigga like he lost his damn mind.

"What about her?" He starts to chuckle.

"Just wanted to know what was up with her. Really want to know if she wit' a nigga and to make sure I'm not steppin' on any toes with you if I holla at her." I damn near fall over laughing at the nigga.

"Come on Lil C, you know damn well it ain't nothing like that with lil sis and me. I don't know who she wit' but she ain't what you want."

"Damn Cargo man, tell me something. I wouldn't be asking if she wasn't what I wanted." I laugh at his ass again.

"Alright, dig this. Tanielle need a man to come in like a stalker, sneak her from behind. Like snatching her without warning in the middle of the night type shit. Give her that T cut across the chest down her stomach. Rip her heart out and replace it with his. Dick her down so good it closes her back up, then cover her in his own flesh healing her leaving no marks behind." I laugh because this nigga mouth wide open and eyes big as shit looking confused as hell.

"What the fuck does that mean Cargo?"

"See, that's what I was trying to tell you nigga. Tanielle is so far out of your league its crazy."

"Thanks for nothin' nigga!" I laugh as the nigga leaves out.

5 RESISTANCE

"Here you go Ms. Vanaria, seventy five dollars has been placed into your savings account. Your balance is on the bottom of the receipt." I thank the teller and start back, before I leave the bank I toss the receipt in the trash. Once I make it to the neighborhood convenience store, Tom Boys, I see it's jammed packed. Everyone is trying to get their checks cashed so they can spend all their money.

I go to the back where they make sandwiches and tell Cho that I need another check. He smiles and I hand him the five dollars and tell him one hundred thirty eight dollars. I wait for him to come from the back with another check. I hate that I have to give her two weeks' worth of my money. Minus of course the seventy five dollars I put in the bank and the five dollars I paid for another check. But I don't let it get to me, I take the check and walk towards Queen Ruby house.

"Esta!" Why me? I should've taken the long way back but no, I had to take the easy way. I hear Melvin call me again and before I know it he's pulling me by the arm. I don't know what's going on but I don't want to go into these vacant buildings with him. I always hated going in the

43

Neighborhood Gardens, it's a playground for fools. Melvin leads me further in and pulls me down the stairs to the basement where apartments used to be.

I cry harder every step he forces me to take, I try to stop walking and he drags me. Then he draws back and smacks me hard and stomps down on my leg cursing for me to get up. I do and he hits me five more times and tells me to shut up. We walk into a vacant apartment and I see the 'Insect Boys'. That's what I like to call them. Ant, Fly, Spider, and Roach, I don't understand why they would want to be called by those names.

"Now look here youngin's, look here. Give me four of them thangs and ya'll can get ya' young asses some from Esta herrre!" I cry hard at the thought and they laugh like there's no tomorrow.

"Man, what da fuck we look like, rapist?" Fly says and throws his hand at Melvin.

"Worm why you beat dis chick like dat? She bloody as fuck and it look like she pissed on herself!" Ant says, they all laugh and I cry louder because I did when Melvin punched me in the stomach.

"Look lil nigga's she good! She good! Give me two fo' me and one fo' my ol' lady and take her." I pull back and scream cry, Melvin punches me in the chest and pulls me back out the door. He punches, kicks then stomps me while I continue to scream and cry. He stops when they scream for him to leave me alone. Melvin drags me by my hair to the door and forces me to stand up. He has the nerve to take his shirt and smear the blood across my face trying to clean it off.

He leads me back in telling me to shut up, the room is quiet, no more laughing and Melvin suddenly stops. I glance around him trying not to cry and count another five bodies that have joined the group of four. I instantly start back crying because maybe one of these men will take Melvin up on his offer.

"What the fuck is going on herrre nigga's?" I hear someone say, I don't recognize the voice and my eyes are starting to swell shut.

"Shit! Dis nigga Worm think we 'bout to rape dis bitch! He out his fuckin' mind," Spider says but this time no one laughs.

"Cargo, let me holla at cha, holla at cha! Look here, all I'm sayin' is, let me get six and you can do whatever you want with her 'til tomorrow. Den if you like what you get, you can give me eight mo' and keep her 'til da next day." I scream out and feel my knees buckle. The last thing I see is Melvin fist approaching my face. I fall hard and that's it for me.

I catch the nigga arm and lock it up in mine before he can hit her again. I look back at the four youngin's who are now standing waiting for me to say something. I look at my peeps and they already know what I'm thinking.

"What da fuck you think you doing nigga?" Worm bitch ass starts begging for me to get at this girl.

"Get her up and out of herrre!" Tiny picks her up and takes her out the room.

"You young nigga's bet not let me find out ya'll taking this type of shit for payment." They all start denying ever doing the shit and say Worm is trippin'. I pull Worm up off the floor and lock his ass up against the wall by his neck.

"Nigga, don't bring this type of shit back around herrre! I don't give a fuck if she willing or not. Who da fuck is she anyway? I ain't never seen this chick around herrre before."

"Wait a minute Cargo man, wait a minute! Dis just a lil bitch I know, she ain't shit man on errthang she ain't." I let the nigga go as he falls back to the floor.

"You nigga's know what time it is. Some retribution needs to be paid for this herrre. It's either from you four or that nigga!" I walk out the door.

"Hold up cargo!" I hear Fly say so I stop.

"What the hell is righ-tri-bu-sion?" Roach says, I look back at my peeps and shake my head at how dumb these lil nigga's are and continue on.

"Nigga, it means revenge, payback, justice! Lil dumb ass nigga, either on you nigga's or on him for the shit he pulled on that shorty," I hear Panther explain, then I hear Worm screaming like a bitch as I walk out the building. Tiny pull up in my whip, I see lil Ma' in the back and jump in. I take her to my spot out in Maplewood and call up Terry then Doc to come check her out.

"What's going on Tristan? Where's this girl at?"

"I don't know Auntie, I stopped the nigga Worm from beatin' on her and he said she was just somebody he know. She looks familiar but her face all swollen and I don't know who she is."

"Worm, as in Melvin? That no good bastard know somebody?" I shrug at her and she takes off into the room. Doc pulls up and I show him to the room and wait to hear what's up with her. After about a hour, they both come out the back so I go over and ask what's up with her.

"She's been beaten of course and has a concussion from the attack. I left some medicine with Mrs. Comb for the pain, she needs to take it easy." I walk Doc to the door as Terry walks over to me.

"Who is she Auntie?" She looks at me like I should already know.

"That's Jasmine Tristan. You asked me about her maybe a year or so ago. Remember the girl you said ran out the gym one morning, you saw her sleeping in the locker room." Damn, that's her? I can't believe that's the same girl.

"You sure? I mean that girl in there looks nothing like the one I saw at the Center."

"That's her alright. I have to get back but I'll be herrre in the morning before she wakes up." I walk her out and can't believe that that's the same girl. I peek in the room and she's lying there, both eyes swollen along with the right side of her face. All night I wonder where the hell she came from and how the hell she know Worm seedy ass.

My head is pounding when my eyes open, I can see light shining down on me from the window. I struggle to sit up and pain rips thru me but I manage to get upright. Where am I and how the heck did I get here? This is not Queen Ruby house, I can smell food and I know for sure that I'm not there. My stomach is in my back and the smell alone is egging on more pain. I scramble to my feet because I have to use the restroom and I can see it across the room. I step forward, it feels like both my legs are still asleep, and I fall pulling down the lamp on the nightstand. Last thing I feel is something slamming into the back of my head and I'm out cold.

What the hell is that? I run into the room and see Jasmine on the floor, the lamp is smashed and she's under the nightstand. I stand the solid wood nightstand back up, pick her up and put her back in the bed. She must've had to use the bathroom, I'm tempted to clean her up but I stop and walk out. Pissy or not, she can get it! I shake my head at the thought of going at her thick ass and call Terry to see where she at. Terry comes and goes in to help her out, I hit the phone to see what's poppin' in the hood.

"Jasmine! Jasmine, baby you awake?" I force my eyes open and see Mrs. Terry sitting on the side of the bed. I throw my arms around her and cry hysterically as she holds me and tells me everything is okay. I sit back and my heads starts pounding again and she gives me some medicine that seems to instantly take effect on me.

"Listen Jasmine baby, you're at Tristan's house, he stopped that crackhead Worm from attacking you. You're safe baby!"

"Thank you Mrs. Terry but I have to get back to Queen Ruby or she'll be mad at me." I struggle to pull the sheets back and she stops me.

"Jasmine, please come stay with me. You don't have to live with her baby. Why won't you leave that fool alone?" I don't respond I don't know if it's the medicine or what but I feel drowsy.

"I can't Mrs. Terry. I need to get back so I can give her my check or I'll be in more trouble than this." She shakes her head and hugs me as I fall off to sleep.

"Look Tristan, I need to take this check down to some Ruby stupid ass so she won't hurt Jasmine."

"What check?"

"The little money she makes working for SLATE she gives to this Ruby person so I need to get down there and give it to her. I'll be back in the morning." A couple hours pass and Jasmine comes out and sits at the table. Debra takes her some food, I head upstairs while she eats. Once I make it back she's still sitting at the table with her head down, sounds like she's crying.

"Yo' Ma', what's up? You need something?" She shakes her head no, I sit across from her as she looks up at me.

"Hey, riddle me this, how you know Worm?"

"He's Queen Ruby boyfriend." She looks away.

"So is Ruby your mother?"

"No, Queen Ruby is my grandmother, my mother's mother."

"What happened to your mother? Where she at?"

"She was killed when I was six." She starts to cry and looks down at the table.

"What about yo' pops, where he at?"

"They both were killed, together." I sit back while she cleans her face.

"What about sisters and brothers, where they at? Do they live with Ruby?"

"No, it's just me."

"How old are you?"

"I just turned sixteen June thirteenth."

"Why do you live with Ruby? Don't you have other family you can go stay with?" She really starts to cry.

"No! Queen Ruby is all I have."

"How long have you been living with them?"

"Since I was six."

"You go to school? I mean what school do you go to?"

"I go to a private school now. Out in the county." Private school? How the hell can she afford that? I ask just out of curiosity.

"Queen Ruby can't read so I had her sign the papers, when the check comes I get it first then pay my tuition. I give her the rest after I get another check from Tom Boys." She looks up at me.

"Why did you help me?" He asked me a million questions why not ask him one.

"Because I wanted to." He starts to chuckle.

"I need to get back so I can give Queen Ruby my check, if not I'll get in trouble."

"Terry took the check down to Ruby already. How much do you give her anyway?"

"One hundred thirty eight dollars, plus the three hundred fifteen dollars I get from the state after I pay my tuition. Why?"

"I just wanted to know. Has Worm ever touched you—touched you?" She shakes her head no so I drop it and don't bother prying. Later that evening I headed back upstairs to see what she was up to. Before I could make it into the living room she jumped up and looked at me.

"Can you take me back now? I really need to go." I don't want to be a burden on him any longer.

He tries to get me to stay the night but I refuse so he takes me back. I tell him to drop me at the Schnucks parking lot and jump out the car. I don't waste any time taking every invisible path I've taken in the past. I ease the door open and walk around the corner to see if Queen Ruby is in. She looks *over at me and sits up.*

"Come herrre bitch!" Why me Lord? I walk over and she smacks me across the face.

"Next time you better bring my money yoself! Now go get dat speaker wire!" I head to the back room and get the braided speaker wire and walk back into the living room. The pain is bone shattering, I take it until she feels the need to stop.

"Sixteen! Happy birthday bitch! Now get out my fucking face." I crawl down the hall as the blood clots into the welts that are forming across my back, butt, and legs. Once in my room I close the door and climb onto the deep freezer. I put the sheet on the top of me and let the top of the ice cold freezer work on the pain. I don't even bother telling her my birthday was in June, it's almost August.

*   *   *

"Has anyone seen her yet?"

"Naw Cargo. She ain't come by herrre yet, we been posted outside the building since you said she got out." Damn, where could she have gone that quick? I find a spot at the bar in Hooters downtown and wait for my peoples to show up.

"What's good Cargo!" I turn around and see my boys, Twin, Mike, Charlie, and Inch. We find a spot off to the side and chill out while the waitress takes our order.

"How that shit go in Miami?" I ask as they all start laughing, I know they must've had a helluva time down in that bitch.

"Smooth! That's a done deal. But man dem ho's down ner, dey a whole otha breed!" Charlie says, we all laugh as they fill me in on all the jump offs they hit up while they were away.

"Cool check, what's the problem on the West Side though? I got word that it's a nigga movin' on yo' shit Twin."

"Yeah okay, that shit ain't gon' happen. The wagon will be around by this time tomorrow so no problemo herrre."

"Whatever you thinkin', let the shit go!" They all look at me like I stuttered.

"Check, on another note, I gotta get gone. Ya'll stay up!" I walkout leaving them at the table and head south. The night is the best time to work. I park the Lexus Coupe and jump into my Ford Taurus. I pull up to Fountain Park and peep Sherm as he sits in front of his trap house. The spot is moving with foot traffic.

After about an hour the traffic thins out then they bring out the count for the night. Sherm still sitting in his whip. I get out, cross over the park, pull up my hoodie and let some of the Gin soak into it covering my arm. I stagger up, the nigga laugh at me thinking I'm about to fall over. I bob and weave over to him and lean on the car.

"Aye big dog, let a nigga hold 'bout two dollas." He continues to laugh.

"Here man, take this shit and gon'!" He let the window all the way down and holds out the money. I reach in and put my nine to his temple.

"You a dumb nigga you know that?" I cut the nigga throat damn near taking his head off and wait 'til his body stops doing the jerk. I stagger up the steps making as much noise as I can to get the nigga's inside attention.

Before I can knock a lil nigga snatch the door open.

"What the fuck yo' drunk ass need nigga?"

"I need like umm, umm, herrre what can I get wit' dis?" I give the nigga the two dollars Sherm gave me. He starts laughing and call three other nigga's to the door. He tells them what I said as they all step out on the porch followed by two nigga's that have come from around the back. I stagger around digging in my pockets tellin' them I just got paid and I think I have some more. All six of the nigga's come closer forming a semicircle around me.

"Let me get all that up off yo' bitch ass then nigga!" the lil nigga that answered the door says as he reaches for my pocket looking back at the rest of them laughing. He turns back around quick because he grabbed the barrel of HK51A3. I smile, pull him around into my chest and let the bitch roar cutting all these fools down.

I let it go once it's empty, this nigga crying like a baby. I give him the gun, he put it up and pull the trigger, he look down and realize it's empty. By the time he looks back up I send his brain waves into the air with three shots in the head and walk back over to Sherm dead ass. I toss the nine in with him on the passenger floor, cut back across the park and ride out.

6 REINCARNATION AND KARMA

"What's up Bobo man? Don't tell me you still don't have word on that mission I sent you on."

"I can't lie Cargo, I thought that shit would be an easy task but I hollad at errbody I thought would know something and still can't pinpoint where she at. I have people errwhere looking, shit, we about to go door to door if you give me the go."

"Nigga please, what the fuck this look like, some movie shit? What about that nigga Worm, have you hollad at him yet? Or that Ruby, her grandmother?"

"I caught Worm ass twice, both times that nigga was sitting on the steps gon' out his mind. I mean this nigga was a thru piece. His gal, I hollad at her tricking down on Broadway behind Saveway. She was high as a kite, only thing she was on was fuckin' and getting paid for it. When I did catch her and she wasn't so lifted she played like she didn't know who the fuck I was talking about.

I was about to whoop her ass, dumb ass was getting' all silly, then she started spittin'. I mean really hawking that shit up from her chest, telling me to get away from her. I had to mush the shit out her ass just so she wouldn't spit in my damn face. But that nigga Worm should be coming by later tonight, I can get at him and see what he know. I told errbody not to sell to him and if he wanted anything he needed to holla at me. Shit, they say the nigga still been getting wasted so he must be getting his shit from somewhere else, I figure from his ol' gal."

"Let me know what happen." I head off to the Center to holla at Terry, see if she heard anything from Jasmine. Before I make it good in the door, heads turn as I walk in and errbody in that bitch come at me for a minute of my time. I hit all the kids off with some dough so they can go get them something to snack on. After hollan at some of the hood freaks I go upstairs to the kitchen, I know Terry should be up here making lunch.

"What's good Auntie?" She walks over with a smile and hugs me. I sit in the chair as she continues getting the lunches ready.

"What the hell you doing Tristan? Get up and help us get this food ready for these kids!" I laugh and join the assembly line. As I put the green beans on the trays Terry puts a hamburger on and passes it to Ms. Charlene for the applesauce cup.

"Hey Auntie, have you seen Jasmine lately?" She stops and looks at me then continues on.

"No, but why do you ask? What is it about Jasmine that has you asking about her?"

"Just wanted to know what was up with her. You haven't seen her around herrre lately?" She stops again and grabs my arm leading me out the kitchen towards the back elevator.

"Look Tristan, whatever it is, leave that girl alone. You helped her and I'm proud of you for doing that but if you are trying to get her involved in anything stop!" I couldn't believe she would come at me like this.

"Auntie I'm not trying to get her involved in anything. I just wanted to holla at her, see if she was okay. You saw how that nigga did her. I'm a little disappointed in you for not checking up on her or calling them people to get her away from them. And you can lose the sour puss face because you've done it in the past. Why are you allowing her to get beat on like that anyway." She tried to walk away but I blocked her in and asked again.

"Jasmine has been thru enough without being placed in some bullshit home. There have been more than enough times that I wanted to get protective services involved but I couldn't. I told you a little about Sharon and how they took her away from Mary dope smoking ass. That baby trusted me when I told her that she would be safer going with them and not staying with Mary.

That bitch was pimping Sharon to every crackhead down here just to get a hit off their pipe. Sharon left and I thought she would be okay when they found her a foster home. Sharon's foster mother knew about her history and figured she was not being paid enough by the state so she started selling Sharon. Sharon called me and was ballin' on the phone when I heard three shots and the line went dead.

When I made it over they were carrying Sharon and her foster mother out, they both had been killed. The neighbors told me that her foster mother had a party and they heard a bunch of arguing. I later found out that the party was a bunch of fools that were there to have their turn with Sharon, seventeen men Tristan! Seventeen men all there having sex with a fourteen year old baby.

Sharon passed out, when she woke up she called me. One of the bastards was furious and killed Sharon and her foster mother. I couldn't do that to Jasmine. All these years that I've seen her beaten and dirty, all I could do was hope for the best. She gave me her promise that if anyone tried to rape her she would come to me. She hasn't come to me so I pray that she's still keeping her word."

My aunt is crying so hard all I can do is hold her and take in all that she has told me. I remember her coming to me so she could give Sharon a funeral. I took care of the arrangements and was surprised that it was only my Aunt and I at the funeral. I sat my Aunt down in the chair once she calmed down.

"Look Auntie, I only want to help Jasmine. I can't stunt, I have been thinking about her every second of the day over the last month or so since she was over at my house. I want...hell, I need to make sure she's okay. I can't find her though, the hood not that big and I know 'bout errbody down herrre but no one seems to know who she is. I can't figure the shit out. She said she's lived down herrre for ten years and no one knows anything about her. I know you have to know something Auntie. Does she really live with Ruby in Eleven Twenty One or what?" She wipes her face and holds her head up.

"As far as I know Tristan, she lives with her over there on two at the end of the hall. Most nights I leave the side door to the locker room open just in case Ruby puts her out. I told Jasmine she could come stay with me but she has never come, I even gave her a key."

"When was the last time you saw her?" She starts crying harder, I wait and she looks up.

"I went looking for her yesterday, Ruby said she didn't live there and not to knock on her door unless I was giving her some money. I told her if she told me where Jasmine was I would pay her, I gave her twenty dollars and she told me she thinks she saw somebody downstairs. She slammed the door so I went down looking for her. I didn't see her so I went home.

I waited 'til one this morning and went looking again for Jasmine. She was in the incinerator room balled up in the corner all beat up and sobbing. I walked her out and she took off once we made it to the front. I was hoping she would come over herrre but she didn't, I planned on looking for her after I left herrre." I waited with her then walked her back into the kitchen as the kids came in ready to eat.

"Aye Bobo, I want you to check all the basement's and shit for that mission and let me know if anything turns up." I head over to Eleven Twenty One to see if Jasmine is anywhere to be found with no luck. I put another crew on lookout for her while I head to Canada to meet up with a new connect to get a shipment in route.

The entire time I'm away I call back to find out if anyone has laid eyes on her. Errbody gives me the same news that she hasn't been seen. Once my business is taken care of I jump back on a flight to the Lou to put an end to all the hide go seek. Monday morning I head out to her school, I sit around all day waiting to see if Jasmine is there or not. By the end of the day I spot two white chicks smiling and coming over to where I'm sitting.

"Hi I'm Claire and this is Sue," the blonde one says, I nod at 'em and watch as the brunette, Sue, tries to get Claire to say something else to me.

"What's your name?" Claire finally says as she twists with her hands behind her back holding her lunch bag I assume. She smiling so hard her face is red and her nipples are pressing thru her satin button up uniform shirt. I don't respond, I feel my phone in my pocket and answer while they continue to wait. Bobo tells me that they still haven't seen Jasmine and are waiting at the bus stop in case she gets off, I hang up without saying anything.

"You have a nice car. This is the Jaguar X-type right? Daddy said he would let me drive his next year. It's a beautiful car, I wonder what daddy would say if he saw that you already had one," Sue says as they both giggle at the thought of her bitch ass father being mad. I continue to watch as the last of the students come out the gate.

"Who you looking for?" Claire asks, "We'll know who you're looking for, we know everyone here," Sue says. Then it hits me that these dumb ass girls may just give me the information I need.

"I'm actually looking for Jasmine. She's about five five, hundred forty pounds, green eyes, honey complexion and wears her hair in a bun." They both look at each other with big ass grins on their faces.

"Oh, Book!" Sue says looking at Claire.

"Book? I said Jasmine." They start laughing.

"Yeah, we call her Book. Everyone calls her Book as a matter of fact," Sue says, they laugh more, I ask them why they call her that.

"One, she's always in a book and two she always needs replacement books. For some reason her books always come up missing and Mrs. Perch always begs Book to replace them. Why are you looking for her?" Claire says, I don't respond.

"Well I hate to tell you but Book called in this morning saying she had the flu. Clair here gave me the message to give to Principal Rogers this morning. So Book will be out for the next four days, she won't be back in until Monday. Although she'll need a doctor's note or the days will be counted against her, I hope she has one this time."

"How many times has she been out?" I slide down off my car towards them as they come closer in front of me.

"She's been attending here since freshmen year. Since then she's missed countless days being ill. Most of the time she doesn't have a doctor's note but they let her slide because Book said she didn't have medical insurance. Also because she has always been ahead in her studies and maintains her grades. The problem is, this is our junior year and if she returns on Monday she won't have any days left that she can miss for the remainder of the year," Claire says.

"I don't know how she plans on getting all the shots she needs if she really is getting accepted to study in Japan," Sue says and smiles when she's finished hatin'. Claire gets her attention as a Lexus pulls up across from me.

"Here, this is my number, call me if you want to hangout," Sue says as they both giggle and get in the car. I jump in and head back to the hood, all throughout the day no one has seen Jasmine. We head to New Jack City for a party on ten at Corona house. She's a neighborhood freak that loves to host parties and shit when she gets her stamps. I chill out and let my nigga's fill me in on all the shit that happened when I was away. I head out to holla at Bobo who I know is behind the building in his usual spot before I turn in for the night.

"Just in time Cargo! Look at who I found herrre." I look down the steps leading to the basement and see Worm holding a book in his hand.

"What the hell going on herrre? Don't tell me you buying books from this nigga?" We all laugh as Worm comes up the steps.

"Look Cargo! Look Cargo. All I'm saying is, dis book is worth at least five dollars. Let me hold something for dat. I can get more if you want." We all laugh harder at the site of his clown ass.

"A'ight Cargo! A'ight Cargo. I know dis girl, Esta. I can take you to herrre and den you let me get a couple for me and my ol' lady. I promise she'll be all you can dream of man. Just let me get a couple and you can take as long as you need with her." I stood back while the rest of these nigga's laugh thinking to myself, who the fuck is Esta?

"Nigga, do it look like we need to rape a bitch out herrre? Man go 'head with that bullshit you spittin'. Besides, didn't Cargo already tell yo' ignant ass not to bring no shit like that around herrre again?" Bobo says while still laughing.

"Check Worm man, where she at?" All these nigga's stop laughing and look at me like I lost my damn mind on even considering his offer. Worm says follow him so I ask again, he say she at his house. We all mob around to see who the nigga was talking about. He gets to the door and knocks then open the door with a key. We all pull out our sluts because that's some set a nigga up type shit. Bobo put his twenty two to his head and led him in the house while he tries to explain what's up.

I walk in after, they check the rooms to see if anyone else is in the house. I look in the living room and see a woman naked on the floor. She too big, fat and funky looking to be Jasmine so I know it's Ruby. She sits up after Worm goes over and asks where Esta is. They start to argue, I look around.

The house is empty except for two crates and newspapers scattered around. The fridge has an empty carton of eggs and a bottle of what looks like pickle juice. The house is clean as hell but something in this bitch stink like fuck! I open the cabinet under the sink where the smell seems to be coming from and see a big ass rat. The damn thing must've been here for a minute because it's covered in maggots.

I hit the light switches and notice that they're no bulbs going back towards the rooms. I head towards the first door and it's an empty pantry with two cans of spam on the shelf. I close it up and go to the next door which is the bathroom and I'm kicked in the chest with the smell that comes out of there. I close it up and turn the corner towards the bedrooms.

Bunch of dirty wet smelling clothes and a shit load of roaches in one. I go to close the door and watch as a mouse breaks out the room. I can't help but laugh 'cause that bitch must've been begging for somebody to get his ass out of there. I make my way to the next door but its pad locked on the outside.

I go back in the front and ask where the key is. Bobo pulls Worm up and Ruby throws the key across the room. I pick it up and go back to the room unlocking it. I hit the switch and the light comes on to my surprise. I see the closet and move the sheet that's acting as the door.

Two long sleeve hoodie sweaters one black the other grey, up top about ten shirts all folded and black. Hanging behind the hoodies is two pair of white girl shoes that look fairly new. I see the toe print and know they're not new at all. I take a look around the room and it's empty except for a deep freezer that's in the recessed part of the wall on the right side of the room.

I step in closer and hear a familiar click and look over in the direction. I see that mouse has been caught in a trap under the heater, he should've stayed his ass in the other room. In the corners of the room I see two other mice that have been caught in traps. I know I'm not alone in here.

I can hear someone breathing and the end of a sheet was pulled off the top of the deep freezer when I first walked in. Whoever's in the room has slid between the deep freezer and the wall out of my view. I go over to the deep freezer and my hand is instantly cooled. The ice has damn near frozen it shut. I open it and see a paper Saveway bag inside so I pull it out, place it on top of the freezer and dump the contents out.

"That's my book bag. Please don't take my books, those are the only ones I have left. You can have anything else in here, just please leave me and my book bag alone." I don't reply, I stand up the items, a toothbrush, two travel size toothpaste, half a jar of hair gel with two hair ties wrapped around it, small one ounce bottle of Tussy deodorant and two books, Advanced Biology, and College Trigonometry.

"Please Sir, I don't know what you want or how much they owe you. Can you please just leave me and my book bag alone and go?"

"It's me Jasmine, Tristan. Come from under that sheet." She doesn't move, I can hear her cry so I move over a little closer.

63

"Peep Jasmine, answer me this. If you had somewhere to go would you stay here?" She didn't say anything but I can tell by the way the sheet is moving she's shaking her head no. That's all I needed to know. I reach down and pick her up with the sheet still covering her up. I walk out the room and head to the door as my nigga's follow behind me asking a bunch of questions. I tell Tiny to run get my whip and meet me in the parking lot.

"I guess dat's the chick? No wonder we couldn't find her, she been locked up in nat bitch da whole time," Bobo says as Tiny pulls my car into the lot.

"I'll be at you cuz, tell them nigga's they can get back to work." I put Jasmine in and pull off.

7 PRIDE

The whole ride I don't know if Jasmine is awake or not, she wouldn't let me take off the sheet that's covering her. I didn't push it, I let her be. I pulled into the garage then carried her to my bedroom placing her on the bed. I left out the room and called up Terry to let her know that I found her and to come by in the morning. I stayed on the phone all night until the sun came up when I heard the doorbell. It was Terry and Doc so I let them in and they went to look after Jasmine. Janine, my housekeeper arrived right on time to make breakfast and clean up as Terry and Doc came back out.

"Jasmine has a minor concussion and two bruised ribs. I gave Mrs. Comb's here pain medication but other than that, Jasmine will recover in no time," Doc says then heads for the door.

"Hold up Doc, she needs a doctor's note saying she has the flu for school." He says he can send one over on Monday. I walk him out as I see Terry coming out behind me.

"Look nephew, I don't want to see you in the news on no kidnapping bullshit because I will kill that bitch Ruby and be in jail. You need to get

Jasmine back home before that bitch realizes her monthly income is in jeopardy. You know that's the only reason Ruby took Jasmine in right? She gets money for Jasmine and once a month they come and check on her. They wouldn't even do that if Ruby didn't send her to school beat up all the fucking time.

Jasmine said her case worker is scheduled to stop by Friday. Ruby knows that if she went to school with her face like that the case worker would come sooner. So you have until Friday nephew to get her back or Ruby will more than likely say you kidnapped her." Terry turned and got in her car and drove off. I jumped on the phone again then headed in to see Jasmine.

"Jasmine, if you hungry it's some food out here for you." I walked away from the door and walked Janine out. When I came back in the house Jasmine was standing by the kitchen island with her back facing me. I walked around to the other side and damn near went into a rage once I saw her face. She picked up on it and turned away from me and began to cry. I can't believe what they did to her.

Both her eyes are swollen almost shut completely, her lip puffy and hanging like it's too heavy. Majority of her arms and chest are black, green, purple and fuckin' blue. I can see welts across her back that look like she was beaten with a flamin' hot whip. I tried to chill out, she looked like Martin did after he fought Hearns on his sitcom. I asked her if she was hungry, she nodded her lumped up ass head. I didn't know what she wanted so I gave her some of everything that Janine made. I placed it on the table with a cup of orange juice and milk. She walked over to the sink, washed her hands and sat at the table. She didn't move or attempt to look up as I watched waiting on her to eat.

"Did you want me to eat alone?" I didn't know what the hell to say.

"You want me to eat with you?"

"If you like, I don't want to be rude and eat in front of you while you watch me." I can't let her sit there when I know she has to be hungry. I also don't want to let her out of my sight so I make me a plate and sit across from her. She says a prayer and we eat. We finish and she asks if she's excused.

"You can leave if you want Jasmine, I won't hold you here and neither will anyone else. I did want to ask you something before you go." She looks at me and asks what.

"Why does Worm call you Esta?"

"They say I look like some Aunt Esta from a TV show called Sanford I think. I've never seen it, have you? If so, do I look like Aunt Esta from there?" Tristan frowns up like he's about to turn blue in the face.

"HELL NAW! They need to stay off that shit." Jasmine thanks me for the food, cleans the table and heads back in the room. The day passes by while I make arrangements and Jasmine sleeps, I check in on her to make sure she's alright every now and then. Two days pass and I find her in the living room, I go over to find out what's wrong with her.

"You alright Jasmine? You need anything?"

"I left my books and I need to study. I know they're probably sold by now because I didn't take them with me."

"Is that all you're worried about?" She looks up at me and for the first time I see some fight in her eyes, like I offended her by asking the question.

"What else should I be worried about? Why are you helping me? Why did you bring me here? What do you want from me?" I chuckled at the sound of her trying to be upset with what I said. She sounded so proper when she said all that it caught me off guard.

"Well you haven't asked where you're at to start. I mean aren't you worried about that?"

"No! Terry told me where I was at. In Warrenton at your house."

"I'm helping you because I can help you so I am. I brought you here because you said if you had somewhere else to go you wouldn't stay down in the hood. I don't want anything from you, I just want to get to know you and see you without your face all smashed up."

"What would you like to know? Didn't I answer enough of your questions the last time I was rescued by you? What else is there to know about me?" She folded over and placed her head in her knees and began to cry.

"Come on Jasmine, you killin' me with all the cryin'. The hard part over, I got you for as long as you need me to be here." I hear the doorbell as I consol her.

"What's wrong with her Tristan?" Dena says as she comes into the living room. I walk over and greet her as she goes over to Jasmine.

"Did you bring the stuff I asked you to bring?" Dena gives me the 'duh' look and holds Jasmines head up.

"Come on Jasmine, I know you probably scared but my mama and my big cousin here won't let anything happen to you. I'm Dena, Tristan called me over to get you all ready so let's go Ma'." Dena stands and pulls Jasmine up to her feet. I head out to make my rounds and meet up with Gauge to make sure the shipment from Canada is all good. I head to my club on Washington Avenue and it's jammed packed for ladies free drink Thursday. I see Gauge in the VIP with the rest of the crew poppin' bottles and enjoying the view.

"Damn Cargo, 'bout time yo' ass made it here man!"

"Yeah I had to hit up dem nigga's out in na county before I came down. I heard that purple shit on the move out there in the streets."

"Dog! When I say a hundred parrots flew off, I mean dem bitches flew off in a couple hours. I told dem nigga's da shit was legit, dey thinkin' it's weak because da shit was purple. One hit nigga's was choking and fallen off da edge takin' flight around nat bitch!"

"Yeah whatever, let them nigga's get a taste and make sure you hold out until all them cages empty. Then let da wind know so it can bust dey heads with inflation nigga." We both laugh as a thick redbone comes over and Gauge scats with her. I sit back and chill with the homies and enjoy my drink.

"What's good Cargo baby, you just don't fuck wit' me no mo huh?" Stephanie says as she walks over and sits beside me. We met at Vashon her sophomore year and started chilling together. I gave her anything she wanted because I was down with her and she took care of a nigga. I can't stunt, she was my gal but I kicked it with hellas over the years we were together. She knew the shit and was alright with it as long as it wasn't somebody from the Lou. Not long ago she told me she was pregnant, I was soup'd and willin' to settle down some with her ass.

I kept her out the clubs and she started resenting a nigga because of it. The whole time I wouldn't let her out my sight because she a party girl and I didn't want shit wrong wit' my shorty. She was supposed to be four, five months pregnant but she wasn't showing like she was. She would always wait 'til I had to go out of town and say she had to go to the doctor.

I followed her one day and that night, she went straight to the club all in some nigga face. I asked her what was up and she finally told me that she had an abortion right after she told me she was pregnant. Said she slept with another nigga and didn't know if it was really mine or not. Like she was doing me a favor. I tossed her ass out and ain't looked back.

"Go 'head wit' dat shit Steph. Ain't shit poppin' wit' me and you ever!"

"Come on Cargo, that shit happened over a year ago. I know you miss me because I sho' miss you." She leans over and licks the side of my neck.

"Look Steph, please don't make me throw yo' ass out of here. You know damn well what's up so what the fuck do you want so you can leave me the fuck alone?" I put my drink down and look over at her.

"Damn Cargo, why you have to act like dat? Look, I need some help wit' my rent dat's all. I mean can you help me out wit' dat and some money for some food for my sisters and brothers?" I knew this girl was a damn fool! I ask her what happened with the nigga she was fucking with, why he not helping her.

"Who Paul? I don't mess wit' his ass no mo, he call his self tryin' to use my momma spot to keep his dope and shit at. I been stopped messin' wit' him." She told me the nigga name was Kelvin, don't matter though. I pulled out twenty dollars and gave it to her, she started acting crazy saying it wasn't enough. I had them put her ass out the club and told Bobo to checkout her spot and let me know what was up.

I was too fucked up to go home so I chilled out upstairs in my loft above the club. The next morning I headed out to check on Jasmine and see if she needed anything. Before I can make it to the car my lawyer calls, says he has the paperwork and I can pick it up. I head down to the court house to meet up with him and get the paperwork. Bobo calls me from Steph house so I go down in the hood to see what's up.

"Hey Ms. Brown, how you doing?" Ms. Brown is Steph's mother, she was willing to take me into her home when we were together. I declined because I had my own spots, I just didn't tell Step at the time.

"Hey baby, it's good to see you. Have you seen dat daughter of mine? Dat girl just out herrre like she don't have a child to take care of." I'm damn near knocked over when she says child.

"What you mean Ms. Brown? Where the baby at? Who the baby father?" Shit, I had to know and quick! Steph never told me she was pregnant and I damn sho' ain't heard shit about her being pregnant.

"Come in, you can see him." We follow her in their apartment, kids are errwhere. The baby is lying on the couch, Ms. Brown goes over and picks him up then hands him to me. I look at the baby then Bobo leans in and take a look. I look at him like he can tell me if he's mines or not. He shrugs his shoulders then we both burst out into laughter. Ms. Brown doesn't know what the hell we laughing about.

"Look, I don't know who Fred's father is. Stephanie went down to Atlanta after you two broke up and came back a couple weeks ago with da baby. She's hasn't been by herrre since, leaving me herrre with another mouf to feed. I don't know what's going on with dat girl." I was still unsure so I asked Ms. Brown if I could take Fred with me for a couple hours. Mainly because after she told me she was pregnant, I figured no need to wrap up. Ain't that a bitch!

She was too happy that I offered. Before I left I sent Bobo to pay her rent for the month and told him to take care of it every month after. I could've paid the full year, she only paid twelve dollars a month. I know if I do they'll go up on her rent so it was just easier to do it that way without messing up her benefits. I called up Mrs. Grant my accountant to take care of her electric bill and Terry to make sure they have food in the house.

By the time I finish, Bobo is back with a car seat he got from one of his jump offs. I roll out to meet up with Doc in the parking lot at the Galleria so he can do a DNA test. After we finish, I head in the mall and get little man errthing I think he may need. Hell, he may not be my child but that won't stop me from pretending that he is. I knock on the door and Steph little bother, Buckle, tells me Ms. Brown went to bingo and said to tell me to bring Fred back in the morning.

I'm cool with it but I need to take care of some business before I leave from in the hood. I stop by Terry house and explain the shit to her then head back on the other end. I see Roach, Ant, Spider, and Fly beating the shit out of somebody. I go over to see what's up and its Worm dumb ass getting the shit kicked out of him by these fifteen, sixteen year old young nigga's. I tell them nigga's to chill out and bring Worm up to his apartment. We all go in and Ruby is pacing back and forth chain smoking and drinking Fifty Fifty straight from the bottle.

"Where da fuck is Esta nigga? She know damn well she supposed to be herrre to talk to dis bitch today. I'm gon' beat da shit out dat bitch when I find herrre stupid ass," Ruby yells coming towards me as Spider steps in front of her stopping her from getting any closer.

"Look, I didn't come here to argue, I came here to kill that nigga if you don't do exactly what I tell you to do." She starts to scream and run over to Worm begging me not to kill him. We all look at each other because no one has even made a move towards Worm. Hell, we all put up our shit after they looked around the apartment and no one else was here.

"Come here Ruby, I don't have all day and it's funky as a bitch in this mufucka!" She won't let go of Worm so Ant and Fly pull her up and bring her over. I tell her to sign all the spots on the forms and fill out the boxes. When she's finished, I double check and they release her as she runs back over to Worm. I walk over and she starts begging me not to kill him again.

"You sad as fuck Ruby! You pick this piece of shit of a nigga over your only grandchild? I mean, what the fuck did she ever do to you for you to treat her the way you have?" She continues to cry over Worm.

"Both you low life mother fuckers listen up because this is the last time I'm going to say it. Stay the fuck away from Jasmine, if she comes here you better not let her in! That punk ass check you get for her won't be coming anymore. I know yo' ignorant ass can't read but you just signed your rights over.

The social worker you waiting on not coming and neither is Jasmine. Leave her the fuck alone or I'll kill both you mufuckas myself." I turned to leave out and not only hear but feel a lugy land on the back leg of my pants. I don't bother turning around or stopping the youngin's from whopping their asses.

8 SOUL EVOLUTION

"Terry told me her oldest daughter was a hair dresser, I didn't know she meant a professional one." Dena laughs and tilts my chair back so she can wash my hair.

"Yeah girl, I been doin' hair all my life. I can cut too! I have a salon here in St. Louis but I make my real money out in LA. I have a fierce clientele child. They pay big bucks out there to have me lay their hair out for them."

"You don't look that old to be doing all that."

"I'm not old, I'm only twenty three!"

"I thought Tristan was nineteen? I thought you said he was your big cousin?" She started laughing and sat me up while she clipped my ends.

"Girl I know. He always have been a big cousin to all of us even though he younger than me and my two brothers. But he's been gettin' it since he was a young buck out in the streets. After I graduated from high school I told him that I was trying to go to beauty school in Atlanta but didn't have the money. Within a week he had the money for my school and a studio apartment waiting for me. He even hooked me up with a job at a barber shop around the corner from my apartment."

"How? I mean he's four years younger than you, even if you graduated at eighteen that means he was fourteen. How is that possible?" She started to really laugh while she set my hair and wrapped thin papers around it.

"Girl they don't call him 'Cargo' for nothing. I don't know to be honest, I never asked him how and I still haven't to this day."

"So you used him? Instead of encouraging him to not be involved in this messed up world you used him?" She stopped laughing and came around into my face.

"Look Jasmine, I know that's how it sounds but I guess it is what it is. Cargo been thru a lot since his mother died and he came to live with us. His father Mack turned over his kingdom to him and opened up all kinds of lanes for Cargo. I mean this is what I overheard happened over the years. Like I said, I never asked Cargo about it.

So looking back and hearing it from you then yes, I should've been the older cousin and kept him away. Reality is, Cargo really didn't have a choice once Mack was indicted. He had to keep the money coming in so his father would have a chance to beat the case." She stopped talking and put the dryer over my head, I pulled it up before she could walkout the room.

"What happened to his father Dena?"

"The police claimed he was resisting and he was beaten to death." She walked out and I sat back and let her words sink into my head. When Dena was finished with me I looked in the mirror and didn't recognize myself. I could barely see my black eyes and my hair was out of this world with color and bounce.

"Okay come with me Jas, I have something to show you." I follow Dena to a room upstairs and wait while she goes in then comes back out. When she opens the door I can't help but cry at the sight.

"This is your room girl! Don't cry, I hooked you up, come on let me show you yo' closet." We walk into this huge closet that's three times bigger than my room at Queen Ruby house. It's filled with all types of clothes and shoes. I even see brand new uniforms for school and I cry harder when she hands me all new text books. I thank her, she says to thank Tristan and that she just used his money to get me what I needed. I couldn't help but laugh.

I sat in the middle of the room all night not worried about any roaches or rats attacking me. The lavender walls have a slightly lighter color blended midway up to the ceiling. There's a real bed that's huge with heavy sheets and ten pillows all different shapes and sizes. I have a desk, a computer, a laptop, a stereo and TV.

I can't close my eyes because I don't want to wake up if this is a dream. I climb into the bay window and watch as the sun comes shining thru. I can't help but laugh like a fool at the thought of not waking up in Center or at Queen Ruby house. I can smell food so I go down to see if I can help cook.

"Good morning Jasmine. Breakfast will be ready in about ten minutes."

"Can I help you with it? I can clean while you do that if you don't need help making breakfast." She laughs and tells me no thanks. I ask if Tristan is in and she tells me he'll be in after lunch. I finish eating and go back into my room. I'm broken out of my studies by the sound of a baby crying. I head down to see where the sound is coming from.

There are too many doors and I don't want anyone to think I'm snooping so I go into the living room. The crying has stopped so I sit and wait, maybe someone will come out with the baby. After a while I go back to my room and grab my book and sit back on the couch and wait.

"Hey Jasmine, you cool?" I hear Tristan say so I stand up from the couch and turn in the direction of his voice. He stops and looks at me like I have a weapon so I put my book down onto the table as he walks over.

"I see Dena did her thang." I turn out of his view as he stops by the chair.

"Not saying anything was wrong with you at first. Just I see she um..." I cut him off and start to laugh.

"I know, I can barely recognize myself. So yes, she did 'do her thang' as you call it." He nods for me to have a seat and follows sitting in the chair.

"I see you found your books."

"Yes. Thank you for everything. The room, the clothes, the books—"

"Don't worry about it Jasmine. You need anything else?"

"No, I have more than enough. I don't know how I'll repay you for what you've done for me."

"Come on Jasmine, don't hurt a nigga ego like that." I try to ignore the way he refers to himself and change the subject.

"I heard a baby crying, I came down to see." He smiles then picks up his phone from the coffee table. A couple minutes later Ms. Janine walks in carrying a baby in her arms. I walk over to take a look and ask him if I can hold him. I sit back on the couch with him and watch as he sucks on his tongue in his sleep. Tristan and Ms. Janine leave the room.

"Have a great night Ren, I'll see you on Monday." I head back in the living room and see Jasmine still on the couch with Fred. Before I can get in she stands and ask where he's sleeping, I take her to his room. After I open the door she stops and looks shocked at the site of the room. She places him in his crib and adjusts the monitor to see him and grabs the other and heads out. I follow behind closing the door.

"I didn't know you had a son." I sit and watch her stare into the monitor at Fred.

"I don't know if he's my son or not. I just found out about him earlier today. He maybe mines and he may not be mine." She looks over confused by what I said.

"You had all that stuff put in there today?" I laugh once I catch on to what she was thinking. I told her how I found out about Fred and how I had the room done when Steph told me she was pregnant.

"So where's Stephanie now?"

"I don't know, when they find her they'll let me know. I plan on taking him back to Ms. Brown Sunday so she won't be worried." I don't want him to take Fred back, I know what it's like to live with a grandmother. I hope he finds out that Fred is his son so he can take care of him. We sit in silence while I watch the monitor and he fiddles with his phone.

"Would you like for me to fix something to eat?"

"I'm sure Janine left some plates in there if you want that."

"I know you probably think I can't cook because Queen Ruby never kept food in the house but I can. I can warm up a plate for you if you like instead."

"Whatever you want to do Jasmine. As long as you eat I'm good." I watch as she gets up with the monitor and heads to the kitchen. Once the plates are heated she sets the plates down and we eat. As I clear our plates Jasmine runs out the room and comes back with Fred in her arms. I take out his milk and bottle while she makes it and feeds him then heads back to his room. I spend the night on the phone and thinking.

I hit my alarm at six thirty, workout in the basement, shower and find Jasmine making breakfast with Fred in his basinet not far from her. I walk over greet her and pick Fred up to feed him while she cooks. We eat and head out for the day, I see a completely different person come out of Jasmine. She looks happy and carefree which worries me because I'm almost certain that it's because of Fred. I'm highly doubting that I'm his father and I don't want to hurt Jasmine when it's time to take him back with Ms. Brown.

Once we return I sit Jasmine down and explain to her that he has to go back home. I try and get her to understand that I honestly don't know if he's mine or not. Instantly her emotions pour out of her expression but she didn't push the issue.

"Jasmine on the real, I been wanting to ask you some shit but don't want to hurt your feelings." Hurt my feelings? I look over at him and put the monitor down on the table turning in his direction.

"The least I can do is answer some questions after all that you have done for me."

"If you don't want to answer then don't and I won't ask again." She says okay so I move in closer and sit on the coffee table in front of her.

"Why did you stay with Ruby when you could have went with Terry?"

"Since I was six Queen Ruby was the only family I had, besides, I couldn't go from one building to the next. Queen Ruby would have found me eventually." I don't know why he thought that would hurt my feelings.

"Has Worm ever tried to touch you or sold you out to——" I can't even get the shit out, I look at her and she looks embarrassed. She falls back on the couch and places her arm over her face hiding from the question.

"Not really. I mean it's not like he didn't try every chance he could to settle some debt he had. But no one would take him up on it because I would cry as loud and hard as I could." She puts the pillow over her head and I ask what's the not really.

"Well, when they would beat me sometimes he would hump my leg or foot or side. Then Queen Ruby would have oral sex with him and they would leave me alone after he had an orgasm." What the fuck is wrong with them mufuckas. She looks over to see my expression then covers her face with the pillow again. I ask if that was all that they had done to her sexually, she said yes.

"Why do you wear your hair tied back all the time? I mean it's really long and thick." I tried to change the subject, I lifted up the pillow and helped her sit up on the couch.

"One day I was in the shower and Queen Ruby kicked the door in, she said she had been calling for me. She took one look at my hair, pulled the shower curtain down and started hitting me with the rod. She drug me into the kitchen by my hair and pulled out a knife from the drawer. She used that dull thing and cut patches and plugs in my head. I walked around with a skull cap for over a year after that." I couldn't help but laugh at how hot that thing was during the summer.

"Jasmine would you like to stay here with me or would you like for me to get you your own spot somewhere?" I couldn't believe what he said. I sat back on the couch in amazement, I heard Fred and almost ran out the room. I stayed in the room with Fred again, I could hear Tristan moving around. At times he would look in to check on us. I stayed still just in case he came over to the bed to look at Fred. I don't think he sleeps for more than an hour here and there at the most.

Sunday morning I took Jasmine over to Dena's so she could get her hair done. I was shocked when she came out, she looked completely different again. Made me realize that with the slightest change she took on a whole other look naturally. Her hair's cut into a bob that was long on both sides.

They both laughed at my reaction, Dena explained how she airbrushed Jasmines makeup so it wouldn't come off. I wouldn't know that she has any make up on. The only way I knew was because the bruising around her eyes had disappeared. We stopped and had lunch at a soul food spot.

On our way out, I got word from Bobo that Steph was arguing with Ms. Brown. I pulled into the parking lot and opened the door for Jasmine as Steph comes storming over to the car.

"Why da fuck do you have my baby?" I look back at her and wait for Jasmine to get out.

"Who da fuck is dat bitch nigga?" I feel Steph move closer, Tiny stops her before she can reach the car. She starts fussing for him to move and for me to give her Fred. I pull him out and grab Jasmine hand leading them into the building not worrying about shit Steph is screaming at me. Ms. Brown comes to the door holding a bloody towel to her mouth as Steph and Tiny follow us down the hall.

"Everything okay Ms. Brown? You want her out of here?" She picks up Fred and sits at the table. I place Jasmine behind me as Steph tries to push past Tiny into the kitchen.

"Bitch give me my son before I fuck you up."

"Stephanie calm down! Why don't you just go back where you came from. You only herrre for money, you know damn well you not worried about dis baby," Ms. Brown says as Fred starts to cry. Jasmine edges forward but I hold her back.

"You damn straight! So either you give me da money or you give me my baby." I can't believe this is Tristan's ex-girlfriend.

"Steph watch yo' mouth and sit down." I move forward and grab her arm forcing her into the chair. I pull up a chair and sit in the middle of them.

"Who's his father Steph?" She starts to laugh.

"Not you nigga! Is that what you thought? I knew yo' weak ass came and snatched him up fo' something. But guess what, he not yours!" Damn I want to fuck this girl up right about now. I look over at Jasmine who's handing Ms. Brown a bottle.

"Who da fuck is dat bitch? I know you ain't had dat slut around my mother fucking son." Jasmine steps back towards the balcony door and looks away.

"How much money are you here for Steph? How much would it take to get you to leave Fred here with Ms. Brown?" Ms. Brown starts to cough and Jasmine starts shaking her head.

"Two hundred dollars! Yeah, a week nigga." Tiny starts laughing at how stupid she sounds. I look over at Ms. Brown and ask if that's how much she's been paying Steph.

"Hell naw! She just dropped dis baby off, he was less than two weeks old and she stole forty dollars from my purse. He'll be a month and a half tomorrow, dis her second time coming by. She come in herrre saying she needed a hundred dollars. When I told her I didn't have it she said she was taking Fred if I didn't give it to her. Den she realize Fred wasn't herrre, she hit me and left out da door." Ms. Brown starts to cough more, Fred begins to cry as Jasmine reaches down to pick Fred up. Steph sees and jumps up out the chair and snatches Fred from out Ms. Brown hands.

"Give me my fucking baby! If I don't get my money he leaving wit' me." Steph backs up against the sink as I stand to walk over to her and Tiny moves in closer.

"Steph, give me the baby before you piss me off, I'll give you the punk ass money just give me the baby." She drops her arm like she's about to let him fall to the floor then pulls him back up.

"Now I need three hundred." I shake my head trying not to kill this chick if she hurts her son. Steph dips Fred down again, this time Jasmine moves in and pulls him out of her arms. She places him in Ms. Brown's arms, Steph grabs Jasmine and Jasmine turns and punches her in the face. She continues to punch Steph as Tiny and I look on. Ms. Brown yells for Jasmine to stop and she does; like a switch was moved to off. Tiny helps Steph up off the floor as Ms. Brown yells for Steph to leave. I walkout with Jasmine and we head back to the house with little words being spoken.

9 ENVY

What was I thinking back there, I know he probably hates me for attacking her the way that I did. I couldn't stand by and let her hurt Fred any longer. Why did he have to leave him there? I know that crazy girl will go back and take him now that he has left. Once we arrive I head straight to my room grab my book and go into Fred's room. I cry myself to sleep praying that he's safe and that girl has not harmed him.

I wake up to Ms. Janine nudging me to get ready for school and come down for breakfast. After I shower and get dressed I look in the mirror and notice the lines going down my face. I cried so much it has smeared my makeup and no matter how much I scrub they won't go away. I hear a knock at the door and answer. It's Dena, she takes one look at me and starts to laugh and I join in with her.

"Jas come on, Cargo told me what happened so I'm here to get you back right. I see those tears then ruined that pretty face of yours." Dena cleans me up in no time and says she's going back to LA for a couple of days. I go down for breakfast and Tristan joins me. We head out so that he can drop me off at school, I want to say something to him but he has already done so much for me.

"You alright Jasmine? I mean with everything that happened yesterday, I know you're upset, you can talk to me you know."

"I'm alright, I apologize for my behavior towards Stephanie yesterday. I was out of line and should've kept my distance." He starts to chuckle while stopping at the light and looks over at me.

"I didn't know you had it in you. I mean I was shell shocked seeing you like that. I thought... I mean you nev——"

"I can fight, well I'm not where I would've been if I would've stayed in training. That's one of the things I remember about my father, he would take me to practice. I continued to practice over the years. For the last three years I stay after or come early for MMA at the gym not far from my school." Tristan pulls over to the curb and looks at me but says nothing, I ask him what's wrong.

"This whole time...why...I mean if you can fight why let them beat on you?" Maybe she likes getting beat on and that's why she never left or spoke out about what was going on.

"Queen Ruby is my grandmother and the only family I have, good or bad. I would never put my hands on her or Melvin, no matter what they did to me. My mother once told me that God will never put something on me I couldn't handle. But your right, I could've fought back, but then what?

I'm sixteen, granted I'm almost seventeen but I can't get a real job or a place to live without Queen Ruby agreeing. When Mrs. Terry helped me get a little money, Queen Ruby took it. Well most of it, so why make things harder on me when I didn't have too?" Tristan looks at me for a minute then slowly pulls away.

"Before I go, I know it's a lot to ask but can you please get Fred from down there? I mean I know it's a lot but please can you go and get him?"

"I know how you feel Jasmine and if he's mine without a doubt I'll go and get him. But I'm almost positive that he's not and I can't take someone else's child away from them." I get out the car and head into school.

I go back to the city, Doc calls and tells me what I already know. Fred is not my child, I put it on the back burner and make my rounds. Before I head back to pick up Jasmine I turn on the news to see what's poppin' in the streets for real. I see a breaking news report about a home invasion out in North County. Three dead in what they call a 'drug related' incident, then I see RaRa picture and know this shit is about to hit the fan. My phone starts buzzing like crazy, I pick up and hang right back up.

I run get Jasmine and get her back to the house. I tell her about Fred and she accepts my decision to not interfere. I head back to the city to meet up with my peoples at the spot. Once they fill me in, we all get out and continue on with our morning.

I pull up to my house on Lord and jump into my ran over Caprice and head to West Florissant. At two thirty in the morning I pull up on Lee, sit and watch as these nigga's celebrate. I wait until they finish and go into the house. By four o'clock I walk up out front knowing all these fools high and drunk.

I don't bother knocking on the door, I head to the back and creep down the basement steps. Once inside I walk around these nigga's are all laid out without a clue that I'm in the house. I see two pounds of parrot on the card table and a box of cigarillos that's almost empty. I know these the right nigga's and it's time for them to pay up. I hit all four without alarming anyone of what's going on. My silencer works its magic. I head up the steps, the kitchen is empty so I continue upstairs.

In the first bedroom I see two nigga's in the bed, I hit them without even trying to see what they were up to. The last room I see a nigga sprawled out across the bed. I go over and beat the nigga until I'm sure he's unconscious. I tie him up and get his ass back up wide awake watching my every move. I pull out a clear bottle from my pocket and show it to him and let him know what it is. He soft as cotton candy, he already crying begging me to stop with his eyes. I pull the rag from around his head so I can hear what he has to say.

"Look man, I don't know shit. Dat nigga Henry downstairs said he had a lick we could get a couple pounds of dat purple parrot. I didn't go in I sat lookout around da corner, dey came out and dat was it."

"Who told that nigga where the parrots were at?" He starts crying again saying he doesn't know so I snatch his head back so he can't move. I took out the eye drop and put two drops under his eyelid. He screamed of course, I put the rag back over his mouth, the smell of the shit is fueling my mission. I asked again with no answer, I put two more drops in the nigga ear.

This bitch passes the fuck out. I spend almost five minutes trying to wake him up. I said fuck it and shot his ass in the head twice and mobbed out. I took the Caprice to the chop shop and caught a cab to Dellwood to get my Expedition and went home.

The summer came and went faster than I thought possible. I dreamed about Fred being here with me so often it's unbelievable. I dreamed of his curly little afro and him sucking on his tongue while he slept. Before my alarm has a chance to go off I'm up getting ready, I don't want to cry about it. I go down and start breakfast so Ms. Janine won't have so much work to do. I don't see why he needs her to clean everyday to be honest.

It's not like this house is dirty at all. She really want to work she needs to spend a day in Queen Ruby house. Now that would be a sight to see, her dealing with those two for a couple days. She would probably quit and never speak with Tristan again. After I get the waffles started I enjoy a cup of fresh squeezed orange juice, this is the life.

"Cooking again I see Jasmine." I turn around and spit orange juice all across the counter and down my shirt.

"Damn baby girl, I know I look good but I'm sweaty and funky as hell!" He thinks it's hilarious.

I can't stop from staring at him, I never paid any attention before but this man has been sent straight from Paradise. His arms are big and tight, looks like his wide, hard, chest is forcing his skin to expand around them. His stomach looks painted on, each muscle seems to be encased in its own slot. The hard dark line running from his bulging breast leads straight down the middle of his body. I can see fine silky hair from his navel disappearing right above his low hanging sweats.

The beads of sweat that he's trying to pat dry only makes his body glow. His bald head even looks beautiful from the beads of perspiration trying to run down as he cleans them up. Never have I noticed his eyes, they're really brown and his eye brows look like they have been arched.

His face is immaculate, smooth, perfect cheeks and he has a thin flavor savor. It runs horizontally under the bottom of his thick lips. Tristan is a chocolate treat that I never even paid any attention to. I guess every time I've come near him I was too embarrassed to take notice.

"What's good Jasmine, you gon' stand there all day with OJ running all over yoself?" I snap out of my thoughts and grab the towel to clean up the mess I made. After the food has finished I head to my room and clean up trying not to think anymore of Tristan. By the time I make it back down he's coming around the corner pulling his shirt on. We sit and eat while he continues to laugh at my reach to him.

"So what's up, you not gon' talk to me at all? I mean now since yo' eyes then cleared up and you see a nigga you don't have anything to say?" He holds a straight face waiting on me to respond.

"You're really conceded you know that?" He starts to laugh, I can't help but focus in on how white, bright and straight his teeth are. His tongue is very attractive and pink, it pulls my eyes in as he continues to laugh at me.

"Serious though, you never answered my question." Please let her say here, I don't want to let her ass go but I'll get her a spot if that's what she wants.

"How tall are you?" I can't concentrate on anything he's talking about.

"Six three!" I'm five four in a half he's the perfect height.

"How much do you weigh?"

"'Bout two twenty! Why you asking anyway?" I already know why she asking I just want to see if she tells me. She's been checking me out since she spit that orange juice out earlier when I came out the gym. She still can't take her eyes off a nigga and I have on all my clothes. She'd probably go berserk if she saw me completely naked. She 'bout pass out at the site of this dick standing tall, I can't help but chuckle at the notion.

"Because you're a very attractive man. Even being full of yourself you're striking. Where's your lady friend? I know you said you ended things with Stephanie over a year ago and all. I can't imagine that you're single. I mean the swelling in your sweats this morning even seeming slightly aroused I can't imagine you being celibate." I can't believe I said that! It's out now so let's see if he's embarrassed.

"I like that in you Jasmine. You keep it real wit' me and I'll do the same. I'm not with anyone, I'm single. I have three chicks I chill wit', they're all married, that way I don't have to deal with all the drama. When I'm away I may or may not break off a couple chicks here or there but I'm always strapped. I never bus in a chick, keep my own magnums and watch 'em go down the toilet when I'm done. Rules of my game baby girl!" Fuck it, why lie? She ain't my gal, I ain't tryin' to get at her...yet and she asked so I told.

"I see. At some point I need to go and check on Queen Ruby, I need to explain and to let her know that I'm alr..."

"FUCK HER!" Tristan yells at me slamming his fist down on the table. He stands up and I follow, he moves around in front of me and I don't know what he'll do but I get ready. He's not my family so I'll do my best at protecting myself from him.

"You stay the fuck away from them Jasmine! I mean it. Don't bring that scum buckets name up around me again. What the hell is wrong with you?

Do you have Stockholm syndrome or somethin'? Why do you always protect that animal after ten years of abuse. Jasmine, the average crackhead treats their pets better than that scum treated you. I'm getting you in to see a professional, you need yo' head checked and fast." I can't believe this girl, after all that piece of shit did to her she worried about her ass.

"Jasmine you can go any and everywhere you want, but you won't go around that bitch again as long as I'm alive!" I don't want to argue with him but that's my grandmother, the only family I have. I hold my tongue and look away.

"Come on so I can get yo' crazy ass to school."

"About that. I've been looking into transportation from here to school and they don't have any buses and a cab ride will be too expensive for me. I figure I can pa..."

"Jasmine come on! I can take you to school and pick you up with no problem. Stop playin' wit' me Jasmine, do you know how to drive?" I shake my head no.

"Well if you want to learn let me know. If not it's all good, you can retire yo' bus pass shorty! I got you." I reach for my book bag but he picks it up for me as we leave out.

"Before I go I was thinking since I'm not with Que...down there I won't be able to get the check before she does. I need to get a job so that I can keep up my tuition. This is my senior year, I can't stop payi..."

"Jasmine get out! Have fun at school and stop comin' at me like I haven't explained to you several times that I got you." I laugh, close the door behind her and watch as she walks into the gate.

"Hey you! I see you found Book." I turn around and it's Sue smiling in my face. I nod at her jump in the whip and pull off.

"So Book, who was that rad guy that dropped you off?" I turn around and see Sue and Claire behind me. These two are the schools gossip queens. They work in the office just so they have the latest juice on everyone.

"I don't know who you're talking about."

"The chocolate Hershey kiss, you know the tall guy with all the muscles. Those dreamy light brown eyes. Are they contacts?" Claire says.

"Yeah, he looks like a model, like Ricky Whittle but way darker and way better. Stop messing around Book, you know who we're talking about. That guy is way too awe-inspiring for you not to know who he is," Sue says, I shrug my shoulders and finish getting my stuff in the locker.

"At any rate, we wanted to know if you were bringing him to the Winter Wonder Dance. If not, please give one of us his name and number so that we can ask him ourselves," Claire says as they both stop laughing and look at me.

"I don't know who you're talking about. If I did and he was all that you described I would want him to ask me to go instead of stalking him. Don't you think that's a little, what do you call it? Pathetic? Maybe pitiful? No, maybe disgraceful? I don't know, but like I said, I don't know who you're talking about ladies." I try not to laugh and walk to class.

Seems like Tristan caused a stir, every snow flake, and ebony wish-I-was-a-model girl in the school asked me about him. I told them all the same thing and was really bored with the conversation. After the final bell, I take off to the gym and get in the ring with Roger, my trainer. I'm too excited because I get a chance to work on my Mauy Thai with him today.

"I heard that the price on nat parrot went up."

"I was thinking since it's more two toned this time to let 'em fly for damn near double. I mean if the colors not that mixed nigga's gon' fly right but when dem bitches dis mixed! Man we talkin' 'bout one feather knockin' nigga's on dey ass."

"I hear you."

"That ain't shit compared to the nigga Vinnie out in Hawaii, nigga said he runnin' out quick! You wouldn't believe how much they goin' for out der." I laugh because I know exactly what they goin' for, six a pound. Vinnie ain't makin' no real money though. He too busy fillin' my pocket up wit' three and a half of that to get it. I mob out and head to pick up Jasmine from school. I pull up and it's a heard of sheep standing around flirtin' wit' a nigga while giggling like crazy by the gate. I see Claire and Sue come out the crowd towards me.

"Hey there you!" Sue says.

"We sort of wanted to ask you something," Claire says, I don't respond but step out the car and lean against the door waiting on them to speak.

"We'll we wanted to know if you we're going to take Book to the Winter Wonder Dance?" Claire says.

"What did Jasmine say?" I was curious of course.

"She said she didn't know who you were and if she did you would have to ask her," Sue says.

"We already know even if you ask she won't go. So we figured we would ask you instead," Claire says as they both start that giggling shit again.

"Why you say she won't go if I asked her?" What can I say, these two will tell me anything I ask.

"Boys have been asking her to all types of stuff and she has never shown up for anything," Sue says, I ask if they know where Jasmine is.

"She left about ten minutes ago for the gym," Sue says.

"Yeah, they say she kicks a ton of tush over there. Jared said he had a match with her and that she fractured his ankle." I tell them to point me in the direction and head out before the rest of their flock comes any closer.

I watch Jasmine thru the window, looks like she's warming up. I slide in when she goes in the back. I ask the white boy at the counter if I can get in the ring wit' her. This nigga say he can't let me because she may hurt me. I had to check the nigga real quick, I drop some dough down and sign a waiver for his punk ass.

He takes me in the back and give me all kind of gear, says it's for my protection. I leave all that shit except for the headgear so she won't know it's me. By the time I walkout she in the ring going at it wit' some Hogan lookin' nigga they keep callin' Roger. The nigga I talked to, Jesse, stop 'em and Roger laughs as I climb in the ring.

What is Tristan doing? I know it's him, I can tell those abs from a thousand man line up. He gets in the ring and all I can see really is his bottom lip. I don't back down no matter how big he looks, I go at him like anyone else that steps in the ring with me. Roger stops us after about an hour and I have to say, Tristan can really fight. I jump down and head to the back before he has a chance to say anything to me.

I can't believe Jasmine can fight the way she just did. After I clean up I get on the phone and call Doc. I now know she needs serious help! Doc says he can set her up and will call to let me know when. I wait out front for her to come out. I can see her at the register trying to pay and Jesse refusing and walking her out.

"What's up Jasmine? What's that all about?" She looks away like she looking for somebody.

"I apologize for attacking you in there, I knew it was you." I laugh at her and move closer to her.

"Why you always apologizing for shit? I just wanted to see how you moved. Plus it gave me a chance to fill you up on the slide." I can't help but burst out laughing at what Tristan says.

"You are a mess, you know that?" He continues to laugh, closes the door, gets in and pulls away.

"How you know it was me anyway?" I look over at her and can see her smile.

"Your abs. In my entire life I've never seen abs like those, I'll never forget them." We both laugh as he continues on. When we get back I run upstairs and do my homework trying my best to forget about Tristan. I can't help it though, the way his body felt is stirring my insides in a way I've never imagined. I hear a knock on the door, I call for whoever it is to come in.

"What's up shorty? I thought you may want to go out tonight. Grab dinner and a movie or something, it's still early, we can hit the mall and get you something if you want." She stands up out of the chair and walks away from her desk and sits in the window. I go over and sit down by her, she looks like she's about to cry or some shit.

"Like a date?" I don't know but that sounded like a date to me. Why would he want to take me on a date? I know he would rather go out with one of the women that he's seeing.

"Yeah, a date. You can't go on a date with yo' boy are something?" I hold her chin up to see if she's about to cry or not.

"I barely know you."

"And yet you live with me. Now what?" I laugh and she smiles and looks out the window.

"Yeah, I know that's weird enough. But I never thought about going on a date with anyone, let alone you."

"Damn! What that mean shorty? I'm not good enough to go out on a date with you?" She starts to really laugh.

"No, I'm not saying that. I mean well, you're you and I'm me. Why would someone as extraordinary as yourself want to go out on a date with someone as repulsive as me?"

"You have an appointment with the psychologist on Saturday, make sure you tell her that." He starts to laugh, I don't understand why he would bring that up.

"Okay, I see I need to explain to you why what you just said was insane. Jasmine, you're beautiful. No doubt about that shorty. I been tryin' to holla at you ever since I peeped you sleepin' in the shower room at the Center. You ran out of there before I had a chance though. Every time I did see you after that, you were all beat up and I still thought you were stunning." I laugh because her face turns red and she covers her face with both her hands.

"Fine Tristan, I'll go but only if you stop the madness." I can't stop smiling from hearing his lunacy about me.

"Good! Now get yo' sexy, thick ass up and get ready. We can leave out in 'bout an hour." I laugh as she groans out of shear embarrassment.

I really didn't want to go to the mall but I went with Tristan because it seemed like he wanted to go. We walked mostly which gave me a chance to see how girls reacted to him in public. Many of them frowned at me and smiled in his face, some of them even approached him when I walked a couple feet away. It didn't bother me any, I was more disturbed by the attention I was getting from the boys.

In the past I always tried to hide and when boys did approach me I ran away. Now grown men who are in their late fifties are winking at me as they pass by. I don't know if it's the makeup or the clothes that has them acting like this.

"Excuse me, is that your girlfriend? Before you answer please let me give you my name and number. Scratch that! Let me give it to you and walk away believing that she's not and you'll call me." I laugh at the audacity she has, that was a cold ass line, I'm gon' have to use it.

"I'm straight sweetheart. She not my girl but I plan on changing that." I walk over to Jasmine before a nigga get his head stomped in for tryin' to holla at her. We stop in Foot Locker, I get me a couple pairs of kicks and get her some.

I ignore her telling me they cost too much and continue to look around. The chick Bree, who works here, brings over some knee high boots with a heel on it. Jasmine looks at them then at Bree like she was crazy for bringing them over. I convince her to try them on, I can't help but laugh when she stands up.

"Tristan, you know it's rude to laugh at people and not with them." I try again and after a couple strides I find it easier to walk in them. I'm quick on my feet and once I figure out how to balance myself I'm strutting all around the store. All the men watch as I maneuver around showing Tristan that I can walk in them. I guess I showed him because he practically begged me to wear them out.

I couldn't take my eyes off Jasmine once she put on those heels and broke 'em in. On our way out I pulled her into Victoria Secret, she was uncomfortable again. I told her I would wait outside while she picked some stuff out. When she was finished I met her at the register, I couldn't help but laugh at her.

All she had was some flannel pajamas, I told her that if she didn't get something else I would. She walked away and I told one of the sales girls to help her find some stuff. I gave her six hundred dollars and told her if Jasmine spent it all I would give her a hundred for helping. It didn't take long, I helped Jasmine with her bags and we headed out.

I don't know why the freaky sales girl kept trying to get me to buy all those nasty looking night gowns. I've never worn that type of stuff in my life and I don't plan on now. I settled for robes, panties, lotions, and bras. I was flabbergasted when they took my measurements, I never knew I was actually a forty two D. She could've knocked me over with a feather when she told me that.

I felt my knees giveaway when she said I spent eighteen hundred and six dollars. I started putting everything back, Tristan came in and stopped me. I tried to apologize but he put his arm around my shoulder and I couldn't concentrate on anything beyond that.

10 GRACE

"**W**hat's up Jasmine? I see you in here getting' yo' study on." I watch as Tristan stands in the doorway to my room. I tell him to come in and turn to see what he came up for.

"Happy belated birthday Tristan."

"Thanks."

"Why don't you celebrate your birthday?"

"I just don't so can we drop it? I would rather celebrate yo' birthday again."

"Don't remind me. I still get sick when I think about that dang nabbit roller coaster going backwards." We spent my birthday at Six Flags and we had a blast.

"As long as you had fun I'm straight."

"I haven't seen you all weekend, I thought you were bored with hanging out with me."

"Neva' that! I just had some work I needed to put in real quick that's all. Check though. I wanted to ask you something, it's been on my mind for a month now." I can't imagine what he waited a month to ask me about.

"So what is it? You could have asked me when you first thought about it you know." I laugh knowing that she'll be all shy when I ask her.

"I wanted to know if I could take you to your winter dance?" Just like I thought, her face turning red and she put her hands up to cover her. I walk over, kneel down pulling her hands from her face and ask again.

"Why would you want to do that? Didn't you attend your winter dance? I'm sure it's the same." I'm so happy he asked I'm trying not to jump out this chair into his arms.

"Because I wanted to ask you. I can't lie, I didn't know anything about it and I imagine you never would've told me. I'm glad those two crazy white girls at yo' school told me about it. They said you would only go if I asked you and they doubted even if I asked that you would go. Word is, you're a hot commodity Jasmine and turn errbody that ask you down." I chuckle and hold her hands in mine.

"So will you let me take you to your winter dance?"

"Yes!" I can't hold it any longer, I throw my arms around his neck causing him to fall back. I can't help but laugh like a fool while hugging him like a maniac.

"Cool! Chill out with all this though." I get out her arms and sit back as she crosses her legs still grinning at me.

"I can't have you all over me like that Jasmine. I'm trying to behave myself and having you in my arms not helpin' a nigga at all." She laughs and apologize.

"Don't trip. Look I have to go out of town for two weeks, but I'll be back in more than enough time for the dance. I called a car service for you, the info is downstairs on the table. Before I leave I want you to know I told errbody in the hood if they see you down there to send you home. Don't think you slick and try that secret ninja shit either.

Ruby and Worm dumb asses have already been warned to stay away from you. I'm tellin' you now Jasmine, if you sneak down there both they trifling asses gon' die!"

"Tristan, why would you say something like that? That's my grandmother you're talki—"

"She maybe by blood but she damn sho' ain't no type of grand or mother and damn sho' not a queen. What the doctor say about that anyway?" She smile and look away, I turn her head back so I can see her eyes.

"Look Jasmine, stay from down there. I don't want to worry about you while I'm away. If those two hurt you I know I'll kill them it's no doubt in my mind that I won't. If you need to go anywhere else call the number and they'll pick you up. Don't worry about paying them and I left you some money and put some into your bank account."

"How do you know about my account?"

"Terry gets your statements."

"How, I changed accounts."

"Okay, but you didn't change the address for the statements. You didn't know that already?"

"I forgot about that." I can't help but laugh loud and hard at such a stupid simple mistake.

"Well you should have enough to cover you while I'm away. If you need anything I have this phone for you. My number is already in it along with

Terry and Dena's number." I give her the phone and pull her up to her feet.

"So when are you leaving?"

"Now! So stay from down there and call me even if you don't need anything." I kiss her on the head and head out.

I can't help but fall back on the bed thanking my lucky stars for Tristan. I spend who knows how long waiting on Ms. Janine to show up so I can tell her. First thing the next morning I have to tell somebody the good news since Ms. Janine didn't show. I'm so stuck on telling somebody that two days have passed by and school is out. Then it dawns on me, Dena! I run to get the phone and call her, she picks up and says she's around the corner and hangs up before I can say anything. I wait looking out the window and see her come up the long driveway.

"Dena, guess what!" She looks surprised by the way I ran down and pulled the door open before she could get out.

"Alright Jas give me a minute to get this stuff in the house then I can play yo' lil guessing game." I grab some of the bags and bounce up the walkway smiling from ear to ear.

"Okay, by the look of that smile on yo' face I figure this has something to do with a big head lil boy." I nod on the brink of exploding.

"Let me guess, you have a date with him?" I nod again and fall back on the couch kicking my feet in the air. Dena starts to laugh at my excitement and sits down beside me.

"So who is he and how does he look?" Then it dawns on me, she doesn't have a clue who it is. I bury my head in a pillow so I can't see her reaction.

"It's Tristan," I mumble into the pillow.

"WHAT?" she yells and jumps up off the couch. I can't face her but she sounded like she wasn't happy for me at all. I peek up at her and see her smiling as hard as I was.

"Jasmine, shut up! I know you not talkin' about Cargo. Girl please stop playin' and look at me." I sit up and nod at her, to my surprise she starts laughing so hard tears stream from her eyes. She keeps saying she can't breathe and hold up. I sit and wait for her to finish unsure if she's laughing at me or with me.

"So you tellin' me that you and Cargo are dating?"

"Well, not really. I mean I don't think so. I mean, he did take me on a date last month. We went to the mall and to dinner then saw a movie. I really don't know."

"Girl, it sound like ya'll datin' to me! Shit, yo' ass already live wit' his ass. This the most I ever known for him to stay out at this big ass house. He usually stay at one of his spots in the city. I asked him why the sudden need to stay out here so much. He talkin' 'bout he wanted to keep you company and not leave you all the way out here." We both laugh, she hugs me and tells me she's happy for me.

"So you say this was last month. Why you so happy now?" I smile hard again.

"He asked me if he can take me to the Winter Wonder Dance. It's in three weeks and he said he would be back by then to take me Dena." I get up and scream running around the couch. Dena is laughing and crying again, I fall back on the couch trying to catch my breath.

"Alright Jasmine, I see why you so happy. I don't want to burst yo' bubble but don't put the perm in before you take the braids out." I look at her not understanding a word of what she said. I ask her to explain.

"Cargo, as fine as he is, has *not* settled down for a reason. Mainly because he's young and he had his heart broken by that tramp Stephanie. With that being said, don't fall for him if you're not sure that he wants to be involved with you." I fallback and scream into the pillow. I never thought about that.

"Dena, why is it like this? I never had a boyfriend or even attempted to have one. I've heard so many stories of disgusting men running over women and women doing the same. I've been through enough Dena, I don't want to have to worry about stuff like that." My happiness is suddenly lost and I cry like Queen Ruby just finished beating me.

"Jas, I'm sorry but it's life. Cargo is a good man, don't get me wrong. I'm sure if he truly wants to be with you and only you, he will. All I'm saying is you need to know for sure if that's what he wants to do. You also need to know if that's what you want to do. I don't want you to break his heart again like Stephanie low life ass did."

"Dena, please don't compare me to that girl."

"I'm not. But I take it you've never had sex before." I jump up and look Dena in the eyes.

"I haven't but eventually if I was his girlfriend, I would have to have sex with him right?" Dena starts to laugh again.

"Jas, please don't make me think about Cargo havin' sex, I'm about to throw up." I can't help but laugh with her.

"But if you do have sex, yo' lil ass may get out of control and want to try all kinds of dick!"

"What? Dena stop, that's disgusting. Why would you say that? I would never do something like that."

"Girl please, dick is like Pringles, once most people try one you can't stop." We both laugh at her analogy.

"That doesn't mean you can't stick with Pringles right?"

"Naw it don't, but it also don't mean that those Red Hot Ripplets won't catch your eye. Next thing you know you den switched up licking the sauce off yo' damn fingers and shit." We both laugh again.

"Serious, I think I need to talk to Tristan. He told me about the women he's seeing and he's probably with someone right now. Dang it! Never mind, I don't want to put myself in any unnecessary pain. I'm not going to the dance with him or anyone else. Thanks Dena for snatching me back to reality."

"Hold up Jas! Don't put this on me. You better not tell Cargo that I changed yo' mind about anything. Like I said, I don't know how he feels about you, what I do know is he ain't ever moved anyone in his house. Only reason I knew about Stephanie is because she came in my shop a couple times and——" This is getting interesting.

"Wait Dena! Start from the beginning, how did you meet her?" She starts to laugh.

"I see you wanna know about the competition."

"She's not competition!"

"I heard that Jas, look at you. Well when my shop, Exquisite Ends, opened it stayed booked. In walks Stephanie and two of her road mutts, they were all talking mad noise about hitting the club later that night. Kim, one of my best stylist and I laughed listening in on their conversation.

Then Stephanie come over and ask for the best stylist to hook up her and her girls. I told her that I was booked, Kim said she could get them. Stephanie offered me two grand to fit them in, I turned her down because the head I was working on was worth more. Plus I had four more that made her money look like chump change. I told her Kim could get them for the money.

The whole time Kim working on her head, they talking about how her man this and her man that. Stephanie was eating it up. I thought she was a fool and needed to watch them ho's around her damn man. Anyway, she say he was planning on taking her out of town once she graduated.

She was too geeked about the shit. I look back at her and ask where she find a man like that. She say he live in her hood, I ask if he go to her school, she say she go to Vashon but he don't. I start naming off all the hoods and she say naw the Cochran. That had my ears up to the max. I ask his name, she say I wouldn't know him so I play her out like she was lying.

Her home girl say, 'Cargo is her man!' I don't say anything, I jump on the phone, tell Cargo to swing by the shop real quick. When he walks in she's in Kim chair behind me so he can't see her and she can't see him. He come closer and the whole shop stop what they doin' staring at him and shit.

She must've got wind because I could see her in my mirror looking around me to see who errbody looking at. Cargo come up on me, I hug him and I hear her say, 'Who da hell is she Cargo?' I burst out laughing at her ass. Cargo whisper to me that I'm wrong for playin' him like that. He go over to Stephanie and tell her who I am. That's how I met her."

"So she's been crazy for a very long time huh?" We both laugh.

"Like I said Jas, you the only one he wanted me to meet, the only one he moved out here and the only one he has really taken care of. Even when he was with Stephanie, as far as I know, he never took her to any of his spots. He spent some bread on her but nothing like he has done for you. Thinking of that, that's why I'm here."

"Why were you coming over here anyway Dena?"

"Cargo said you had the next four days out for holiday and he wanted me to...guess!"

"What? I don't want to guess just tell me." She laughs and walk into the kitchen, I follow behind.

"I played the game with you so guess." Dang it.

"Okay, fix my hair?" She shakes her head no. I start rambling off all kinds of stuff, nails, company, mall, movies she's still shaking her head no.

"Can you tell me now?"

"He wanted me to take you shopping!" I sit at the stool in the kitchen.

"I said the mall already Dena."

"Girl, not the mall. He wants me to take you to New York for shopping." I try to get up and fall back out the stool. Dena is cracking up laughing and trying to help me up.

"Yeah girl New York, we meeting with a personal shopper tomorrow so you need to get yo' bags packed we have a flight in two hours."

"You're serious Dena? Stop playing with me, he does not want me to go to New York and shop." She starts pulling me up the steps.

"I'm serious as hell! Get this, he gave me a spending limit, guess how much."

"I'm not playing that game anymore so just tell me." We get in the room as she laughs heading into the closet with me behind her.

"Tell me Dena!" I pull her around to face me, she gives me a credit card and turns back around so I ask her again.

"He said and I quote, 'I'm like Master P, ain't no limit!' that's what he said."

"Who the hecky is Master P and what does that mean Dena?" She really gets a kick out of that and says I need to work on my cursing.

"Jas, it means you can spend how much you want."

"Well we can just stay here because I don't want to spend any of his money. He's done more than enough for me."

"Un-un! We going and you spendin'!"

"No. I'm. Not!" I left her right in the closet, she walked out and asked to use the phone he gave me. I give it to her and she goes back into the closet. When she comes out she hands me the phone, smiles and goes back inside. I look down and it's Tristan so I ask hello.

"Jasmine, can you please go with Dena and at least enjoy New York?"

"Tristan, I don't want to go and I most defiantly don't want to spend your money. You've done way too much for me."

"Come on shorty, work with me. Just go, you don't have to buy anything just go have fun, sightsee do whatever."

"No Tristan. You said I don't have to go anywhere if I don't want to. I don't want to go."

"Cool then. I'll just come back on the next flight and chill out with you. No problem."

"Wait Tristan, I'll go. You don't have to come back, I'll go to New York with Dena." I hear him laugh, he must've been pulling my leg.

"Thanks Jasmine, have fun. Put Dena on the phone for a minute." I give Dena back the phone as she rolls out a suitcase. I don't know where she found that at, after she hangs up I ask her where it came from.

"The cabinet. All of your luggage is in there. Come on we ready."

After I check in at the Windsor Court I head to the penthouse and chillout. Right on time, I make it down to the restaurant and see Santana coming in the door. We chomp it up for a minute and take a seat so we can get down to business.

"Hey bru, doing big chings all over. Only problem I see is you not showing love done here in N'awlins."

"Come on Santana man. You the one said the price was too high for you. Now you wanna say I'm not showing love." We laugh as the waitress gives us our plates.

"Awrite den I'm makin' groceries wit' you!"

"Cool and only because it's you it's the same as staying here for eight nights. Penthouse baby!"

"It don' madda, let's pass a good time to dat." I don't know what the hell this nigga just said. I write it down on the napkin in front of me and show it to him. We kick back and finish our meal. I don't stick around with Santana long, once he heads to the Casino I bounce out. When I make it to the lounge the card game is in full effect. I survey the room for a minute as the big ass security locks us in.

"Aye big man, how much they playin' for tonight?" He look over at the table jockey then back at me.

"Two fifty to get in." I get in and kill these nigga's at they own game. It's all about numbers when it come to cards. These nigga's been eating too much seafood, they heads all murky. A yellow skinned French lookin' nigga they call Roup makes small talk. I guess he figured he could throw me off my game. It don't make me no difference, like I said, it's all about numbers. After I hit the nigga's for a mil they get antsy like I'm supposed to stay. I tell 'em I'm out and big man walks me out.

I don't make it down the street before I see a car following me. I pull up to the stop light, it's the nigga Roup flaggin' me down and shit. I pull over he get to rappin', I think the nigga was asking me to hit up some party. He said, 'pass a good time' so that's what I figured he was talking about. I told the nigga I was looking for some powder and didn't have time. This nigga say he the one I need to holla at and to pull on the side of the row houses wit' him.

I follow behind him, his potna' get out and open the trunk, Roup get out as I walk over to see what he got. We shoot the shit for a minute, this nigga ask me if I wanted to sample it. Really? I told him have his boy sample it, that nigga eyes were already heavy as hell. He was too hyped when he heard what I said. Roup tried to play like I was five o. I pulled out a tester bag put the shit in and once it changed colors I told him I was ready to make groceries.

His potna was still itchin' to do a line so I told him I would pay for his man to sample it for me. Once he did, this nigga damn near fall back against the wall and slide down sittin' on his ass. I go over smack him on the face a bit see if the nigga still alive, he can barely hold his eyes open though. Roup standing by watchin' tellin' me the nigga 'bout had one too many hits. I go back over to him and we laugh at his man.

"On the real Roup, only time I seen a nigga do that shit is when I was in Missouri. I didn't know ya'll nigga's had it like this down here."

"Good thing I'm back here right?"

"Straight? Where you from nigga?"

"Here but I been in Kansas for a while. I have family in St. Louis who get me what I need so if you want some more you can get with me. I know it's a bitch coming from Florida going all over trying to get a deal."

"Shit, it wouldn't be a problem if this is the shit out of St. Louis or wherever them nigga's in Missouri gettin' it. But nigga you from Kansas that ain't Missouri, maybe this ain't what I'm looking for. You did say yo' mans over there had more than enough."

"I can get you up with my people for two hundred large. This nigga Freddie K from St. Louis can get whatever you need. But I can save you the hassle of driving from Florida to St. Louis without a doubt!" I look in the trunk again and tell the nigga bet. He hold out his hand and I send a front kick to the nigga chest sending him into the wall. He pull out his strap but not before I lock his hand up forcing him to drop it. After I get his ass in the sleeper he start trying to negotiate.

"Nigga shut up! Next time yo' bitch ass accept stolen goods you better know where they came from." I snap his neck and let him fall to the ground. His man slept through the whole thing. It was nothing to aerate his cranium. I put the gun in Roup hand and dipped out.

11 MAGNETIC AFFINITIES

"Okay Jas, it's time for you to go in, I'm tryin' to hit the clubs tonight."

"Have fun with that. After two days up here I'm beat anyway, plus I need to get some studying in before the weekend is over." We hug and I go upstairs to my room, once I get in I notice the TV is on.

"Dang shorty, 'bout time you made it back." I can't believe Tristan is here, I go over and sit on the couch as he sits up.

"What are you doing here Tristan? I thought you were out of town."

"I am out of town, I thought you were smarter than that. I know you don't think you still in St. Louis right?" We both laugh, I grab the remote from behind her and turn off the TV.

"I mean what are you doing in New York?"

"You know why I'm here." I tell him I don't know, he laughs and sits back.

"Well?"

"I told you that I would come hangout with you if you didn't want to go shopping. The whole time you been here you won't go in one store and you won't talk to Ann. So I'm here just like I told you."

"That's not really what you said. I think you're here because you missed me." I start to laugh watching his expression.

"Yeah I did miss you and the other reason I told you. There's also another reason that ties in with your reason." I wait to hear what he has to say but he gets up and walks in front of me and sits on the table.

"The whole time I been gon' you haven't called me once. What's the deal with that?"

"Oh, that's all?" He looks at me like I need to hurry up and explain it to him.

"Well I didn't call because I figured you were out selling drugs or killing someone, maybe even both and I didn't want to interrupt." All of a sudden he burst into loud thunderous roars of laughter. I was serious with what I told him, I walk into the bedroom leaving him to finish laughing at me.

"Damn, you straight put a nigga on blast like a mug! Come here though." I sit her on top of the desk and stand to the side of her.

"On some real, I said call me even if you don't need anything, you interruptin' me by not callin'. I'm smarter than you think, if I don't answer then know I'll get back at you."

"I can handle that. I'm getting into the shower now, can you give me a second?" I slide down off the desk.

"Cool, I'll be out front, take yo' time, enjoy." Okay book, note pad, and pen. Everything I need, I sit on the sofa while Tristan watches the TV, well I think he's watching the TV. Tristan looks over to see what I'm doing.

"You need some help over there?"

"What do you know about human anatomy and physiology?" I can hear him chuckle.

"More than you do!" I ignore him and when I'm finished I close my book and put everything on the table.

"So what you wanna do now?" I sit up to see her face.

"I'm kind of tired, I really just want to lie down and watch this one channel, Discovery Health. There's a medical examiner that does autopsy's and figure out how someone died. Do you have that channel back at your house?"

"Our house and yeah, I know the show you talking about. So you goin' in the room or you chillin' out here?"

"I guess in there, like I said I wanted to lie down. I could lie on this couch across from you with no problem. But the thought of a bed is still new to me and I want to enjoy it while I can."

"You make a bed sound like a luxury item."

"It is a luxury item for someone who mainly slept on the top of a deep freezer, or shower dividers, or park benches, or bu..."

"I get it Jasmine, I'll chill out here."

"I thought you said we were hanging out?" Why she playing with me?

"I thought you said you were going in there to lie down."

"So come on we can hangout in there." I grab my stuff up before he can answer and go in the room. He sits on the end of the bed while I get comfortable at the top. After a while he lies back with his head on his arms. I nudge his arm getting his attention.

"This is a big bed, you can get comfortable."

"Comfortable means me holding you in my arms so I'm good here."

"I haven't been held in anyone's arms since I was six. I'd like that if that's what you're offering." She damn straight it's an offer. I pull off my shirt leaving on my wife beater and pants then pull her into my arms. I'm tryin' my damndest not to get too close, I can feel her thick ass brushing against my stomach.

"You alright Tristan?"

"Yeah why?"

"Because you said hold me. Seems like you're trying to keep as far away from me as possible. Aren't your arms tired from stretching out like this?" I can't help but chuckle at what she said. I pull her all the way into me.

"Now stay still because I'm not touching you."

"You may not be touching me but that gun is." I can't help but giggle at what I said. Tristan laughs and tries to ignore my comment. We watch a couple episodes of the show and I check to see if she's still awake so I can bounce out. When I move she lifts her head and looks back at me, I stop and she lays back down.

"So how did the ladies treat you?" I can hear him try to hold his laugh.

"Straight, why?"

"Do they know back home?"

"Why would they care, those women are married and have other things to think about."

"So why haven't you found someone who would care?" I roll her over so that I can see her face.

"What's this about? Rap wit' me on some straight shit."

"I was just wondering why you're not with someone exclusively, can you be with one person?"

"I see where this is going. If I was with you then I would be with you and no one else. I'm single so of course I'm doin' me right now. Check this though. If we were together then I would expect for you to only be with me and I would only be with you. It's as simple as that. Hell, I don't have time for games, if we were together we may as well be married." She start to giggle. I ask her what's funny.

"You don't see the irony in that? Your sleeping with three married women already. So your theory is absurd."

"I see that but I'm not the one that's married to them or anyone else for that matter. Every time I'm wit' 'em really, I ask them what would their husband think about me dickin' them down. They all play it off with some bullshit. If I was married to either one of them that shit wouldn't go down. Like I said, I'm not booed up so it is what it is."

"So if you were in a relationship you would just up and leave them alone? What about when you're out of town? I mean it all sounds like a bunch of bologna."

"When did I start lying to you? I don't recall the exact date."

"You haven't, I just think you're being a hypocrite to expect your wife or girlfriend to do the opposite of what you're doing."

"I'm serious about that. You don't have to worry about none of that anyway. You wanna finish watchin' TV or what?" I rolled back over, he holds me tighter than before.

"Why did you say I don't have to worry about that?"

"Because if or when the time comes, I can show you better than I can tell you."

"What if I wanted the time to come now?" 'What has come over you?' I scream in my head but it's too late, I've already put the words into rotation.

"Then I would have to tell you A. you're not ready and B. you still have a year worth of sessions with the psychiatrist." She doesn't respond, I feel her exhale hard and pull my arm down across her chest. After a minute I feel her body melt into mine as she sleeps, not long after I can hear her mumbling.

I listen in and she has a full blown conversation with her parents. I wish I knew what they were telling her. If I did I would know how to react when she brought it up to me. Once the sun starts to show I head down to the gym and get a much needed workout.

I'm surprised when I awake because Tristan is nowhere to be found. I shower and study until I hear someone knocking on the door. I go over to answer and it's Dena. She looks like she's had a rough night.

"Dena, why didn't you tell me Tristan was here?" She stands back on her leg.

"Jas stop playin', Cargo is not here."

"We'll not now but he was here last night."

"So you havin' little freak nasty dreams about Cargo huh?" We both laugh.

"No, I'm serious he was here."

"No, I'm serious he's not here," she said it in the same tone as I causing us both to laugh harder. There's a knock at the door so I go over to answer but it comes open and Tristan steps in.

"I told you he was here!" Dena walks over to him and ask what he's doing here, he says I know why he's here.

"For real Cargo, what you doin' here?" Dena says when I shrug letting her know I don't know why he's here.

"We'll seeing you couldn't handle a little task of shopping on someone else's dime, I came to chill with Jasmine. I told her if she didn't go shopping I would come so I'm here."

"That's not exactly what you sai—"

"Yeah, yeah, yeah. Check Dena, Ann waiting down in the lobby for you, you know what to do so get dressed. Why are you two still in robes anyway? Ya'll leave out tomorrow, what ya'll was gon' do, sit around all day doin' nothin'?" Dena runs over and hugs me and heads for the door.

"Wait, Ann? What does Dena know to do?" Dena turns around with a huge smile on her face looking at me.

"I'm about to shop 'til I drop. Don't trip party pooper, Master P over there not." She practically ran out the door.

"So what we doin' today?"

"When do you sleep?"

"I couldn't really tell you because I'm sleep not looking at the time." She start giggling like crazy.

"Tell a nigga somethin', what we doin'?"

"Why do you refer to yourself as a nigger?" She sound crazy as hell when she say it.

"Don't change the subject, it's just like sayin' homie, potna, ace, shorty, bruh, so what we doin'?"

"Either way if your parents wanted you to be called any of those I'm sure they would have named you accordingly. Dena brought over some movies we were going to watch. She said I had to see these they were classics." He ask the titles.

"Menace to Society, Boys n' Da Hood, New Jack City and Colors. They all sound funny to me, have you seen them?"

"Of course! I'm surprised you haven't. You're probably the only black person that hasn't."

"My parents didn't allow me to watch TV. The only time I did watch was at the Center, a couple videos they showed during camp. Other than that, I've never really watched TV."

"Damn! I practically grew up off TV but I rarely watch it now. Anyway, here or in there?"

"Here for now, my stomachs growling lik..."

"What the hell you mean? You hungry? It's almost eleven in the morning you still haven't eatin' anything? Hold up!" He storms into the room I don't know what the big deal is. When he comes back he wants to know what I want to eat and if I want to go out to eat. I tell him I want to stay in and get room service so he orders. Not long after they bring in all kinds of food. We eat in silence, every now and then I look up and he's staring at me. They come to get the carts shortly after we're finish.

"Look Jasmine, my bad spazzin' out on you like that. You have to understand, the thought of you being hungry or needing anything pisses me off. There's no reason for it. Just eat and if you need anything let me know or get it."

"Okay, I can do that if you do something for me." If I do it or not she better. I ask her what.

"Come on, let's watch the movies." I put in the movie and watch as he sits back on the end of the bed. I close the curtains making it dark in the room then turn the air to sixty degrees. I get back up top pulling the sheets back waving him over.

"Before you get in, lose the pants and both shirts!" He starts to laugh and shake his head no.

"You said you would do something for me."

"You trippin' but remember, it's not goin' down." I laugh my ass in the bed, she move like she wants me to put my head on her chest.

"Come on Jasmine, I told you what was up."

"Just lay down, I know this will get you to sleep so try it. What's the worst that can happen?"

"I know what can get me to sleep and the worst that can happen already." I move over to him and squeeze his head into my chest as he suddenly pulls my leg forward catching me by surprise. I'm wrapped around him the entire movie and don't want to move a single muscle. I change the channel and look down to see if he's awake and to my surprise he's not. Hours pass and I'm awakened by someone knocking on the door, Tristan's still sleep. I ease out the bed to go answer and it's Dena.

"What's up Jas? Where Cargo at?" I smile at her.

"He's sleep. What's going on, you need me to wake him?"

"He sleep? That's a first. What you up too?"

"Lying down. I was asleep until you knocked on the door." She looked around then pulled me by the shoulders closer to her.

"Tell me you two didn't...I mean ya'll weren't—"

"No Dena, we didn't have sex and we were not about to have sex. We both feel asleep that's all."

"Okay. I'll stop by later Jas." I close the door and go back in, Tristan's still asleep. Once I get close to the bed he moves the sheets back and I climb in. We get back into position and I fell him nuzzle his head into me and inhale deeply. I try not to laugh too hard at the way he sighs after he exhales pulling me closer to him.

By the time I get up I look and I'm still wrapped up in Jasmine. I guess I was looking too hard and for too long because she slowly starts to come to.

"Damn shorty, you straight put a nigga to sleep on some ol' caked up type shit." I can't help but laugh with him as I unwrap myself from around him. I can barely pull my leg away before he stops me pulling me closer to him again.

"Chill out, let me post up here for a minute. A nigga may have found his dream crib." Slowly opening my eyes I feel so rested I don't want to move. Leaning over Tristan's head I see the alarm clock, it's seven at night. Slowly I meticulously run my fingers down his shoulder blade stopping at where he's holding my leg.

As I head back to where I started I can feel him smile into my chest and groan as if he's saying no. I call for him a couple times softly as I run my fingers behind his ear to the top of his head. I know he's awake, I know how it feels when you're sleeping and think something is crawling on you. He squeezes me tightly lifting his eyes to mine.

"Come on shorty. You wanted me to get some sleep now you don't, which one is it?"

"It's after seven, we both need to eat."

"Seven? Jasmine you got a nigga good Ma'. As much as I wanna stay right here I'm gon' get up. Damn shorty!" I pull her in wanting to bury myself into her permanently. She starts to laugh, I let her go and climb out the bed pickin' up my shit.

"Hurry up Ma'. We goin' out to eat, I think we stayed in here long enough. I need to get my head right real quick, I'll be back in about an hour. You and Dena be ready to go eat." I jump on the elevator and get in my room, a quick call downstairs to the concierge, I hear her knock on the door. After she gives me some courtesy head service I jump in the shower.

"Jas, while you two were up there cuddling I been out working. Have fun at dinner with Cargo boo, I'm in Manhattan and I think I found me a new friend. Don't wait up and you damn sho' bet not do what I plan on doin'!" I can't believe she hung up on me, she doesn't have to worry about me doing anything she plans on doing. I hear Tristan calling for me so I join him and we go to dinner.

I'm laughin' so hard at my damn self once I roll over and see the clock. She must be hypnotizin' a nigga, I don't even remember when I fell asleep. It's quarter to eight in the morning. I get her up and head out, I make it back just as room service is bringin' up the breakfast I ordered. I call Dena to bring her ass over to see what happened to her last night.

"I gotta roll so I'll see you Jasmine in a week and Dena I'll see you when you get back from LA." I watch as he heads to the door.

"Jasmine, don't forget what I said about callin' a nigga."

"Right!" He stops and closes the door walking back into the room.

"Come here real quick Jasmine." I get up off the couch as Dena laughs and wags her index finger at me.

"That didn't sound too convincing, don't have a nigga missing you and worried. What, I ain't good enough for you to call but you can call Dena?"

"No Tristan, I'll call you." He leans down and puts me into a big bear hug, I can't stop from laughing even after he lets me go.

"Good. Now that I have yo' word be safe, stay out the hood and I'll see you when I get home." Tristan pecks my cheek, walks to the door again and looks back at Dena.

"Good lookin' Dena, I got you fosho now!" He closes the door and Dena is jumping around with her arms extended in the air.

"What are you so happy about?"

"While you were playing house I told you I been working. I found a hot spot not far from Cargo club that I went to the other night. Last night I met up with the owner of the building. He said he needed to speak with Cargo, I told Cargo about it when he called me this morning. Well it sound like I'm about to have a new salon in the big apple boo boo!"

12 WISDOM

"Dena who am I going to talk too if you're going to be gone for an entire month?" I can't help but want to cry, my worse fear of being alone with no one is finally setting in.

"Stop that Jas! Don't cry like I'm not coming back. Cargo will be back in less than three days. I'm sure when he gets back you gon' forget all about me being out in LA."

"How can I forget? You and Tristan are the only two people I can call friends. Now both of you are leaving me."

"First of all Jas, I'm too old to be yo' damn friend! We family and you can call me any time you want. So fix your face, have a good day at school and stop thinking everyone is leaving you. It's not like I can take you with me, Cargo would be too mad if you ditched school. Now go ahead before you're late."

I spend the next three days moping around alone, even Ms. Janine's not around to keep me company. The only things that kept me busy was my books, training and a driver's ed course I signed up for. I spoke with Tristan once and avoided his calls because I didn't want to miss him or ask him to come back. I've only been going to the house in the wee hours of the morning to get a couple hours of sleep. I don't know what time he'll be arriving, I stayed up as long as I could waiting on him. At midnight I turned off the TV and went to bed thinking maybe he would stay in the city.

As soon as I touch down in the Lou I shoot out to the house to check on Jasmine. I been calling like crazy and she's not answering. I should've pushed back Janine vacation so I could've sent her over to check on her. Terry and Dena are both out of town and I wouldn't dare send anybody else over to my spot. I go in and head straight to her room, I check around and decide to check the nursery, it's the last place to look.

I go in and don't know why I didn't check here first. I back out jump in the shower and go back in the room. I pull her into my arms and smile for hours because she's still here safe and sound.

"Morning hard head." I thought I was dreaming, I felt Tristan move my hair and I knew I was awake.

"Morning. I thought you were going to stay in the city."

"Nope! You ready to go to breakfast?" She tries to roll over I hold her in place.

"It's Saturday, I want to sleep in. I'm tired."

"You need to get up I'm hungry and I can hear that you are as well so let's go." We stopped at Ihop, I told Tristan I wanted to try it, he acted like he couldn't believe I had never been before. I ate almost everything they had on the menu, he was a good sport and helped me. We even stopped at a carnival, it reminded me of the time I spent in Disney World. By the end of the night I was exhausted, Tristan must've carried me in. I woke up the next morning in my bed and he was nowhere to be found.

When he did show up he told me to get dressed because we were going to a house party. We drove for an hour out towards Kansas City, when he turned off I could see nothing but hundreds of cows. There was a big three story house not far from where the cows were, he pulled down the long road and stopped in front of the house. It didn't look like a place for a house party, but I've never been to one so I didn't know what to expect.

I asked who's house it was he said I'll see and guided me inside. There were people everywhere who all seemed shocked for a second then they began to speak to Tristan. He told them all that he would be right back without breaking his stride. Before he turned a corner he asked if I was ready. I didn't know what I should be ready for.

He laughed and walked into the kitchen, I saw Mrs. Terry and Dena, I wanted to go over and speak. Tristan held my hand tighter and moved to a small table where three women sat. He leaned over and kissed and hugged all three of the women and came back to my side.

"Jasmine, this is my grandmother Loraine, my great grandmother Ma' Bell, and my great great grandmother Ma' Earlean. Ladies this is Jasmine." I can't believe it. Here sits three generations of his family and all of them seem so loving. I feel the tears break free from my eyes and I hug all of them like they're mine. When I'm finished Ma' Bell sends Tristan out the room, he pulls a chair over for me, kisses my hair and leaves.

"Baby we know what those tears are all about. You better believe we consider you family already. We been hearing about you for years and I'm happy baby that you're finally here," Ma' Bell said. Mrs. Terry came over and held me in her arms, I feel at peace instantly.

"Listen suga', I'm a huned an eighf yeazs blessed, I wuz forced inchu slavery so I'z knowz what cha gone chru. When my baby came for my advice after he shaw youz sleeping in dat place I made him take me to Terry! I wanted to find doze suckas and give dem a taste of der own medicine. Baby I knowz what chu goin' chru right now. You safe and don't eva forget dat!" Ma' Earlean said. I had no idea she was one hundred and eight years old, she looks no day over sixty. She stood up and everyone in the house seemed to get quiet. She walked out the room and we all followed.

I met everyone in Tristan's family and they all welcomed me to be a part of it. I felt the love in the room and could see it in all of their faces. After we ate I headed out to the yard, I can't cry again. Seeing their family reminds me so much of my parents and what my life should've been like. The more I think about them the faster my tears stream.

"What's wrong Jasmine? They givin' you a hard time? Just let me know who and I'll go take care of it." As I wrap my arms around her shoulders she turns and buries her head into my chest. Once she stops crying I help her clean her face and we head back in to enjoy the party.

*   *   *

The Winter Wonder Dance was in full effect by the time we arrived and I was too happy with the dress Jasmine chose. Looking around the room all I can see is butt naked ho's ready to be unleashed in the streets. Man I hope I never have a daughter, hell, I'm glad I don't have a sister. By the looks of what these chicks have on there is no way in hell I would let either of mine out like this. I couldn't help but laugh because by the look on Jasmine's face she's thinking the same thing.

"You want to take pictures?" I smile at the thought of taking pictures with Tristan. Less than an hour into the dance I'm already annoyed waiting in line for pictures. Even though these females have dates of their own they act like they can't take their eyes off mine. After we took our pictures Sue and Claire had the nerve to come over and ask Tristan to take one with the two of them.

I wanted to give the two of them a good curse. Tristan found it amusing and didn't bother to answer them. All night it seemed like every time I looked up Brandon was looking over at me. Tristan had been asking me to dance, I told him I'd rather watch. He must've grown tired of watching with me because he pulled me onto the floor.

"Tristan, I can't dance." I had to tell him before we looked like complete idiots. It's bad enough we have constant eyes on us, I don't want the entire school laughing at me.

"It's cool I got you. Besides, I'm happy you not like these gals in here. I figure the least I can do is dance with you seeing it's my fault we were running late." The second I saw Jasmine come into the living room I turned right back around and jumped in the shower. I needed to beat some shit out before I would be able to resist.

Even with her being covered her girls are holding on to her strapless dress for dear life. The sage color brings out her eyes, plus it's fitted around her waist and flows to the floor. I could take my hands and easily use my index and thumb to determine her waist size, I'd probably still need to overlap them if I did. She killing every chick in here, her hair and makeup is on point.

"Why did you have to take another shower anyway? You looked exceptional as always to me." Exceptional is the only word I can think of at the moment to describe Tristan. I'm sure if I took a poll from all the girls in school they could come up with all types of words to describe him.

"Stop playin', you know why I had to take a shower. The same reason I been takin' a cold shower every time I wake up with you in my arms. You look gorgeous Jasmine." Tristan pulled me into his arms as we continued to sway back and forth.

"So who is ol' boy that won't stop lookin' at a nigga over there?" I look around slowly to see who Tristan is talking about.

"Oh, that's Brandon. He's the star quarterback." No wonder the nigga look like he lost the game. I guess it's too bad I intercepted his ass and I don't plan on fumblin'. The nigga must've seen Jasmine look over at him, I can see him coming our way.

"Excuse me. I was wondering if I could have a dance with Jasmine. If that's okay with you Jasmine."

"Naw! Not tonight homie. Come back in about two hundred years and see if you can then." I can feel Jasmine giggle as she put her head into my neck.

"You don't have to be like that man. It's a dance, at least let Jasmine decide."

"No thank you Brandon. Maybe in four hundred years you can pry me out of this man's arms." I never looked at Brandon, I can feel him leave. I looked up at Tristan and he was on the verge of having a laughing fit. It seemed like Brandon started something, everyone decided it was their turn to give it a shot. Several females came over after Sue and Claire. I told Tristan I was going to the ladies room just to get a moment to get my head together.

As soon as Jasmine stepped away these chicks came like I was giving away free weaves. I didn't say shit to them and I'm starting to think maybe I should've goin' off on a couple. These chicks didn't even hear my voice and was offering the pussy up to me. I walked out into the hall to wait on Jasmine.

"Hey you!" I turn around and see the nigga Brandon and three of his boys walking down towards me. Damn, I don't want to go to jail for killing these lil nigga's tonight. I watched as they came closer sealing their fate.

"I just want to know why ya'll old nigga's always try and come thru and snatch up our gals. Don't you nigga's have better shit to do then hangout at high school? I bet yo' old ass didn't even make it to high school or hell, dropped out if you did." They all started laughing at what Brandon said. I didn't say a word, I chuckled and stared all the dumb ass nigga's down.

"What the fuck so funny nigga? We ain't here to tell you no fucking jokes. You better be lucky we don't whoop yo' ass and drag you the fuck up out of here." I watched as the big black nigga puffed up and stepped forward like I was supposed to be scared.

"Man this nigga so scared he don't even know how to talk," the taller skinny nigga said.

"He was talkin' mad shit when he was with my soon to be girl," Brandon said.

"Look, you bitch ass nigga's betta go on back in the dance before I send some shit to ya'll bodies that make ya'll dance involuntarily!"

"Nigga my uncle wil—" A heavy set white lady came around the corner and asked why we were in the hall cutting Brandon off. They turned and walked away, the lady looked at me waiting on me to answer. I watched as Jasmine came around the corner, we walked back inside the dance.

I was ready to get out of here, I told Dena that these heels would bother my feet. Being five inches taller did have its advantages though, looking at Tristan up close was worth it. After I told him I was ready to go he asked if I wanted to go to all these after parties and hangout places. I should've known these sneaky girls would invite him.

"You can go if you want I'm ready for bed, they invited you not me." I had to laugh at the thought of leaving her in the house while I chilled with those lame ass people. Hell I own my own damn clubs I could chill there if I wanted to.

"I'm good, we can go back to the house." When we made it to the parking lot I put Jasmine in the car because I noticed Brandon and a couple other nigga's heading over. I walked around to the driver side and opened the back door waiting on them to make a move.

"There that nigga go right there Unk, I told you he had to be the nigga pushin' the Jag." They stop and I close the door laughing shakin' my head at how much of a bitch Brandon is.

"Damn lil nigga, you den ran and got yo' uncle on me. That's some weak ass shit!" Charlie laughs and comes over to dab me off.

"What's up Cargo? I was stoppin' by to give my nephew here some change to kick it wit' tonight. He come talkin' about a nigga sellin' woof tickets and shi—man hold up!" Charlie walks back over to his nephew and his friends, they all leave except for Brandon. I see Twin and Mike roll up and park two cars down and walk towards me.

"What the fuck? I didn't know this was a hood reunion out at this bitch!" Mike says as we all start laughing. Charlie and Brandon walk back over to join us. Brandon looks like he's seen a ghost.

"Damn what's up Charlie? I know you didn't call Cargo about some young nigga fuckin' wit' yo' peoples," Twin said.

"I guess this nigga thought we was gon' let some shit go down and just watch." We all laugh harder, Brandon looks away to his boys who are waiting on him at the other end of the parking lot.

"Naw man, this dumb ass boy was talkin' 'bout Cargo," Charlie explained, they all looked at me then at Brandon and busted out laughing.

"So hold up Cargo, did this nigga come at you like he said he did?" Twin said as they all looked at me. I looked at Brandon, he dropped his head not meetin' my eyes.

"What that nigga say he said?" I wanted to know what the nigga was feedin' his uncle.

"Big boy shit, like he was about to smack you but you flashed a burner and the teacher walked out before he took it from you." We all laughed at the thought of that being said. I knew the nigga Twin was exaggerating but the shit was still funny.

"Come on Twin, don't make this shit worse. Look Cargo, this nigga didn't mean no harm and he damn sho' didn't know who he was talkin' too no matter what the fuck he said. Speak up nigga!" Charlie pushed Brandon forward into the middle of the circle we unintentionally had formed.

"I didn't know who you were Cargo Sir. I was out of line for even comin' at yo——" I heard enough and Jasmine's still in the car waitin', they can't see thru the tent so I need to wrap this shit up.

"Look here, I'm out! Charlie yo' nephew gon' get you in some shit, you two nigga's too running to save his ass." I stand up from off the side of the car and head to the door, Charlie ask if we straight.

"Hell yeah nigga! Ya'll stay up, I'm out." I jump in and pull off, Jasmine didn't say a word, I look over and she knocked out.

13 SLOTH

"You know Tristan, I wanted to ask you something weeks ago. I was debating on talking to you about it in New York." I'm all ears, I ask her to talk to me.

"Well you helped me out a lot, you let me win at the gym, we've been on countless dates and you took me to the dance. I asked Dena if we would be consider a couple or dating."

"What did Dena say?"

"After she finished laughing she said it sounded like we were, the same as I thought. Then it hit me that we couldn't be dating and I'm more like a community outreach project for you. Either way it doesn't matter what she thinks, the only thing that matters is what you think." I felt him look over at the side of my head, I didn't want to look and see his reaction. He tapped my shoulder so I looked over he was turned staring straight at me.

"Why you say that?"

"I've never had a boyfriend but in my mind if I did he wouldn't be involved with anyone else. So I figure you're doing all this because you felt bad for me and we're from the same community. Hence community outreach project."

"I ain't gon' stunt I do like you. I feel bad for a lot of people in the hood but I didn't feel bad for you. I feel bad for that damn Ruby and bitch nigga Worm, that's why they still breathing. I told you already I could show you better than I could tell you."

"Well to me we're dating. I know you said I'm not ready and I'm not saying I'm ready to have sex because I think I should wait until I'm married. But I'm ready to date. I asked Dr. Cooper about it, she said it's normal at my age to want to date." Tristan found that entertaining.

I waited as he took his last shot and everyone cheered as the ball went in the hoop. The Dave and Buster worker explained which prizes to choose from, I didn't want anything. Tristan decided to let the watching kids pick something and ended up paying for a couple things for them. We didn't walk far, just far enough to be sort of alone, we sat at a table.

"So you talking to your psychiatrist about me?"

"Not really." I ask her again because she looked down like she wasn't sure about her answer.

"I told her what you said, about me not being ready. She wanted to know how old you were and I told her twenty. She said maybe you're not ready to be in a relationship and it's normal."

"Well if it's that simple I'm not ready." I feel my heart sink into the pits of the underworld. I need to leave before I cry right in the middle of this place for all to see.

"Jasmine, don't take it the wrong way. All I'm saying is, I don't think you know what a relationship is. I think you see it as someone goin' upside yo' head whenever they feel the need. If we dated and that's what you want I couldn't give it to you, that ain't how I roll."

"I don't think that but I do think your saying that because you don't want to give up your philandering ways." Tristan's eyes go wide and he pulls his lips to the side watching me.

"Come on shorty, what you really tryin' to say?"

"I'm saying we're dating so it's time to show me!" I know what she's asking me I still need to hear it so I tell her to make it clear.

"Like I said, I'm not ready to have sex but I don't want you to have sex because we're dating." I think I really shocked him with my admission this time.

"That's it? Check, take this." I pull out my phone and give it to her.

"Don't you need your phone." Tristan places three more phones on the table.

"I have my phones. That's sort of my black book. You know where I store all my jumpoff numbers and shit." I tell her to check it out, she ask why they have two names.

"None of them know my real name, the other name is the name I told them. The two cities is where there from and where I told them I'm from." She looks for a second then drops the phone into the glass of water on the table. She ask what are the other phones for.

"One for you, and the other for my family and business."

"By business you mean drug stuff?" She always keep it on the up and up wit' a nigga.

"Naw, I don't talk about anything illegal over the phone." Tristan asks if

I'm ready to go I agree so we head back to the house. Before we go to sleep I can't help but ask.

"So what do you think about what I said Tristan?" He smiles into my chest as we laid down together.

"I like the way you say my name. You make it sound like I'm a white nigga or something." I pull her into me tighter as she laughs.

"Like I said, I can show you better than I can tell you." I close my eyes and give Tristan a tight squeeze.

The holidays were all a blur to me. Tristan took me to all his families gatherings, I've never experienced anything like it. When my parents were alive we never spent the holidays with family, it was always with my mother and fathers co-workers. Attorneys and doctors all talking about work, I would play with the other children.

Chillin' in the office at my new club in the county, Meechie come in and tell me it's two cops wanting to speak with me. I ask the nigga why, he say he don't know. I ask the nigga if they asked for me by name, he say they wanted to speak wit' the owner.

"Man the owner not here! Tell dem nigga's to call the owner if they want to speak with the owner."

"I did, they said if they didn't speak with someone in charge they would shut down the club until they do."

"Rose Man!" This nigga start buggin' up laughin'.

"I guess the Rose Man is in charge of the roses huh. Hell, if they don't want to speak wit' him, I'll get Dj Spike and Macho the cook." I wait while he goes back and talk to them, Meechie comes back clownin' because the nigga's were pissed. I head out the backdoor talking to Big Hen before they have a chance to come back.

"Aye, hold up!" I see these two clown ass nigga's, Pig Brown and Pig Franklin coming towards us.

"So you do speak English huh lil nigga," Pig Franklin says.

"Sumus deprenditur?" I ask them in Latin if we are under arrest, they both laugh. We don't see the shit funny so we just stare at the nigga's.

"Nigga please, cut the act, we just heard yo' ass speaking English so I know you understand and can speak it," Pig Franklin says.

"It's been a couple years nigga, I'm surprised you still alive," Pig Brown says.

"Hell, I'm shocked the nigga been laying low and not once been brought in the station. Hell, I should have known something was up when Chief Jeffery was lookin' out for his ass," Pig Franklin says.

"My name is Brandon Hen, I'm a bondsman and work a——" Big Hen starts to explain to them.

"Nigga shut yo' black, fat, pork skin smellin' ass up. We already heard that bullshit before. Fuck you and what you do nigga," Pig Brown says walking towards Big Hen.

"Look nigga, we here to rap wit' you about security for this here spot you got poppin'——" Big Hen burst out laughing cutting Pig Franklin off.

"Damn nigga, these two morons act like I haven't told them that I already have that job. I'm too fucking big for them not to see me standing here. This nigga just gon' try and take my fuckin' job in my got damn face. Ain't this a bitch," Big Hen says lookin' at me like the two pigs not even standing there. Pig Brown is hot, he raises up a big ass flashlight as Big Hen prepares for what he's about to do. Four Excursions pull up but no one gets out. The window on the third truck opens a little.

"Aye youngin', come holla at me for a second," I hear from the window. Pig Brown tells us not to move and to get on the ground.

"Nigga it's wet as a bitch out here! If we not under arrest why the fuck would we get on the got damn ground?" Big Hen says, Pig Brown pulls his heat out pointing at us as both their phones ring like before. Whoever on the other end is yelling so loud Pig Franklin pulls the phone back then lowers the volume. Pig Brown is furious still pointing his burner at us.

"Sir. I understand Sir. It's away Sir." Pig Franklin reaches over and lowers Pig Browns hand that's holding the pistol. Pig Brown pulls the phone away putting his heat back in the holster then puts the phone back to his ear.

"It's away Sir." They both turn and leave without saying another word. I walk over to the truck and hop in as Big Hen heads back inside the club.

"What's good fam? It's about time yo' ass came out of hiding." Bateador laughs and daps me off.

"Yeah man, good lookin' on that pull. I knew you two could be counted on." I knew the nigga was talking about the Judge me and Ghost got at.

"I don't know what you mean big dog. I still don't understand how that shit went down though." He turn up the radio and we mob out. We head upstairs and after he knocks Pandillero opens the door and we speak. We all jump back on the elevator and go on the roof.

"Damn it's good seeing you two nigga's. I should've known ya'll would pull thru. 1 can't stunt, for a minute there 1 didn't know what the deal was and Ghost wasn't making shit any better. 1 thought that mufucka was gon' go postal around this bitch." We all laugh and take a seat.

"Look youngin', don't worry about finding anyone or trying to take care of who did the shit." 1 can't believe what Pandillero said.

"So ya'll just gon' let the nigga breath after they shot ya'll the fuck up? Where the fuck is Treasure at anyway? You just gon' let a nigga walk and he shot yo' wife?" 1 was lost and 1 don't understand what the fuck they're laughing at.

"Calm down lil nigga," Bateador says. 1 ask him what happened.

"Remember 1 told you about not going thru the bullshit 1 did finding the right one?" 1 nod at Pandillero not knowing what that has to do with shit we're talking about.

"Hear me out. 1 put T thru more than enough shit over the years and to be honest, 1 don't know how the fuck 1 didn't see what 1 was doing. 1 know you've heard the saying, 'There's nothing like a woman scorned', right. Well take it from me, that shit don't even explain the jist of it." They both laugh again.

"So what happened man? Tell me the deal without all the riddles and shit."

"T!" Pandillero says then sits back, Bateador chuckles.

"Treasure what man, come on tell me what's the deal."

"Treasure shot us nigga," Bateador says, 1 fall back into the chair really not understanding what the fuck is going on. We sit in silence, 1 sit back up.

"So why would Treasure shoot you two?" Pandillero looks out into the sky.

"You can only put someone thru so much bullshit before they snap man. That's my wife and I love her more than I love myself and that's on errthing I know. Truth is, I wasn't taking care of my wife like I should have been. She needed me more than I ever thought she did and I was too blind to see it." Pandillero stands up and walks to the rail.

"Look Cargo, this a family thing. Not saying you're not family because you are. If not you damn sure wouldn't be hearing any of this right now," Bateador says, Pandillero walks back over.

"So with that being said let the shit go. I'm gon' holla at Ghost myself because if anything happens to my wife I'll see to it that everybody pays the price."

"I understand where you coming from Pandillero. I just don't understand why she would do some shit like that. I mean what the fuck is up with that? I couldn't imagine my girl putting rounds in me and my brother and still protecting her." They both laugh.

"That's because you ain't found the one yet lil nigga," Pandillero says.

"Treasure not my wife but I know fosho if something happen to her it's going down! Trust and believe, if Sammy did some shit like that, if I survived I wouldn't have it any other way. Like he said, you find the one you'll know what we talking about."

"You nigga's crazy as fuck but hell, it's ya'll call so it is what it is. Just so you nigga's know that funeral was off the fucking chain packed. Ya'll know they had it at that big ass symphony place off Grand. That shit was jammed packed wit' mufuckas. But get this. You nigga's had a mix tape playin' in the background. The shit wasn't funny at the time but errtime I look at the damn gift bag with the cd, I can't help but laugh and play the shit." We all laugh hard at the thought.

"Man the Reverend said about two minutes worth of shit and shut the fuck up. After that, errbody was going up telling how they met ya'll nigga's and all the shit ya'll did helping them. That was the realist fuckin' funeral I ever been to in my life. I thought the Reverend was gon' preach and tell a bunch of bullshit and lies but he didn't."

"Nigga you crazy for that shit. My mom's know the deal, she damn sure know I'm no fucking Saint by any means. I'm glad you found the shit amusing though nigga," Pandillero says as we continue to laugh.

"Come on nigga before we have to go looking for T ass." I stop laughing and look at the nigga.

"She here?" They continue laughing as we make it back down to his spot. Bateador goes down the hall as we step inside Pandillero spot. We walk in and he calls for Treasure but I feel something poke me in my back.

"Don't move!" I turn around anyway and damn near fall back.

"Damn Treasure, what the hell wrong with yo' eyes girl?" Pandillero laughs and walks over to her huggin' her, she mugs me and pulls her top lip to the side.

"That's all you have to say Cargo? What's wrong with my damn eyes? Ain't shit wrong with my eyes bastard! What's wrong with yo' face?" I can't help but laugh at her nasty attitude.

"Chill out T, you know damn well he just fuckin' with you," Pandillero tells her and walks into the kitchen. I hug her and she hugs me back then pushes away from me.

"Don't be tryin' to fill me up lil nasty!" I laugh as Pandillero looks over at me. I put my hands up and join them in the kitchen.

"It's good seeing you too Treasure. What's with all the attitude? You ain't ever came at me like this before. I thought you loved me." We all laugh again.

"I'm sure Treasure does love you nigga. I just tolerate you becau—" Pandillero kisses her stopping her from talking. I can't understand why she's speaking in third person or what she was about to say. I head into the living room and flip on the TV, Pandillero comes in and Treasure says goodnight going in the back.

"See what I mean?"

"Hell naw Pandillero, I don't see what you mean. What's wrong with Treasure, why she acting like that?"

"You know how you get into character when you out doing what you do?" I nod at him.

"Well when you in that zone that's a whole other personality that you take on. You following?" I shake my head yes.

"T sort of does the same thing but she doesn't put on a costume when she does. That person in there she calls Taz and that's the one that shot us." He leans back in his chair chuggin' his water back.

"So you saying she has multiple personalities? That's why she said the shit about Treasure and her tolerating me?" He chuckles and I grab the water he sat down for me and think about what he said. We watch TV for a second and shoot the breeze before I decide to bounce out. Before I jump in with Big Hen, Bateador come out the building telling me to hold up.

"Look Cargo, meet me at the Center tomorrow, I need to holla at you and Ghost." I tell him okay and roll out.

14 ONE

"Tristan, guess what?" I can't help but laugh at how excited Jasmine is coming in the room.

"I got accepted at SLU!" I'm bouncing up and down excited that I was accepted close by. Tristan hugs me but doesn't seem as happy as I thought he would be, I ask him what's up.

"I'm happy for you but I thought you wanted to go overseas to that school in Japan." I can always tell what Jasmine feeling, her facial expressions can be read by a blind man.

"I did but..I thought..I mean it's expensive and I can make it happen if I go to SLU, that's all." Tristan sounds like he's disappointed that I'm staying and not moving across the world.

"Stop playin' Jasmine, I know you didn't do all that work on getting those scholarships so you won't go over there. If it's the money you're worried about then you can stop worrying, I'm sure I can afford it. So tell me what's the real reason why you want to go to SLU all of a sudden?" Jasmine tries to walkout the room but I pull her into my arms as tears roll down her face. I walk her over and sit her on the desk and stand in front of her dabbing her eyes with tissue.

"I don't want to leave you Tristan. That's the reason I don't want to go across the world. I love you and don't want to leave you here." I look up at Tristan and see his big smile then he starts to laugh and hugs me.

"Jasmine, you crazy as hell you know that?" I bite the side of her neck and she's a wreck laughing begging me to stop.

"You need to live your life sweetheart. Don't let me hold you back from doing what you want to do."

"You're not holding me back. But I understand." I slide down off the desk and leave out of Tristan's room.

A little over two weeks before I graduate I'm sitting in the middle of the bed waiting on him to come in. He took off after our last talk and told me to call him but I told him I wouldn't. That was over a month ago. The whole time he's been gone all I do is worry about him not coming back.

Dena's busy getting her salon together in New York so she's only been by once since he's been away. When I hear the alarm chirp, I jump off the bed and run downstairs. As I make it to the bottom of the steps Tristan is there smiling at me. I can't help but jump into his arms laughing because I'm so happy to see him.

"I guess you missed me huh?"

"Of course I missed you crazy."

"If you missed me that much you should've called me." I carry her up to the room and sit her on the bed. She won't let me go, instead she pulls me onto the bed with her while she laughs.

"I've been tremendously worried about you, I hope you never leave for that long again." I roll over away from her and she sits on top of me with her arms crossed pouting. I pull her chin down easing her pout away as she giggles.

"I've been worried about yo' fine ass too." She laughs and falls into my neck with her hands covering her face.

"You call me crazy." Tristan puts his arms around me and holds me tighter.

After a second I can feel my insides warm up, Tristan starts to slowly caress the dip in my back. Before I know it I peck his neck and he stops for an instant then continues. He squeezes me tighter then let's go. I sit up and look at him as he opens his eyes with a smoldering look on his face.

"I want to kiss you Tristan." He smiles and flips me over onto my back. I put my arms around his neck as he presses his lips to mine forcing me to close my eyes. He moves to position himself between my legs, I put my feet on the back of his thighs.

'You better stop now nigga! If not you bound to do some shit you may just regret.' I thought as I pulled Jasmine lip into my mouth sampling her sweet taste. Her bodies starting to slowly move up and down, I press down more to hold her still. Her moans are becoming louder, the second her mouth opened I eased my tongue inside.

'Please don't stop! You taste so good Tristan.' I wanted to tell him what I was thinking but I thought if I did he would most defiantly stop. When his tongue went in my mouth all I wanted to do was swallow it. It's like he's checking my teeth with his tongue and it's so freaking amazing, I reciprocate but after a couple seconds he groans and takes back over. After I got the hang of it we went back and forth letting each other have control, I couldn't believe how good it felt. Tristan was trying to pull away but I didn't want it to be over so I held on. I hear him chuckle so I open my eyes as he pecks my lips a couple times smiling down at me.

"You getting mannish you know that right?" I can't believe he said that to me. I pull my hands down covering my face as he laughs moving my hands away.

"I'm sorry I didn't mea—"

"It's all good Jasmine. I been wanting to kiss the women I love for a long time now." I'm so happy to hear Tristan say he loves me that my eyes start to leak. Tristan kisses them both then all over my face and neck causing me to laugh.

"I love you too Tristan."

"You love me enough to chill out and let me jump in the shower so I can get in the bed with you? I need some sleep like crazy and I know you can help me out with that. I'm glad you out of school for the next two days, I need some sleep bad."

"I'll be right here waiting on you to get out. You want anything to eat or drink?" Tristan smiles and says no. He leans back down and sucked my lip back in his mouth then released it and sits up. As he heads out the room I can't help but roll over clutching the pillow feeling all bubbly inside.

By Friday Tristan's phone is ringing off the hook. Whoever is calling has him worried but he won't tell me what's going on. He spends all weekend on the phone or the computer leaving out the room whenever I'm around. Sunday he tells me he has to make a run and he'll be back before I know it. I asked him to stay, of course he goes anyway.

While Tristan is away I hang out with Dena and spend as much time away from the house as I can. Since I'm practically out of school and Dena is working in her salon, I head to the riverfront. I never knew how horrible the parking was until I had to find somewhere to park. It took me almost thirty minutes to find a spot and it was all the way by the bars. I could've parked close to the water but I was scared the car would flip over on the incline. I was enjoying my time sitting out reading my book until a familiar face came in front of me.

"Damn Esta, look at you all grown up and shit!" Melvin sits down beside me and reaches for my hair. I move away and tell him not to touch me.

"Why you actin' like dat Esta? Come over here and give me a hug." I pull away and go to stand up but he grabs me holding me still. He smells just as filthy as he looks, I push off him more when he puts his tongue in my ear. While I struggle to get him off we both fall to the ground, he grabs my ankle and I jerk away. I scramble to my feet and take off running as Melvin chases behind me. I'm shocked that he's as fast as he is but I can hear him slowing down.

By the time I reach the car I don't see him, my hands are trembling so bad I can't get the key in. I'm crying so hard I put my head on the steering wheel trying to calm myself down. Melvin starts banging on the window so I start the car and pull off before he shatters it. I make it home so fast I don't know how I made it without getting stopped by the police. I jump out and run inside needing to clean the touch of Melvin off of me.

When I open the door Tristan is standing there talking to Ms. Janine. I burst into tears and run right past them both up to the room and slam the door. I can hear Tristan knocking on the door but I don't answer. I get into the shower with my clothes still on. By the time the water heats up I hear the door come open and Tristan is asking if he can come in.

"Baby what's wrong? What happened to you?" I don't answer, I sit down and bury my head into my knees and continue to cry. Tristan comes over and tries to turn the water off but I tell him to leave it on.

"Tell me something Jasmine? I can't make it right if you're not telling me what's up." I move her hair back and help her stand up, I almost laughed because she could barely get up at first. Her hair so long she was sitting on it and I guess didn't realize it. Her shirt and skirt are soaked leaving little to the imagination about how curvy she is.

"It's nothing Tristan, please just give me a second." I can't look at him until I wash off Melvin. He backs out the door as I take off my clothes and scrub my body.

While I'm waiting on Jasmine to finish up I have a million and one things running in my head. I'm glad Ghost cool but damn this shit has errbody and they mama calling me. When Jasmine comes out she crawls in the bed, I ask her to talk to me but she won't. After I get out the shower I join her and hold her while she sleeps.

After graduation Tristan throws me a big party at his club and it's filled with all his family. We have a great time. A couple days later he says he has to take another trip. By the time he comes back he looks exhausted but happy for some reason. The following week he tells me he wants to take me on a trip with him. When we arrive I feel like a new person the moment we step off the plane.

"I can't believe I'm in Africa." Tristan smiles and opens the door for me and slides in. Once we reach the Corinthia Hotel I'm still in shock that I'm actually here. The driver pulls off as they help us in. The room is beautiful and I can't stop from smiling, the smell on another hand is something you have to get used to.

"You tired?" I can tell she is, seem like she moving in slow motion around the room.

"A little I guess. I don't know why though, seem like I slept the entire way over here." I walk over and sit next to Tristan on the couch.

"It's natural baby. Go 'head and change, I'll get us something to eat. I need you to get your rest because I want you to meet a couple people in the morning." The second her head touches my chest she's knocked out. I wait a minute on her to get good and sleep before I leave to check on my people.

When I wake up Tristan is holding me in his arms staring into the ceiling. I don't think he's been to sleep for a second but he insist on getting a move on to meet with someone. We headed to a little shop and sat down waiting for his guest so we could have breakfast. Tristan stood up so I turned to see who he was looking at.

"About time you two made it. We were just about to go up to get ya'll," Tristan said as they walked over. The girl was really pretty and the guy was striking. The two of them together was intimidating looks wise to say the least.

"Jasmine this is Tanielle and Marcello. I would like for you two to meet Jasmine." Marcello shook my hand and Tanielle hugged me, I was surprised but I hugged her back. She's all smiles the entire time we ate breakfast. We talked so much I think the guys let us walk ahead of them on purpose. After stopping in a bead shop I had to pick her brain while we were alone.

"How long have you known Tristan?"

"Seem like forever. Cargo's like a brother to me." She turned and looked at me then started to laugh.

"Is that what you really wanted to ask me?" I burst out laughing.

"No, I wanted to know if you've been with my man for real." She laughed right along with me.

"Girl naw! Like I said he like a brother to me. We've never dated or anything else. Besides, I got a man." She turned around looking out the door.

"Do you live here or did Tristan bring you here to meet me or what's the deal?" Tanielle starts to laugh.

"Naw. I guess you can say I brought all of you here."

"Why you say that?"

"I was sort of fired and needed some time to think. Cargo came and checked on me twice, I didn't know though so I guess he brought you back to surprise me. I think he was surprised to see Marcello had beat him to the punch." All I could think of was her saying Tristan coming to check on her twice. No wonder he was so freaking tired when he came back.

"So what job did you get fired from?" She grabbed my arm leading me back out the store towards Tristan and Marcello. She hugged Marcello and looked over at Tristan as I walked over to him.

"Cargo, Jasmine wants to know what job I was fired from." They all started laughing, Marcello and Tanielle walked off towards the hotel. I can't believe Tanielle ass played me like that. Jasmine doesn't know what's going on but I don't want to get into it with her at the moment. We make it back in, change and relax as the sun falls.

"Come up here. Big Daddy wanna feel your fine, juicy, thick ass pressed against him." Tristan holds his arms open and I gladly mount him giggling as he tightens his embrace. Mesmerized by the angle of his face I kiss his chin, he lowers his eyes down on me.

"What was so funny about me asking Tanielle what job she was fired from? I thought she was upset about it but seeing her laugh it off has me wondering why she wanted you to tell me and not her."

"I'm sure she would rather tell you herself but she knows that I wouldn't want her to tell you without you hearing some stuff from me first." I try to sit up and see his face but he holds me in place.

"Does it have something to do with what you do?"

"You can say that."

"What do you do exactly Tristan? I've been wanting to know for a long time now."

"I'll tell you as long as you tell me what had you so worked up that day you came in the house." I really don't want to open that can of worms. Literally! I agree anyway.

"I own several night clubs, repair shops, I get most of my money from the land I own and leas—"

"Tristan, you know what I'm talking about. Are you going to tell me or act like I'm working for the DEA?" I chuckle and kiss her forehead, she always cuts straight to the point.

"Chill out. You sure you want to know? I mean if I tell you I can't ever let you go." I don't want him to let me go if he tells me or not. But if this guarantees he won't that's even better. I tell him yes. He pulls me up a bit more and kisses my ear making me laugh and heat up at the same time.

"You can say I'm in the shipping and handling business. I move large shipments of product of all kinds around." The sound of his whisper into my ear is doing something to my lower province. The movement of his hands down my lower back and slightly following the start of my bottom is causing me to lose focus.

"So how does it work?"

"Easy, it all depends on what I want. I'm not using real names only because like I said, I can only tell you about me."

"Okay continue." I give her a simple rundown of what I do.

"I don't know, sound like a bunch of trust and faith that everything goes accordingly."

"Baby please, I don't trust or have faith in none of them nigga's. I have people errwhere watchin'. But still, they watch and give me the scoop just for a couple dollars, it's all a win-win for me no matter how the shit turn out."

"You say all that like you're not at risk. What happens when you don't pay your connect?"

"Most of those nigga's don't know me for real."

"How's that possible? And why do you say 'most' of them?"

"Before my father was sent up we went to somebody funeral. It was people errwhere. I stayed in the limo the whole time watchin' my father talk to all these old school nigga's. Before we arrived my father told me to pay attention to everyone he shook hands with. I did. After he shook hands with them he threw up a sign to me on the slid.

When he got back in I showed him errthing I wrote down, we went over it and he told me that he told them that a pen pal would be in contact with them. That pen pal was me. I sent them all notes saying if they wanted to be my pen pal to send in an attorney to meet up with my father. My father let me know which ones sent one, I met up with the attorneys giving them a letter to the connects. It's been on a poppin' since then."

"So what about the others?"

"Yeah them. I see you following along huh? Anyway the connects I've personally met I really haven't. See I send word to 'em and if they agree to meet up with me I usually go in disguise, you remember you met Bridgett?"

"Yeah, she works out in LA right?"

"Yeah that's her, she taught me a few tricks. Whenever I want to meet up with them I use what she taught me. Sometimes I'm fat, ugly, old, you name it I can create it, if I need to I'll fly her out but I rarely have to. I go meet the nigga's and set the shit up."

"Is that all?" She asked like she was out of breath.

"I also kill for a living." I can feel her smile into my neck, I don't know if it's from me touching her and she didn't hear me or what. I ask if she heard what I said.

"Yeah I did. You say it like you're a hit man and not someone trying to protect his 'product' as you refer to it."

"I'm better than a 'hit man' as you call it Jasmine. So much that no one even tries to fuck with my product." She tries to sit up again I let her go, she pulls me up so we're face to face.

"You're serious?" He nods in agreement. I don't know whether to be scared for myself, for him, or turned on. The swelling in his boxers is pushing into me making me want to adjust my body, I ask him to explain. He moves his lips not far from mine.

"I kill people and get paid for it. I've killed who knows how many all over the place." I move back to read her face, oddly enough she doesn't look too fazed by what I told her.

"Is that the job Tanielle was fired from?" He chuckles and holds my waist.

"I can only tell you about me Jasmine. You can ask her if you want, maybe she'll tell you what job she was fired from, maybe she won't." I wonder if Dena knows any of this? Maybe not, I hope she doesn't.

"Is that what you were doing when you were away for so long?"

"Yes and no." She slaps my shoulder, I laugh at her impatience.

"Did you just hear anything I told you? Here you are hitting on me and shit." I lean in and kiss him holding his face in my hands, his left hand goes up my back while his right pulls me into him.

"I'm not afraid of you so just tell me and stop making me guess at what you mean."

"You know you taste good and you feel even better." She laughs I flip her onto her back.

"Tell me." I ask her what while I kiss her neck and grind into her. She tightens her legs around my waist giving me better access, she ask how many and why.

"I don't count baby. Probably about twenty one or so that go round. That was a big trip, not my biggest but we had some complications so I had to do a little more."

"You did all that for someone?" I'm trying not to claw his skin off but the rocking motion is making my panties feel wet.

"I did it for the pleasure of doing it, getting paid is a bonus. I offered to do it for free." I feel her body tense up, I stop sucking marks into her chest causing my dick to jump. 'What the fuck nigga?' this nigga yell at me, I try to shake him out of my mind and stop what's about to go down.

"Is this how you plan on living the rest of your life?" Tristan climbs off of me and sits on the end of the bed. I go over to him moving my legs around him hugging his back.

"What's done is done. But I meant what I said about loving you Tristan. I love you and I'm worried more than ever about you, heck I'm terrified for you now. I don't want to ever lose you but the way it sounds I think I need to reconsider." Tristan sighs then stands up heading to the terrace. I give him a minute then walk over in front of him pulling his face down to me.

"I love you Tristan, you're all I have and losing you is something I don't want to do. If this is how you plan on living your life I can't ask you to stop for me. I don't want to but I think I need to..I mean I.." Tears fall from Jasmine eyes, it's hard to see her cry over me and what I do. I kiss her and tell her I understand. I never thought I'd see the day I would even consider hanging up my coat for a woman. Holding Jasmine in my arms looking out into the African night has me thinking that it's time to do just that.

15 VIBRATIONAL ATTAINMENT

"**S**o are you excited to go to Koro tomorrow?" Tanielle asks me while we shop, or should I say pretend to shop. She's not picking anything out along with me, seems like we're both putting up a charade.

"How do you get fired from killing people?" I must have surprised her with my question, she turned around fast. Slowly a smile spreads across her face and she starts to laugh.

"You figured it out. I like that Jasmine."

"I didn't figure anything out, I just thought I'd throw it out there and see what you say." We both laughed moving on to another stand.

"I don't know how, that's why I came here to figure something's out."

"So what are you going to do now?" Tanielle looks up and blows out like she's tired.

"Like I said, I'm trying to figure something's out. All I plan on doing at the moment is spending as much time with my man as I can."

"Maybe I need to get lost for a couple weeks and figure out what I'm going to do next." I can feel the tears start to fill into my eyes, I look away when Tanielle comes in front of me.

"I don't want to get in your business but I hope you're not planning on leaving Cargo."

"I don't know what to do. I don't think I can ignore what he does. I want to because I love him but I don't know what I'll do if something happens to him. I think I need to learn how to make it in the world without depending on someone to take care of me."

"Here I thought my life was complicated. I'm the last person to even bring this up but have you told Cargo how you feel?"

"I can't even tell him that I want to take some time off of school." Tanielle steps back crossing her arms in front of her looking at me like I upset her.

"Why would you want to do that? School is something that should be number one in your life right now. Matter fact, you're about to tell Cargo right now!" She storms away towards Tristan and Marco. I walk almost run standing in front of her stopping her from going any further.

"Look, you have to understand I want to tell him I just don't want him to think I'm doing it because of him. School has bee—" She nods, I know it's because they're coming closer. I quickly ask her not to say anything. Tristan puts his arms around my waist and kisses my neck, I plead with Tanielle using my eyes.

"Let me holla at her for a second baby." I kiss Jasmine again and step around her.

"Come on Jasmine, let's wait for these two at the Mugran Restaurant," Marco says. He pulls her in saying something making her laugh then walks over to me heading towards the restaurant.

"Whatever you about to tell me Ghost let it go."

"I wasn't about to tell you anything Cargo, she was."

"Looked like you were trying to force her to tell me something though. Ghost, don't mess this up for me, I'm doing a damn good job of that all by myself."

"I can't believe I fell for all that bullshit you were spitting Cargo! What was it you were saying? I remember you said, 'I plan on marrying her Ghost on errthing I do!' and 'I love that girl more than I love to breathe, you don't find a love like that anywhere,' what happened to all that?" I laugh at how crazy Tanielle is trying to make her voice sound like mine.

"All that's true and that's exactly how I feel." I put my arm around her shoulder walking her back.

"Why you just sitting back letting her get away then Cargo? I mean if you feel all that for her, how can you let her go?"

"You getting on my nerve you know that?" We both laugh.

"I can't hold her ass hostage."

"What's the problem then?"

"You tell me Ghost!" We stop walking and stare at each other.

"Why the fuck did you run off Ghost? What was the problem?"

"You know what the problem is. I'm out! One second I'm doing what I love and now I'm fucking out with a man I don't even know."

"That sound like we have the same problem then."

"How Cargo? You been stalking Jasmine for years now. Ya'll been living together for almost what, two years? Stop bullshitting a bullshitter nigga! You scared." We both laugh again.

"Damn straight, I'm scared as a bitch. I never thought I would feel like this about a woman. Dem nigga's warned me and I don't know if I'm putting too much into it or if I'm open. I mean she straight got a nigga wanting to turn over his kingdom!" Ghost burst out laughing.

"I know, I can't believe I'm saying the shit either. But I plan on hollan at them nigga's when we get there on it for real. You know how much sleep I get now?"

"Sleep? Since when? You lying yo' ass off now Cargo."

"No shit, I sleep so fucking good with her it should be against the law. We don't even have sex, my joint be rock fucking solid and I still fall asleep like she drugged my ass." We continue to laugh as we look around for Jasmine and Marco.

"What do you do Marco?" He pulls out my seat and sits across from me.

"Nothing illegal if that's what you want to know. I never have played that game and don't plan on playing anytime soon." I giggle at his honesty, he orders our drinks.

"I'd like to get you a graduation gift. I asked Cargo, he said I'd have to ask you what you want." Tristan never said anything to me about this, it's weird for Marco even to ask seeing I just met him.

"How'd you know about me graduating?" He laughs a little and takes a sip.

"I was calling Cargo trying to find Tanielle, he said he'd look into it and to stop calling because he was at your graduation." He laughs shaking his head at the memory.

"Thanks for the offer but I don't want anything, so thanks. Tristan keeps trying to get me an expensive car, I told him I'd think about it but now I really know I can't accept it." He looked like I said something that surprised him and asked me why.

"He's done more than enough for me. I'd rather do something for him but I don't know what to give someone that has so much. Shoot, everything I have is his so I really don't know how to repay him for what he's done for me."

"Why can't you accept him for the man that he is and let him take care of you? I mean as long as he loves you unconditionally and provides for you. You can repay him by accepting his love and letting him love and provide for you. What's so wrong with that?"

"You may know more about the man that he is than I do. I don't know if I can put my heart into his hands and not worry that I'll lose him. If I had my way, we'd both live until we're old and grey. But the chances of him even being around to see thirty seem farfetched because of the man that he is."

"I get that. But most relationships fail because of three things, trust, money and sex. If you can't trust the person you love than you really don't love them at all. That means no secrets and being open about what's going on in your head. I'm sure Cargo has more than enough money and I'm not going to speak on the last one."

"Thanks Marco. I know I need to talk to Tristan ab—"

"Damn, Marco! I leave you alone with my gal for five minutes and you manage to talk me into the fucking dog house." We all laugh as Tristan slides into the booth beside me.

After we arrived on Koro we were taken to a huge two story beach home.

The driver took Tanielle and Marco off, I figured to where they would be staying. I pulled Tristan all around the place, he gave me a brochure that had all the details about the house in it. It's thirty four hundred square feet with four bedrooms all with separate full baths in the rooms. The master bedroom is the complete upstairs and has a porch wrapped around to see the ocean.

The kitchen reminds me of Tristan's kitchen back home so much I asked if he designed it. Once I looked around closer, I found that everything about the house said Tristan. Before I had a chance to ask him he said he had a meeting to go to and was out the door. I go upstairs in the master bedroom, I figured I'd put away the few bags that we have. I was floored when I walked into the closet and saw all the clothes and shoes already there.

I sat back on the bed wondering who it all belonged to. Then I decided to go to one of the bedrooms downstairs just in case we were sharing the house with someone else. After putting away our things in the room there was a knock at the door. By the time I made it to the door and opened it, no one was there. When I stepped back inside the house, I couldn't help but scream at the figure sitting on the couch.

"Stop all that damn screaming fool! For somebody who's supposed to know how to fight, you sure do seem scary!" I don't know who she is but after I looked at her belly I figured she wasn't a threat.

"I apologize. I mean you scared the heck out of me. How'd you get past me anyway?" She started to laugh and walked into the kitchen so I followed behind her.

"Easy, I used my key." She looked into the fridge pulling out some waters and asked if I could cook, I told her yeah.

"Well what the hell you waiting on? Can you have a little bit of hospitality and feed a pregnant women?" I can't help but laugh.

"You have a key so I can only assume this is your home and those are your things upstairs. But I think I can find something in here to whip up for you." I don't know if she found what I said funny or not because of the blank look of devious surprise on her face.

"Who are you anyway?"

"Jasmine, anybody ever tell you, you look like a darker Mila Kunis, but have a body like the younger Lisa Raye?"

"I don't know who those people are. I was told that I look like Aunt Esta, Tristan said they were lying." She laughed so loud I thought she was about to give birth right in the chair.

"Girl please, don't let that bitch ass Worm lie to you like that! Who do you think I am anyway Jasmine? I know who the hell you are, don't tell me Cargo hasn't told you anything about me."

"Actually I think I would have remembered him bringing up someone with yellow eyes. Is your iron low?" She blinked a couple times and asked me what I said. I asked her again and she looked like 'The Thinker' for a second then snapped out of it and said she'd check.

"Anyway I'm Treasure, Deangelo's wife. You know if you want me to I can take care of Ruby and please say yes because I've been dying to." I was frozen in my place, I turned around and she looked so serious. What type of people am I dealing with? Do they all get a kick out of killing people?

"Please don't harm her. I hope you're not serious and I don't know what

Tristan has told you but she's the only family I have so please don't. My mother told me, 'God won't put anything on you, you can't handle,' and I'm a living testament to that." She found that hilarious, tears were pouring from her eyes and she was holding her belly.

"Child please, Cargo thought you was his hidden secret and wouldn't say a word about you. As far as Ruby and family in the same sentence, I have to agree with Cargo, even dogs are treated better. That shit you spittin' about a make believe God, you can miss me with all that. Think about what you just said. Sound like your God is evil as fuck.

Why allow a six year old to lose her parents by her uncle's hands? I mean why allow you to get beat with a speaker wire for ten years? He let you get beat on not only by Ruby funky ass but also by that nigga Worm. To top it off, let them molest you to the point it should be considered rape. If that's how your God operates, leave me the fuck alone." She found what she said even funnier. I didn't reply, I finished up making spaghetti and meatballs with garlic bread and a salad in silence. After she set the table, I pulled the bread from the oven and made our plates.

"You may as well make two more, maybe even four." I looked over at her she was walking to the door. When she opened it Tristan was coming inside followed by three other people.

"Treasure not over her trying to bully you is she baby?" Tristan said hugging her then walking to me doing the same and then kissing me, I shook my head no, he led me into the living room.

"Jasmine, this is Deangelo, Treasure's Pandillero wife, Corey, they're brothers and Sammy here is Bateador wife. Everyone this is Jasmine."

"I guess what they say is true, all fine men do run in packs." I had to tell the truth, these men were freaking mind-boggling attractive. I wonder if this is what I can expect when Tristan gets their age. We all laughed, Tristan pulled me into his arms.

"Alright lil girl! Don't fuck around and ge——" Treasure started to say but Pandillero bit the side of her mouth causing her to laugh.

"It's nice to finally met you Jasmine. Excuse my wife, she knows you meant no harm," Pandillero said.

"Hell, I'm mad we just now meeting you!" Bateador said giving me another hug.

"Girl don't mind Treasure crazy ass, say what you feel because yo' man can give these two a run for their money any day," Sammy said, Bateador turned around stalking back towards her as she laughed and hugged him telling him not to be jealous.

"Trick please, Cargo alright but that got damn Ashley, the youn——" Pandillero lifted Treasure up as she laughed.

"Naw, you thought it was all hehe and haha when she was giving her praises to yo' ass." We all laughed.

"We don't want to hold ya'll up, we getting out of here before I have to punish my wife," Pandillero said letting Treasure down to her feet.

"No we're not! I'm hungry as hell and I know Sammy big ass hungry. And by the smell of it, I'm about to taste just how fucking good that food is that Jasmine made." Treasure walked off pulling Pandillero into the bathroom. Bateador and Sammy sat on the couch, Tristan walked with me back in the kitchen.

"You alright baby?"

"Yeah, why'd you ask me that?" Tristan pulled me into his arms and kissed me like we were alone.

"Just making sure, I'm seeing that the new Treasure can be a bit aggressive." I kissed him back and told him I was fine. We all sat down at the table with small conversation. Seemed like the only one who did anything illegal at the table was Tristan. Something about Pandillero and Bateador told me that is wasn't so long ago that they stopped doing illegal things.

Then again there was Treasure, she seemed like this lady I saw on TV from Miami, Griselda Blanco. Or maybe this woman originally from Norway, Belle Gunness. Everything about her screamed that she was ruthless and I couldn't figure it out. Death, that's it, she gives that feeling of entering a funeral, she's nothing like Sammy. Everything about Sammy says she's excited to be having a baby. She has a calm motherly glow about her that makes you see the love her and Bateador share. I can see that Treasure loves Pandillero immensely but something says if he crossed her she'd kill him in cold blood.

"Why you so quite over there?" Treasure said swirling her fork in my direction.

"I was just wondering if this was both of your first born." I must have said something funny because everyone was laughing at me.

"Girl, hell naw! Those two freaks have nine fucking kids already. Ain't no telling how many her fertile ass carrying now," Sammy said, they continued to laugh.

"Shut the flap jack up! Is she serious?" I had to know, they don't look that old to have that many kids. Pandillero explained the order of their kids along with names and ages. The oldest girl, set of boy twins, and two sets of triplets born a year apart. They didn't want to know the sex or how many they're caring now.

Bateador has a daughter by his deceased fiancé and this is the first child for Sammy. I was so surprised by all the information I was wondering if I could have that. I'd love to have as many children as Treasure and Pandillero. After dinner we sat on the beach continuing our conversation until Sammy said she was getting tired.

"I hope you all don't mind but I put our things in the bedroom in the back." I guess I'm the joke of the night, seems like whatever I say they all laugh at me. I guess they figured it out because Pandillero and Bateador stopped laughing and apologized.

"My bad baby girl, I see Cargo hasn't told you but we own the island and have our own homes. Cargo can fill you in on the rest," Pandillero said, we said our goodbyes and watched them leave.

"Sorry about that baby. I should've told you before I left." We sat down on the couch, I pulled Jasmine on my lap, she asked me what I needed to tell her.

"The house is mine, it's a gift from Bateador and Pandillero. Everything here is actually mine."

"They must be filthy rich to not only have an entire island but also give a house away. With a full wardrobe and furnishing. Shut. Up." I was beyond words.

"They are and not just a house but they gave all of us houses. Those clothes are mine and yours. Don't get it twisted, we still have to pay a pretty penny in fees and shit but it's cheaper than you may think." She was even more surprised by what I told her. I kissed her again pulling her closer to me.

"Tanielle and Marco too? Dang!" Tristan chuckled.

"You as well."

"WHAT?" They don't even know me, why the heck would they do that? He must mean here with him, I asked him if that's what he meant.

"No. You have your own house down the way on the other side of the ridge. They wanted to give you a graduation present so that's what they did." I stood up and walked to the bathroom closing the door behind me. I need a long hot bath because I'm really hallucinating and it must be from all the flying.

I didn't know if Jasmine was upset, in shock, or tired, I heard the tub filling up so I head out to talk with Ghost. When I made it back I sat out back thinking about all that has happened since we made it in. After I jumped in the shower I headed upstairs to see what Jasmine was up too. When I walked in she was cracking up laughing watching 'Sanford and Son'.

"I see you found Aunt Esta huh?"

"Yeah and I have to say you're right, I look nothing like her." I kiss her on the forehead as she sits up.

"Can I talk to you about something real quick?" Jasmine turns off the TV and turns around facing me.

"Can I go first?" I tell her sure, she moves back resting against the headboard across from me.

"I've been wanting to tell you that I'm going to take a break from school. I'm signing up for some online classes for about a year before I go full time. I'm also going to work part time in the Mayor's office or the DA's office. I'm still waiting on someone for Mr. Pierce office to get back with me.

Please don't think I'm doing all of this because of you. I do want to stay close to you but I also need to find my own footing. Working will give me a better insight on if I want to spend the rest of my life being an Attorney or not." Tristan is still and I don't want to look over to see his reaction so we sit quiet.

"Jasmine, are you happy with me? I mean do I make you happy?"

"Of course Tristan. I haven't been this happy since before my parents were killed. Even then I was a different kind of happy, nothing like how you make me feel." I move over and sit on him pulling his arms around my waist.

"After everything I told you about me, has that changed your mind about me?"

"In some aspects yes it has. I can't lie and say that it hasn't."

"So if I told you I wouldn't change who I am or what I do, would you ride with me or do you want to go your separate way?"

"Baby I love you so much if you told me that I would nag you everyday to stay by your side. It would get to the point where I would cuff you to the bed, chain all the doors and board up all the windows to keep you safe. I don't want to lose you Tristan. If you were to say that and I did that then eventually we would lose each other. I don't want that baby." I kissed him begging that he understands where I'm coming from.

"I love you too Jasmine and I want you happy, if not going to school and working makes you happy than I'll support that. I would rather you go to school and not ever work a day in your life but like I said, it's up to you. If you want to go to school in Japan than I'll go with you. Hell, I'll go wherever you want me to go with you, I wouldn't have it any other way. Just promise me that if I'm not making you happy you'll let me know."

"Only if you promise me something." Here she go with this again. I ask her what.

"That you'll have sex with me."

"What?" I bury my face between her breast flipping her over on her back making her laugh.

"Shit, I thought you'd never ask." Tristan's playing around shaking his head between my breast making bubbling noises. I can't stop laughing at him being silly.

"Jasmine stop playing, you want to be married before you have sex remember?"

"I know what I said but I'm so freaking turned on whenever I'm around you it makes no sense."

"No deal! You've sacrificed enough for me young lady. Your virtue will remain in tack until you get married like you said." I climb off her and roll on my back looking over at her.

"Can I see your phone?" I give her my phone, she jumps out the bed heading downstairs. I go down because I could have sworn I heard a car pull up, by the time I make it down Jasmine's nowhere to be found and the car is pulling away. I go back upstairs grab my phone and call her on my phone she has with her, no answer. I'm tempted to jump in the car and go after her but I know she's safe. Hell, we're at the safest place in the world and I know they have eyes on her.

16 FELLOWSHIP

"Thanks Bateador for helping me out with this, I hope Sammy's not too upset that I woke her up."

"Sammy not sleep, her and Treasure over there gambling playing Pokeno with Treasure staff. She called me and told me to help you out with this."

"What's Pokeno? How much do they play for?"

"It's basically bingo but their crazy asses have anywhere from one to two million dollars on the table with all the side bets."

"Get the French toast out of here! Do you know how many kids that type of money will feed in the Cochran?" He's laughing, I'm serious.

"Yes we do. Believe it or not the money they win will go to one of their charities. Is that what you're into?" I ask him what and he explains.

"I want to become a prosecuting attorney, I'm actually waiting to hear back from Mr. Pierce office, he's the DA back in St. Louis. But my passion is helping foster children. I'd like to eventually open my own homes for them to live until their adults. I have a plan back at Tristan's place that I've been working on for quite some time now. I don't want to bother you with my silly dreams though."

"That don't sound silly to me. Matter fact, I'd like for you to speak with Sammy and Treasure, you'd be surprised what those two can do. Tomorrow before the party I'll tell Cargo to bring you over to Pandillero house so you can meet Ethan. I know you don't know it but he's Treasure's best friend. I'll make sure you get that job with him if that's what you want. Hell, if you want you can work at McGovern, Taylor and Joseph, it's based in Georgia."

"Are you saying the two of you are also lawyers? Skittles!" This is out of this world crazy.

"Exactly! You have a funny way of cursing you know that?" We both laugh as he pulls up to the shop, after we're finish he takes me back and wishes me good luck.

I look over at the clock and can't believe Jasmine has been gone for over an hour. I'm pacing back and forth debating on if I'm making the call or not. I feel like I'm about to put out an all point's bulletin on her ass. I know she safe but damn! If this is anything like she feels when I'm away I see why she said she would put a nigga on lock down. This side of the wait is harder than I ever thought it would be. I hear a car pull up, shoot down the steps, Jasmine's coming in the door but waving bye looking back.

"Baby what's up with that? I thought yo' ass was trying to leave me or something. You got me thinking all kinds of shit running out of here like that." I pull her up into my arms she laughing kissing me and shit like it's funny to have me worried.

"I was the same way when you took a month away from me. It was so bad I had to stay away from the house so I wouldn't worry so much. Every time you leave on your missions I feel like I'm about to go mad waiting on you to come back in one piece." I kiss all over his face and giggle. He looks like a baby that's lost his favorite blankey.

"Where you been baby?" I let her down and she puts the bag she has behind her back, I can hear her ruffling thru it.

"Tristan, you know I love you right?"

"Yeah baby, I love you too. What you hiding in that bag?" She looks serious pushing me back to the couch, I sit and she kneels between my legs.

"Tristan, I love you and couldn't imagine my life without you. I would do anything for you and whatever it takes to make you happy. I promise that I'll let you lead staying by your side and always be honest with you. You're my first love, my protector and my soul mate. No matter what you do or what you've done I'll support you and encourage you. Tristan, I want to know if you'll marry me?" I'm so nervous I open the ring box and it snaps shut before he can see it. I manage to get it open and hold it out to him.

I can't believe she really did all this. Her hands shaking and I can feel her heartbeat pounding away up my leg. I pull her up onto my lap and kiss her hugging her so hard she asked me to ease up.

"You know I'm supposed to ask you that right?" We both laugh and she asks me again.

"Are you sure this what you want Jasmine? Please don't tell me you're doing this because of what we talked about before you left?"

"Tristan! I'm serious. Is this your way of saying no?" I can't believe I didn't think this thru. I never thought about him saying no. Here they come, I feel the tears start to fill my eyes. I don't know how much longer I can hold them back.

"Yes baby! I'll marry you. I love you and you're my heart and soul. Jasmine, you were made in the spitting image of my heart and I never want to let you down or let you go. Being with you has made me look at my life in a different light. I want to do the best that I can by you and I'll do whatever it takes to make sure you're happy. So yes baby! I'll marry you." My baby has tears coming from her eyes, I know she's happy.

"Thank you Tristan." I chuckle and kiss her tears away.

"No thank you, Mrs. Warner. I've been making plans all day to take you to Paradise Island in the Bahamas when we left here. I guess you beat me to the punch." I'm so happy I can't help but cry more, I don't want him to see so I hide out in his neck.

"Let's go to bed baby. You know you don't have to cry right? I'm still taking you. And since you taking a break from school we can stay at least a month." I put her in the bed and hold her in my arms happy as a horse getting head.

"Mrs. Warner, Mrs. Warner, I know you can hear me. We need to get out of here." I feel so warm and happy I don't want to get out of Tristan's arms. I don't know how I ended up on top of him and I don't care to get off no time soon.

"Good morning baby."

"Good morning wife!"

"What time is it?"

"Almost five."

"Baby it's too early, didn't you get any sleep?"

"My wife already neglecting her duties. You know I need to hear your heartbeat and feel these thick ass thighs wrapped around me in order for me to sleep."

"It won't happen again baby." I kiss his chin then his chest.

"It's all good, as long as I can have you in my arms it's all fucking good!" I pulled the sheets away and shuffle us out the bed. I take her to the bathroom sitting her on the countertop.

"If you want to make it to your meeting we have about thirty minutes before you're supposed to be there. I see you've been just as busy as I have. I thought I was the only one here to take care of some business but you sure surprised the hell out of me."

"What? I'm here because you brought me here not for any business. What business are you talking about?" Tristan laughs and starts the shower for me.

"Bateador called me a minute ago about taking you to Pandillero crib." I jump down and start stripping off my clothes, Tristan acts like he's about to run out the bathroom. I giggle at him as he closes the door.

"Cornpuffs! I didn't think he was serious. That was only what, four hours ago and he wants me to go over this early in the morning? Do any of you sleep?" I yell out to Tristan but he doesn't answer me. I scammer to get ready in record time and we're off heading to the house.

"Frankenberres, this house is enormous! If this is their island why do they have a gated entry? And what's the deal with all the security around here?" I can tell Jasmine is nervous, she's looking around in every direction. When we pull up and make it inside she can't stop talking about it. Ms. Jackson walks us back to the office, I stop Jasmine at the door.

"Alright baby, I'll be waiting on you when you finish." Jasmine throws her arms around my neck making me laugh at her nervousness.

"Jasmine, you'll be alright they won't bite. Go in there and do what I know you can do baby. I love you." I pull her arms away and open the door for her.

"Hold up Cargo! Come in here for a second," I hear Pandillero call out to me. We go in and he points me to a sofa in the back of the office.

"Jasmine, this is Ethan Pierce, Ethan this is Jasmine Vanaria soon to be Warner." Treasure introduces us.

"Thank you Mr. Pierce for meeting with me on such short notice. I've been trying to meet with you for months, so thanks for taking the time out to meet with me. Thank you all for meeting with me."

"Don't thank me Mrs. Warner, I get a ton of applicants and I've been a little preoccupied. Had I seen you're application and recommendations I would have made sure you were hired." I can't believe it, I feel like I'm about to pass out in front of all of them. Not to mention the fact that Mr. Pierce is positively more handsome in person. The photos I've seen don't do him any justice, they were dead on, fine men do run in packs.

Looking around the room there's nothing but dreamy models all around. I can't help but feel a bit insecure in their presence. We all sit down and it hits me that their all here. To my left, Pandillero's at the head of the table, to his left sits Treasure, Mr. Pierce, Sammy then Bateador parallel to Pandillero. Tristan is sitting behind me on the sofa making me the only one on this side of the huge mahogany conference table.

"Like I said Mrs. Warner, had I seen your paperwork you would already be working in my office. There is one thing I would like to address." Mr. Pierce leans in closing the packet in front of him. I assume it's filled with my background.

"I have to be honest and point out that if you worked in my office I wouldn't have time to babysit or play favoritism. It's hard work and I would demand that you keep up and take this seriously." I agree and assure him that I wouldn't expect anything less.

"One more thing, you seem to be surrounded by people with cloudy backgrounds in th——"

"City!" Sammy looks over at him, Treasure burst into laughter, Bateador holds his head back towards the ceiling, Pandillero is looking down shaking his head. Bateador looks to Mr. Pierce with fire in his eyes.

"Nigga please! Don't make me remind you of your fucking cloudy background," Bateador says. They all laugh except for Bateador. Pandillero looks over at Mr. Pierce, before he can say anything I speak up.

"Mr. Pierce, I understand your concerns and I've given it great thought as well. When it comes to backgrounds mine is not as transparent as it could or should have been. I'm sure that your concerns lie with my husband and where my loyalty lies. If that's the bases of your concerns then I'll be honest with you.

I choose my husband over any job and anyone in this room, that includes him. What I mean is, we all are work in progress, the man that I'll spend the rest of my life with is as well. I'll do everything I can to make sure that we both go forward leaving the cloudiness behind. It's work in progress Mr. Pierce, I understand if you don't want me working for you. Thank you again for meeting with me."

"I guess she told you," Treasure says to Mr. Pierce.

"Mrs. Warner as an attorney the company you keep can send you to prison for life. That goes for anyone actually, attorney or not. But in this field everyone around you will be scrutinized and held to a different set of rules. Meaning, more time for them and for you if anything goes wrong. I want you to be aware of that and take it into consideration. I admire your honesty and your loyalty but at this time I won't be able to offer you a position."

"I understand Mr. Pierce and thank you again for your time."

"City, do us all a favor and get out!" Pandillero says and everyone laughs again including Mr. Pierce.

"Whatever nigga, I don't have time to be playing around with any of you corrupt psycho's anyway." They all laugh again. Mr. Pierce says his goodbyes hugging Sammy then Treasure.

"I'll see you later Treasure, don't let that nigga keep you too long either. Now where the hell are all my kids at?" Mr. Pierce says as he leaves out the room.

"I got yo' kids nigga!" Pandillero yells behind him as they all laugh.

"Fuck what City punk ass talking about. I know Bateador offered you a position at our firm in Georgia. Cargo said it's up to you on what you wanted to do. So if you want it it's yours." I looked back at Tristan but he looks into the air causing me to laugh.

"Before you answer that we would like to talk to you about your foster home ideas," Treasure says passing me a folder.

"I hope you don't mind, we had your plans faxed over this morning and looked over them," Sammy says. I don't know if I should be upset that they went thru my stuff or happy they have it for me to refer to. I look back at Tristan and he hunches his shoulders like he didn't know.

"First and foremost, I don't think you should work for anyone. I'm not saying don't follow your dreams of becoming a lawyer by no means. What I'm saying is you should do both but make this your first priority since your taking a year off," Sammy says.

"I believe you can do more than that. Don't take a year off, go to school full time and work on getting this off the ground. I know you can also work part time at the law firm but if it's too much than it is what it is," Treasure says.

"Whatever you choose Jasmine it's up to you. We wanted to speak with you to make you an offer. Before we do we'd like to hear exactly what you've been working on so the floor is yours," Bateador says. I go into telling them my ideas. They ask questions and say things to each other in Italian. Two hours later I conclude my presentation.

"We see an opportunity here that we haven't taken into consideration. What you've come up with is something that will not only benefit our communities but can change many lives. We looked at the numbers and they are steady on the rise. It's a laboring task that would require time and hard work to make it happen," Treasure says. Pandillero says something to them and they go back and forth in Italian again. Every now and then I hear Tristan behind me chuckle and make a whistling noise like he understands what they're saying.

"This is our offer, please hear us out before you make a decision, you don't have to decide today we won't do anything regardless. It's up to you seeing this is your vision," Bateador says I agree.

"We can hold your position as CEO and Founder for as long as you want with these condi..." I let Pandillero continue on and can't wait for him to get to the point.

"Or we're willing to buy your ideas from you." Pandillero stands up coming towards me with a sheet of paper placing it in front of me.

"If you take the first option this will be your annual salary until all of the expenses we invest plus twenty percent. Or we can become silent partners for ten percent of the annual income of the business." I look over the spreadsheet and can't believe that so much money would be generated from foster homes. He sits on the side of the table and flips the sheet over.

"This number here is what we're offering to buy your ideas. It's negotiable so think about it and let us know. Like Bateador said it's your idea so we won't pressure you or steal it," Pandillero says then he walks back to Tristan and everyone else gets up saying their goodbyes.

"You alright over there?" Jasmine is quiet and staring at the paperwork in the folder they gave her. When we get to the house she runs into the bathroom, sound like she singing to the porcelain. When she comes back down I pull her in and laugh because she has a wet towel on her forehead like she has the flu.

"What was so funny in there? Did you understand what they were saying?"

"Yeah. I was laughing because Treasure was saying she was hungry then

Sammy said she always hungry. Those two were going back and forth about who eats the most. Pandillero and Bateador were ignoring them trying to figure out an offer to make you. Every now and then, Treasure and Sammy would add to what Pandillero and Bateador were saying then go back to arguing.

Those two are a trip but they heard everything that those nigga's were saying. Then Bateador told them to stop arguing and they would eat soon enough. Treasure told him to shut up and Sammy told her to watch her mouth. I swear I don't know how they do it."

"What do you think I should do?" I sat up looking at Tristan.

"Whatever you want to do baby. You don't have to do anything at all, you know that right? If you want to do it on your own time at your own pace I'm behind you. We're not hurting by no means for money so you don't have to worry about that."

"I was serious about what I said about you, you know? I know you said that you would continue on doing what you do and all. But I was serious Tristan. I don't want to worry about you and we're going to be together forever. So don't be surprised when you wake up chained to the bed and all that other stuff I told you." Tristan explodes into laughter, maybe he thinks I'm playing but I gave him fair warning.

"I hear you. I came here to put some things in motion anyway. Back to you though. What you think about what they said?"

"It's making me sick just thinking about it." I wasn't expecting that, I asked her why she said that.

"Not in a bad way just in an overwhelming way. It's making me think about so many other possibilities. I would've never thought that all this would happen to me. Me Tristan! It was not long ago I was beat up hiding on the side of a deep freezer I considered a bed. Now I'm engaged to a drug moving hit man who loves me as much as I love him. I'm turned down on a great job only to be offered my dream career.

Then my dreams are handed to me on a silver platter. The offers! What the fudge is the deal with that? How did they come up with all of that in such a short period of time? Do any of you sleep? I mean one hundred forty seven thousand a year? Barnes and Shoble! Or the second offer of four million just for an idea? Get the hockey stick out of here! I think I'm about to pass out." Jasmine has me laughing so hard I feel like I'm about to burst. She fell into my arms like she really passed out on me, she is really something else.

At the party I feel like I'm at a GQ mixed with Ebony photo shoot. Everyone is dressed sharp and look like they could be found on a runway. Not one of them look as though they participate in anything illegal but something is telling me looks are deceiving. When Tanielle and Marco arrive everyone is clapping and welcoming her back.

Tristan introduces me to everyone all around the room as his wife. I can't get enough of hearing him say it. Tristan says he needed to go talk with Tanielle, I try and sit at the far end of the long table in the center of the room. The table is big enough to seat at least thirty people and the spots are labeled. Around the perimeter of the tent I sit at the high bar style two person table.

"Jasmine, I'm so happy for you girl," Shameka, Prime's girlfriend says sitting in the stool across from me.

"Thanks so much. I'm still in shock myself."

"You know all these people?" Shameka asks looking around the room.

"Hecky no! I just met them."

"Girl, I met a couple of them a while back at a party but most of them I just met tonight. I mean I've never even seem them before but Ashley swears most of them are from the Cochran." I had to ask her if she was from the Cochran, she said yeah.

"I guess that's one thing we all have in common then. Is it weird to you how welcoming they are? I don't know about you but they all seem to act like I've been a part of the family forever."

"Hell I thought you knew them, but fuck yeah! That's a trip. And it feels genuine like they really do make you feel like family. But I can say without a doubt looking around it's some fine ass brothers in this fucking family." We both laugh loud and slap hands in agreement.

"I can't fib Shameka, it's hard to even look at some of them in the face without feeling like I'm drooling." I had to catch myself from telling her how gorgeous her guy is. When Tristan introduced us I tried not to stare at him but got slam he's fine!

"You don't have to tell me. Ashley has to close my mouth for me because I've been so hypnotized by these men here. Please tell me you met muthafuckin' Yoppa and Rider! Girl, I thought I would pass out, those men are so gorgeous. Then I met that Pandillero and Bateador. Girrrrrrrl! When I sa—"

"When you say what?" Sammy says catching us off guard.

"No disrespect Sammy but yo' man and Pandillero are so fucking fine, like I was just telling Jasmine, Ashley had to close my mouth for me. They fine as I don't know what." I'm in shock that she actually admitted that to Sammy.

"I know right," Sammy says we all laugh again.

"You better not let Treasure hear you sayin' that shit. Her silly ass will be trying to get you back fucking with Prime."

"I sure the fuck am going to be fucking with Prime blue eyed, bowlegged, bright skin ass, see how yo' ass like it. It's a gift and a fucking curse to have men as fine as the ones we have. Take the shit from me because when you know better, you do better," Treasure said putting her arm around Sammy waist as we all laughed. Two men that must've just arrived walked over stopping before they were too close.

"DAMMMMMMMM!" they said at the same time.

"What the hell do you two wanna be mack daddies want?" Treasure said.

"Damn Treasure why you have to come at us like that? Can't you at least introduce us to these fine ass women before you throw us out there like that?"

"My bad. The pimp talking is Blane. The pimp salivating is Shane. Blane and Shane these fine ass women are spoken for. Did I get it right?" We all were laughing at her introduction.

"Thanks a lot fat ass!" Blane said giving Treasure a hug.

"She such a fucking hater it don't make no sense. It's all good though, because as soon as Pandillero divorce her ass I'm gon' wife her up," Shane said putting his arm around Treasure and Sammy.

"First of all, he wouldn't dream of divorcing me nigga and if he did he would wake up, smack his damn self and apologize for it. Second, yo' ass wouldn't know what to do with me if he did. Now go 'head and take Ghost ass with ya'll, I know that's what ya'll came back here for." We all laugh and they walked away with Tanielle. We all continued to talk, before I know it, it seemed like every woman in attendance was in the back talking. Pandillero walked over hugging Treasure from behind. As I look away seems like everyone is coming to get their other half.

After dinner the party was in full effect, the music was pumping and we all had a blast. Jasmine seemed to warm up to everyone, she was happy without a doubt. Bateador came dragging me around the back of the tent into a smaller one. I look around and they have a full blown craps game going.

"Damn this shit look like we back in the hood in the horseshoe or some shit." They all laughing having a good time.

"Only difference is we shooting for Put up or Shut Up prices youngin', you in or out?" Pandillero say callin' out his five on his roll. I jump in the game and we clownin' each other like the good old days.

"Who you lookin' for?" I hear someone say as I make it out the front of the tent. When I turn to the side I see a guy, of course he's fine surround by seven other people. As I approach them I notice that Mr. Pierce is among them. I speak and introduce myself to them all.

"Damn nigga, you on the clock?" Tony, Treasures brother says looking over at Mr. Pierce.

"Please call me City or Ethan." I tell him he can call me Jasmine. I'm surprised to see and to hear that City is one of what they refer to as Big Eight Hundred. Must be some back in the day thing because they all seem a bit old to be a part of a group with that type of name. I'm so comfortable talking with them and getting to know them, I forgot what I actually came out for.

"Do you all know where Tristan is hiding?" They all laugh.

"Yeah, dem nigga's all in there. Just walk back and I'm sure you'll hear their ghetto asses." We all laugh and I go in the direction that James pointed me to. I make it in, I'm surprised to see that the majority of them are crouched down. When I make it in further, I can see that they're throwing dice with a mound of money on the floor. Blane stands up and walks over putting his arm around my shoulder.

"Damn, I was waiting on you to come find me. Fine don't describe you by no means Jasmine." I laugh at what Blane says as Shane grabs my hand and kneels in front of me.

"Jasmine, don't let that nigga fool you, I'm the right one for you. Marry me instead of Cargo ass." The room is laughing as Tristan smacks his hand away and moves Blane away from me.

"You nigga's play too fucking much! Leave my damn wife alone." Everyone laughs more. Tristan kisses me again like we're the only ones in the room. Before I can pull away I feel my feet leave the ground and he's carrying me out the tent.

"What's up baby? You ready to go?" I laugh as he puts me down.

"No, I was just coming to see you. If you're ready to leave then we can."

191

"I'm good, you wanna dance?" I show her my two step, that real back in the day G shit. None of that punk pussy shit these nigga's be doing today, I hit her with that right foot boow, left foot boow. Jasmine laughing like crazy as I walked her around the tent.

"Damn, how the fuck this nigga pull a woman as fine as Jasmine?" Damon say.

"These nigga's lucky as a mufucka when it comes to sexy ass women on the real," Darrius said.

"Nigga please, these nigga's be begging and pleading for those fine ass sistas to put up wit' they asses," Tony say.

"Naw, fine women with good heads on their shoulders like that bad boy shit that's all. Sooner or later they'll get tired of the thug life and either the nigga gone change or he gone lose her," City says.

"Any of you other Eight Hundred nigga's have anything to say right about now? Last I checked all you nigga's came here with somebody so find ya'lls and stop hating on me and mine. City, don't think you slick either nigga, we all know you hoping Treasure 'get tired' as you call it." We all laugh and dab each other off. I walk inside with Jasmine as they continue to clown City behind what I said. I pull her on the dance floor and rock with her.

"How long have you known City?"

"A minute now why?"

"Why didn't you say anything when I brought up working for him?"

"I knew he would be here so I figured I'd introduce you but you beat me to it." I giggle at the thought.

"You weren't offended by what he said in the meeting?"

"Hell naw! City can play like his shit don't stink all the fuck he wants. Besides, I didn't want you working for him anyway." I'm cracking up laughing at the look on Jasmine face.

"Why?"

"Because I don't want you to work at all. If it makes you happy I'd rather you work for yourself and not somebody else. Don't get me wrong, City like that older brother who always has something to say about what you do. Matter fact, come're for a second." I walk Jasmine back out to where City is and tell him to holla at me for a second.

"What's up Cargo?" City nods at me with dreamy eyes, I have to look away because I don't want to look like Shameka described.

"Go ahead and tell her." City laughs and shakes his head then ask Tristan if he's sure.

"Alright Jasmine, I was all for hiring you without even looking at your application. Cargo my lil brother, no matter how fucking hard headed he can be. The reason I said I couldn't hire you is because this nigga asked me not to." I turn and look at Tristan and I'm instantly upset and ask him why.

"Let me answer that for you Jasmine. Until this nigga get his shit together, you don't need to be anywhere near a law firm and that's 'keeping it funky' as Treasure would say."

"Can I ask you something City?" He stops laughing and looks at me and says sure.

"Eight Hundred, I only saw seven people, who's the eighth person, Tristan?" They both laugh.

"That would be my best friend, she crazy as hell, shit, with her alone we should've been called the Lunatics." City kissed my cheek, told me not to be upset and walked away.

"Please don't be mad at me baby." I can't help but laugh at the sound of Tristan's voice and the sad face he's put on.

"I'm not mad but I still want to work so if that's going to be an issue then we need to discuss it now."

"It's not an issue at all. But I would rather you work in Georgia if that's the case until I get my shit together. Come on so we can get back on the dance floor." I walk her back inside.

"So City likes Treasure?" I thought it was something up with those two.

"Baby stop, City is in love with Treasure. A blind goat can see that." I laugh and kiss her neck.

"How did they meet? I know Bateador said they were best friends but I don't understand why Pandillero would let a man such as City be his wife's best friend." Tristan wide eyes me and chuckles.

"Whatchu mean, 'a man such as City' Jasmine?"

"Come on, like you said a blind goat can see that City is a looker. Not to mention every freaking man that you've introduced me to. I told you packs but now I see it's more like boat loads." We both laugh, I ask him to tell me.

"They grew up together that's why Pandillero don't trip off it, but believe you me, he know what's up on City part. Treasure, you seen how she is with that nigga, she ain't going nowhere. City man enough to respect that and keep it friendly. That's why he said that shit about getting tired and I said what I said. Enough about them though."

17 UNCONDITIONAL LOVE

"**B**aby when you said leave I didn't think you meant leave and fly to the Caribbean." I'm wrapped up in Tristan's arms leaned all the way back in the seat.

"I could tell that much by the look on yo' face when we pulled up on the runway." After we landed we pulled up to this big gated two story Tuscan Villa. It's amazing inside, five spacious bedrooms and a private master bedroom. It has a huge walk-in river stone shower and a gigantic master closet. There's also a separate one bedroom, one bath guest house out back. The flooring's consist of travertine stone, hardwood and ceramic tiles.

"Don't tell me this is your house as well. And please whatever you do don't say it was a gift or that it belongs to me." I laugh all the way inside the kitchen with Jasmine by my side.

"Naw baby it's City's crib. He said he left something for you in the living room too." I take off running to see what City could have possibly left me. When I read thru what it is I fall to the floor in tears clutching the papers in my hands.

"What's going on Jasmine?" I pull her off the floor and sit with her on my lap on the couch while she cries into my chest handing me the papers.

"I hope this not what you're crying about baby. Anybody else would be running around jumping for joy if they had this here in their hands." I don't understand what's going on.

The papers City left is actually a trust left to Jasmine by her parents. There's also a couple letters addressed to her from them that she hasn't even opened yet. After taking a second look at the stuff, I would love to tell Ruby fat nasty ass what she missed out on. They had been trying to contact her letting her know that she needed to sign the paperwork seeing that she was Jasmine's guardian.

She missed out on two houses, four cars, a boat, a law firm and a medical center named, 'Jasmine's Healing Hands'. Some quick addition of several insurance policies and the net worth at the time of their death, Jasmine has at least twenty two million. I bet Ruby would kill herself if she found out about this shit here. My baby cried so much she fell asleep. I put her in the bed and let her rest while I jumped on the phone.

"What's good Cargo man? Don't tell me you calling me on some Marco shit." I fall out laughing at Bateador ass.

"Naw man, I was actually calling to speak with Treasure about the package City left for Jasmine." Bateador told me to hold on.

"Damn Cargo, don't tell me she split out on yo' ass already."

"Come on Pandillero, you know she didn't. I was calling to see if I could holla at yo' wife about the package City left for Jasmine." He start to laugh.

"I told City punk ass don't just drop that shit on her. By the sound of your voice she didn't take the shit that well did she."

"I really don't know for real. Shit, she cried herself to sleep so I don't know how she feel about the shit. In the mean time I wanted to holla at Treasure see if she can pull the numbers on it and track everything down for her." He laugh.

"Any other time youngin' I would put you thru. Don't tell her I said this but T on punishment right now." We both hurt laughing.

"Naw on the real, I'm trying to do some de-stressing for her right now. Like I said don't tell her because I know she gon' be pissed about not helping. I can't do it myself, I can but I know you want it like yesterday. I got Bateador on the phone with Prime now, he'll hook you up so holla at yo' brother in a few if he don't call you back in say an hour or so."

"Thanks for looking out and I hope Treasure crazy ass chill out, I know she be on that secret agent shit. But thanks man, I should've hollad at Prime first anyway."

"It's all good youngin' you know if I could I would and T will be alright if she sit down more. But I'll holla at you later. Call me if you need anything, hold up to. How many times I have to tell you, you can call both of us direct?"

"Why change something that's not broken man?"

"Eight up Cargo!" I hang up and go back to sit with Jasmine.

"Tristan you up?" I roll over to see.

"Of course I'm up, my wife went to sleep on me over eight hours ago, plus it's almost ten and we both need to at least stretch before we call it a night."

"I broke my promise huh? Come on, let's see if you can get a couple hours in." We move into position so my head is against her chest and she puts her leg around me as I grab her ass pulling her closer.

"You wanna talk?"

"I really want to curse, scream and fight but I don't know why or who I should take it out on."

"Well I'm here for you and if you want, you can take it out on me if that'll make you feel better with what you're going thru."

"Thanks for the offer but not over this, it's not your fault I'm feeling like this. But if we don't find an alternative occupation for you then I'm sure I'll take you up on that." I'm all smiles pulling Tristan's head into me.

"Well damn, put a ring on a nigga finga and you just lay down the law on him huh? You don't have to worry about my occupation, I told you I was making moves and I plan on doing just that. On the real if there's anything I can do to make it better for you then let me know." Jasmine giggled and pulled away looking down at me.

"We can have sex, I know that will take my mind off what I'm thinking about right now." I chuckle and bite down on the top of her right breast as she laughs.

"That would only take your mind off it for now, we need to deal with what you're going thru. Good try but you wanted to wait until you were married and that's just what I plan on waiting for." Jasmine groans making me laugh.

"You promise?" I don't know why she asked, I told her of course I do.

"Can I see your phone?" Before I can answer she tries to reach behind me to grab my phone off the nightstand. I roll her onto her back as she laughs.

"What you think you doing? I'm not letting you out of my sight so whatever you thinking let it go."

"I'm sure I can call Sammy and she can find someone to marry us right now." Tristan laughs and kisses all over my neck.

"You know we would never hear the end of it, Ma' Earlean will come after us both. If you want to ditch your only wedding then let me know and I'll make the call right now." I looked up at Jasmine she had on the pout face.

"I'm starting to think you just don't want to have sex with me Tristan, if that's the case then let me know. Now's the best time for bad news, I know when it rains it pours so lay it on me."

"I wanna have sex with you more than you think, I can't wait to pop that cherry!"

"Tristan!" I laugh as she puts her arms around my neck pulling me down on her.

"Don't Tristan me. I wanna be the first to taste the pussy, feel the heat from the pussy and break the pussy in. I can feel how wet yo' panties getting right now and you just don't know how bad I want to slurp those juices up. By the way, when we get married, all this sleeping in a gown and panties ends!" I'm in tears laughing at what he's saying he wants to do to me.

"On errthing baby, I want to make love to you. Jasmine serious, you sure you wanna get married and it's not just so yo' hot ass can get a fix?"

"Tristan, I'm sure I don't want to marry you just to have sex. I'm so serious we can have sex right now so that I can prove it to you." I damn near die laughing at Jasmine and get the hell up off of her.

"You slick as hell, you know that right? How you gon' try and run that shit past me like 1 don't know what's up?" 1 get up and follow behind Tristan as he goes towards the bathroom.

"Just like 1 did. What are you about to do?" He laughs and stops at the door giving me a slow teasing kiss, by the time 1 open my eyes he's looking down at me.

"I'm about to get in the shower." 1 ask if 1 can go he laughs and says no.

"Can 1 watch?" He really thought that was funny.

"Don't worry 1 got you, but not today. I'll be out in a minute so can 1 ask my wife for something to eat?" Jasmine starts to grab the helm of her gown and 1 laugh and stop her.

"You were just talking all that stuff a minute ago. 1 thought you wanted something to eat?" Tristan looks shocked at what 1 said and closes the door, 1 laugh and go to the kitchen to make him something to eat.

I'm in the shower and my dick so fucking hard 1 think my shit about to break or explode. 1 don't know what's going on with Jasmine but got damn, 1 don't know how much longer 1 can resist. The way she coming at me, if she keep it up we not gon' make it until after we get married.

Hell, it's hard enough being around her now and not going at it, 1 have a feeling she about to turn up the pressure. By the time 1 make it out and in the kitchen she's on the phone, sound like she's talking to Prime girl. 1 kiss her and she ends the call turning around into my arms.

"Your food is almost ready, steak, mac and cheese, and broccoli, you want anything else?" Tristan is just looking at me with a sexy grin on his face running his hands up and down my back.

"That sounds good, I'll be in the living room." I need to get out of here before I fuck the shit out of Jasmine all around this bitch.

We spent two weeks doing everything and going everywhere we could think of on the island. At night we sleep in each other's arms almost like we're afraid to let go. He treated me to a spa day, I didn't really want to be away from him for four hours but he said he wanted me to relax. I felt like my entire body was a feather and would fall to the ground by the time I was finish. I was lying out in the shade when I heard Tristan chuckle walking up to me.

"Damn baby what they do to you? You look like you high as shit over here." I'm so relaxed I can barely laugh as he gives me a kiss and sits beside me.

"You ready to go?" She shakes her head no like she can't talk, I laugh and swoop her up into my arms.

"Thank you baby because I'm not sure I can move a muscle, all I want to do is sleep for some reason." I cuddle up into his neck as he laughs walking me back. When we make it in he sits me on the couch and I'm out like a light. I wake up in the bed and he's watching TV with the volume muted.

"I don't want a big wedding. As long as you're there I'm fine with it. Do you want a big wedding? I know you have a big family and extended family so if that's the case, like I said I'm fine with that as long as you're there." He chuckles but doesn't look back at me and something hits me like a brick.

"Tristan. Do you want a long engagement? I mean how long do you want to wait until we get married?" He turns around looking at me, I guess he heard to worry in my words.

"I'm with you baby, as long as you're there I'm straight. You ready to eat? You've been sleep for a minute." He picks up my foot and licks the arch of it followed by a kiss as I laugh.

"I'm fine, you need to rest." I motion for him to come closer and he does, I pull him down with me.

We spent the next week having a blast enjoying our time together. We're getting all dressed up so we can go out to dinner for the evening. When I come out the bathroom Tristan's eyes are big and his smile is even bigger. I turned embarrassed at the way he's looking at me. He laughed and kissed all over my neck telling me how beautiful I am.

"Come on baby before I forget what I said about waiting." We make it downstairs and I look at Jasmine, she looks like she's about to fall over.

"What's going on?" Tristan's smiling at me then goes to his knee.

"Jasmine, I love you more than life itself. There's nothing in this world, galaxy or anywhere else that will change how much I love you. I've searched for you for years and now that I have you, I'm not letting you go no matter what. I told you before you're the image of my heart but I stand corrected because you are my heart Jasmine.

I'll protect you, provide for you, be there for you at all times and love you because you're my heart. I don't want to go on another day, hour, minute, or second without you being my wife. Jasmine, will you marry me?" She's crying, her hands are shaking and all she can do is nod yes. I slip the ring on her finger as she laughs and says yes over and over again.

"Tristan, I love you baby," I whisper into his ear as he hugs me. I look around the room and everyone is here. Shameka, Prime, Tanielle, Marco,

Treasure, May, Pandillero, Sammy, Flight, Bateador, Dena, Mrs. Terry, Cap, Ma' Belle, Ms. Janine, Ma' Earlean, both girl Ashley's and Lorraine. He leads me into the living room as they all part and I can see a Reverend standing waiting on us. I look up at Tristan and he leans down in my ear.

"You sure you don't want to wait, because once we say those words it's forever. Even after death you're not leaving me and I'm not leaving you? Now's the perfect time to tell a nigga before the Reverend ask you." I kiss Tristan and everyone tells us to wait until the Reverend tell us to. We both laugh and listen to what the Reverend says. When it's time for the rings I go to try and take it off so he can put it back on but he pulls my hand up and kisses it.

Prime passes him another ring box and I almost faint because the ring is enormous. Sammy passes me a box and it's the same ring that I gave him before. I didn't notice that he didn't have his ring on. I'm starting to feel bad because here I am with three rings on one finger all the diamonds are bigger than the first one. We kiss and everyone is congratulating us but we pay them no attention. Tristan pulls away.

"Don't worry about the ring baby. Ego thru the roof right now with you rocking those twenty one carats. Only time you taking 'em off is when we go to get them banded together as one." I don't want to let him go but everyone comes over hugging us and wanting to look at my rings. We had a blast with everyone and after dinner it seemed like the room went quiet.

I looked back and Tristan was coming towards me with a cake in his hands as they all started to sing Happy Birthday to me. I had forgotten all about my birthday to the point I had to check the date for myself. They thought it was funny but I was serious, it's midnight and my eighteenth birthday. We walked everyone out after a few and we're left standing in the house alone.

"I hope you ready because I'm about to tear yo' ass up." I laughed at Tristan, kissed him and pulled away heading up the stairs.

"You said I could see you in the shower and it's time to pay up." I can't help but laugh and run up the steps behind her. She serious as hell about what she said to, I don't give a fuck that shit sexy. The second I stripped down her eyes were big as hell and she didn't want to look away from my dick. She reached for it and I made it jump causing her to jump as I laughed at the look on her face.

I put on a show for her making sure she can see everything I'm doing. I look over at her, she keeps crossing her legs and adjusting in the chair I pulled in for her. When I was finished she wrapped a towel around my waist as I kissed her taking off her clothes. I sat down in the chair, she looked everywhere except at me like she's shy.

"What you waiting on Jasmine? Don't hold up the show standing here, gon' get in and let me see what it do." I'm so nervous I should've thought this out beforehand.

My heart is pumping, my body is shaking and my kitty is soaking wet already. I put my arm across my chest and try to cover my bottom with the other. Tristan stands up grabbing my hands. I look down because that long, thick, one eye'd destroyer is looking dead at me.

"Don't hide from me baby. You're beautiful and sexy as all out. I don't know how many times I have to tell you that before you believe what I'm saying. Hold yo' head up and get in the shower, show daddy what's up with all this." I smile and walk into the shower as he sits back in the chair. I let the water pour all over me from head to toe slowly turning so that Tristan can see me.

I take my time with the sponge, it's strange because I feel like what I'm doing is dirty but in a good way. Good thing the shower's huge because I dropped the sponge. I turned and that's when I noticed Tristan stroking himself. I turned around and bent all the way over to where I can see him between my legs upside down.

"That's it!" I can't sit here any longer watching Jasmine. I get my ass up with the quickness and don't let her ass stand back up. I press her ass right up against me not letting her move. I can feel her juices against me, that shit driving me mad. I have to get a drink, I feel dehydrated as a mufucka holding her here.

"Stay still or I'll have yo' pussy drippin' wet 'til you beg me." He sounds so serious. I want to move just to see if he'll do as he said. I can see him go down on his knees, I feel way to open for his face to be that close to me back there. It's like he's in a trance, he's just looking at me for way too long. Tristan's licking his lips rubbing down my bottom to my thighs then back up.

He moved closer and the feel of his tongue against me made me flinch but he held me still and continued. I closed my eyes tight, I can't breathe or think about anything besides the feel of his tongue. Tristan's kissing me there like he has done so many times before when he kissed my lips. His teeth brushed against my pearl making it tingle.

His lips wrapped around it easing the sensation. My right knee's wobbling and shaking, I can't stop it from moving on its own. He sucked hard and I feel like my insides will come out right into his mouth. The sounds are driving me to move my hips, I want him to get it all whatever it is.

Jasmine's moaning and shaking making me want to seek and annihilate her ass. Her legs are shaking so hard her ass is clapping right in a nigga face. I don't want her to go just yet, I stopped and pulled her up into my arms putting her in the bed. She pulled my face to hers kissing me not wanting to let me go. I had to strap up but I damn sho' didn't want to stop. I move us over so I can get my joint together. I feel her reach for my hand so I look at her as she slowly opened her eyes.

"I want to feel you inside of me. I don't want that between us. Ever," she said it like she's out of breath but I know she's just as turned on as I am.

"GOT DAMN!" I didn't know if I said something wrong or not so I asked him why'd he say that. He slowed down and looked at me with desire in his eyes.

"Jasmine, you're about to get pregnant, I hope that's what you want because after what you just said I'm never putting one on." Tristan kissed me with so much fire it heated up my pearl even more as he moves down and presses against me.

"You ready baby?" I nod letting him know I'm more than ready.

"SHHHHIT!" She so damn tight, hot and wet I don't know how I'm going to do this shit. I get in a bit more and her body tenses up so I stop and tell her to relax while I sucked her breast. I need a minute to recoup, I let one go, that shit happened just getting the head in. My dick act like it don't give a fuck, it wanted to let go again. I can't have her thinkin' I'm a two second ass nigga so I have to chill and try to calm the fuck down.

"Relax baby, I'm not going to hurt you," he says as I take a deep breath. He's holding his self up on his forearms and he's shaking, beads of sweat are popping up on his forehead.

"Mmmmm, ahhh, ahhh!" she yells as I push through declaring her mine. I stop and let her catch her breath.

"Mmmove...Tris...now!" Before I can tell her to take a little more time to adjust she pulls me down and kisses me. Her right hand finds my back as she pushes her hips forward while pulling me down. We fall into a steady rhythm with her pushing forward meeting me, after a minute I can't handle all the juice running from her down on me. I pick it up and ride her hard as she gasp for air and claws at my arms and back.

"OOOh...shhh...Tristan!" I don't know what happened but something inside of me blew the heck up. My legs are flapping against his sides as I jerk and search for air. I don't know how long he was staring at me but when I opened my eyes he was looking.

"Please do it again!" She don't have to ask me twice. I go back to moving, watching her bite on her lip. She's in a zone throwing it back, Jasmine leaking so bad I can feel it on my nuts. She so fucking orgasmic I couldn't have ever imagined that a women could get that many off.

She going back to back and every time her damn walls snap the fuck back pulling tighter around me. The shits bananas. Each time it's like a category three thousand hurricane sucking me in, grabbing hold of me not letting me move. Her walls throwing my dick around inside her making me want to never get out. I snatch her leg up into my arm and bang out.

"Shit, this pussy good! I'm cumin' baby!" I don't want it to end. It's feeling so flapping good I look up and Tristan's looking down at me. I feel the explosion again and he stopped and jerked a few more times. My insides are hot. I can feel him gush inside of me, his body is still but his penis is moving.

He collapsed onto his forearms trying not to crush me but I pulled him in not caring. I need to feel all of him all over my body inside and out. We're both breathing harder than ever, Tristan looked over at the sound of his phone ringing. I'm too shocked that we've been going at it for over two hours and it seemed like I would never stop.

"You tired?" Tristan laughs and looks up at me.

"I'm exhausted but not tired. Why?" Jasmine smiles and rolls over on top of me brushing the sweat away from my eyes.

"I want to shower with you and do all of that again." I giggle at the look on his face. He laughs and picks me up carrying me into the shower.

*   *   *

After I made a couple runs I head back to the house to pick up Jasmine and give her her ring now that it's finished. When I make it in I see her and Dena sitting in the living room laughing at the computer. Once they notice I'm in the room they both burst out laughing after Jasmine slams the computer shut and walks over to me.

"What ya'll up to?" Jasmine kisses me and Dena continues to laugh but they both say nothing.

"What's that?" I see the bag Tristan's carrying, he must have forgot. He sits in the chair and pulls me on his lap digging inside the bag.

"This is yours. It's to let all dem nigga's know I got three rings around yo' ass and they ain't got shit coming." We all laugh as I put her ring back on her finger.

"You ready to go? I want to show you a couple spots today before it gets too late."

"Baby, when you said you owned a few businesses I didn't realize that I didn't know what a few was. We've been back for almost a month and every day you're taking me to another one. Can't you just get a list and I can see them that way? I would rather stay in." Dena is cracking up laughing along with Tristan, she says she's out and heads to the door. Tristan walks her out and comes back in.

"You not slick Jasmine, trust me, I'm getting some pussy from yo' lil mannish ass as soon as we get back. So come on, you know we have to make a stop first." I laugh and go with the flow. After we stop at the mall we head to the other side to meet up with the guys.

"Baby, why do we always meet up with them just so we can go into the city? Do you do this all the time? I mean why do you have so much security if you're so good at what you do?" I kiss Jasmine on the temple and laugh at what her crazy ass talking about.

"Trust me, I'm better than good at what I do. The game has changed and I'm not risking you getting hurt so that's why I have so much security. It's for you." Jasmine stops in the middle of the food court looking at me.

"Why? Tristan, I can take care of myself, I don't need four car loads of people to protect me." Tristan pulls me into his arms and kisses me holding my hair in his hand. When he pulls away I don't want to open my eyes it's feeling too good.

"I love you."

"I love you too Tristan." Now that's how you end an argument before it even begins. We keep walking and get in. When we pull up at the club we get out and go in the back entrance. I take her to my office show her the safes and how to open them all up. I give her the rundown of how things work and point out some key people on the staff.

She asks questions and I answer, after about two hours we head down to join the party. The club is packed wall to wall, my baby turning heads from the second we stepped off the elevator. Before we make it to the table I pull her around into my arms and rock with her as she laughs and grooves with me.

"You know I still can't dance right." Tristan nods but continues to move tapping me on my hip to the beat. I can feel all eyes looking at us like it's unusual to see two people dancing in a club. Tristan turns me around into his arms and I laugh and put my rump right into him.

"Excuse you lil gurl, get up off my man like dat!" I look over and see a fairly attractive girl off to the side of me. She's a couple inches taller and really skinny. Her hair is spiked all around and she has two gold teeth on the bottom of her central teeth. Tristan chuckles like it's funny and turns me so that I can't see her anymore.

"Damn Cargo, it's like dat? I can't even dance wit' chu?" I turn around and put my arms around his neck as he smiles and bites my bottom lip pulling it into his mouth. I can see her move forward and reach for him so I step around him and look at her.

"I don't know you and you don't know me. Can you please let it go for tonight so we all can have a good time without any altercations?" Tristan still hasn't said a word, he pulls me against him and holds my waist.

"Who da fuck iz you? If you don't get up off my man nobody in dis bitch gon' have a good time. You can bet dat!" This chick Carmen about to get her damn wig split if she keep this shit up. I'm trying my best to ignore her ass but she makin' it hard as hell for me to do right now.

"You want to see something? It's really cool," I asked her, she rolls her eyes still upset like I'm getting on her nerves.

"I wanna see you get da fuck up off my man. Cargo what's up? Why iz you all ova dis bit—" I feel Tristan tense but I held onto his arms not letting him move. Before she can finish Roman and Aaron are standing in front of her.

"Can you two escort this lady out, she's had enough for tonight." I wave her fair well as she continues to cuss and scream while Tristan is laughing into my neck.

"Now that's some G shit baby. Come on here." I walk her off the dance floor to the VIP. It's not long before I see my nigga's come up the stairs headed our way.

"Damn Cargo, long time no fucking see nigga," Twin say as we all dab off and I walk them over.

"Yeah whatever nigga. Spring, this is Twin, Mike, Charlie, Inch, Bobo, and Tiny. Everybody, this is Spring." I watch as they all shake her hand and check her out. I notice the look on Jasmine face and know I'm about to hear it. I can see she tucked her hand behind her back and I smile at her.

"Well fellas,...we out." They all look at me like I'm crazy, I moved Jasmine in front of me and walked her away to the elevator. The second we stepped on I pulled Jasmine into my arms and tongued her down stopping the elevator lifting her into my arms.

"I love the fuck out of you baby. I was trying to wait 'til we made it home but I can't, I need my pussy now." I'm so turned on for some reason, I helped him unbuckle his belt and can't wait for him to get in.

"You know this dick is yours right?" I sucked the side of her neck as she moaned yes and scratched down my back. She riding like there's no tomorrow, we're going at it.

"Ooo...Tristan...I'm, I'm...right there...ummmm...SHIT!" Hearing Jasmine curse for the first time made me nut so hard I feel like I'm about to pass out.

I can barely hold myself up let alone hold her in my arms without crushing her. I squatted down taking her with me while I regained my strength. When I did look at her she had her hands to her mouth with her eyes squeezed shut, I'm cracking up laughing. I stood back up and helped her down, my dick still hard; it was a bitch trying to put it away.

"Come on potty mouth so I can wash yo' mouth out with soap." Jasmine put her face into my neck as we both laughed waiting on the elevator to open up.

18 BODHISATTVA

Once we cleaned up we headed back down to the basement to leave out. Big Hen was waiting as we walked out to the cars. Before we could get close we saw the lights come on as a black three hundred pulled up on the side of us. Pig Brown and Pig Franklin jump out and walk right over to us. Jasmine steps completely behind me putting both her hands thru my arms on my waist.

"Well lookie fuckin' here. What's good man? Long time no see," Pig Franklin says.

"Who dat chick hidin' behind you?" Pig Brown say, Big Hen moves closer.

"Look here, my name is Brandon Hen I'm a bondsma—" They both start laughing, I pull Jasmine arms forward so she's pressed firmly into my back.

"Man shut the fuck up!" Pig Brown says cutting Big Hen off.

"Baby girl, I'm Officer Franklin, I need you to come from behind him and let me see yo' hands."

"It's against my religion to let a man see me without proper covering. I have my hands visible so you both can see. If we're under arrest I would like to grab my niqab from out of the truck."

"Who said anything about you being under arrest? Why every time we see you two ya'll think we want to arrest ya'll? I thought I told you last time what was up young blood. Now can you holla at me on some real shit and stop with all the silent treatment or the no English bullshit?" Pig Franklin says, I look over at Big Hen.

"Since you're not placing us under arrest I'm going to reach into his pocket so don't shoot me." They both laugh at Jasmine as she reaches into my pocket. She pulls her phone out and I can hear her mumble into my back but she's been on her bluetooth the whole time. I chuckle as she turns her phone around, I grab it and hold it out for one of the pigs to take it.

"This is District Attorney Pierce, Officer Franklin please tell me that you and Officer Brown have probable cause for stopping my client. While you're at it, have you allowed her to put on her head dressing? She's already told you that it was in the vehicle and seeing that you two ambushed them and are not planning on arresting them don't violate her rights any longer." Pig Brown's so mad he walks away, Pig Franklin gives me back the phone and laughs. I help Jasmine in the truck and we pull off.

"Once again Cargo, you've out done yourself. Even yo' girl got pull on some real quick thinkin' type of shit for real. I would've never thought of the religion thing but that shit was dope. Then to jump on the phone and let the DA do all the talking, never cease to amaze me nigga. Never cease to amaze me!" We all laugh. I tell her to put her ring back on and not take it off again. I can't help but stare at my wife feeling lucky as hell. Once we step in the house I pin Jasmine against the door pulling her legs up into my arms.

The next morning I jump out of bed and get to cooking before Ms. Janine can make it in. I hear Tristan go down to the gym, not long after I'm hurrying to finish up. I can hear the shower going so I run past Ms. Janine coming in the door saying hello quickly and take the stairs to join him in the shower.

"What you doing all that running for? I was willing to wait until you made it in here." Jasmine laughs and gets in with me.

"Good Morning."

"Every morning I wake up with you is beyond good baby. We still have a couple spots to hit up but I'm not taking you back out until I figure out what those punk ass nigga's want. You surprised the shit out of me last night with how you handled all of that."

"So you about to tell me what's the deal with all that?" I pull her in knowing exactly what you she really asking me but I ask her what anyway.

"Who is she Tristan?" I step in front of him and wash my hair while he plays with my nipples making me laugh.

"Her name is Carmen, I used to mess with her but cut her off like the rest when you sank my phone." Jasmine laughs as I help her rinse the shampoo out of her hair.

"You sure? I mean that's been a long time ago and it sounded like she didn't get the message that she was cut off at all."

"I guess that's the problem. I didn't leave a message, I just stopped fuckin' wit' her and never looked back. If you want I can holla at her and let her know the deal." Before I know it I reach down and grab a hold of his penis and his eyes spring open wider.

"You said this was mine, if you want to talk with her this needs to stay here with me." I turn Jasmine around and pin her against the wall of the shower.

"It is yours, just like this here is mine." My finger is covered the second I rub her lips and stroke her clit.

"You don't have to worry about her or no other chick, all you have to worry about is keeping my ring on yo' damn finger." I get in and Jasmine is cumin' all over me with just a few strokes. After we dress we head downstairs and eat breakfast.

"Now ya'll just taking it too far. Why every time I come over here and ya'll eating Jas have to be sitting on yo' lap?"

"Stop haten Dena. What the hell you doin' over here this early anyway?" Dena makes her a plate and we go back to eating. Tristan keeps telling me all the things he wants to do to me and what he plans on using to make it happen.

"I'm here to take Mrs. Warner's giggling ass with me to the shop so she can figure out the hair and makeup for this second wedding."

"Dena, it's not a second wedding it's more of an introduction to let all these crazy girls know who my husband is." We all laugh and Tristan kisses me.

"Cool. I'll let them know that ya'll riding with them today."

"Hold up potna! I don't want to be with those two Damon looking ass nigga's, why can't we take yo' car?" I knew that's what Dena was getting around to.

"I get that." We both look at Jasmine trying to figure out what it is that she gets.

"The Damon thing. He's in that move with the little pimp, I get it. But I don't need Roman and Aaron tagging along with us all day." We crack up laughing at Jasmine.

"So what you gon' say if somebody roll up on you and ask you what's up baby?"

"Easy I'll say, 'Nothin', jus' clapping hammers at niggers and slangin', what it be like wit' ya'll?' did I get it right?" They both laugh like I said it wrong. Tristan's face is in my neck and he's bugging up laughing at me.

"Hell naw! Cargo we gon' need more than two of those nigga's, we need a fleet if Jas crazy ass gon' be out there talkin' like that." We laugh harder and my baby looks like she doesn't understand why.

"I got you baby. Just stick to the religion bit and keep yo' phone on just in case."

"Cargo, we should take yo' car for real. Don't act like that," Dena says looking like I'm really hurting her damn feelings or something.

"It's not my car for the thousandth time Dena, it's my wife's along with any and everything else. So go ahead and take the Bently they can follow ya'll."

"No, not take the Bently we can take my car."

"What? Jasmine, did you just hear yo' damn husband say we can take a damn Bently? Why can't he take the Fortwo?"

"Because I'm a grown ass man and too fucking big to be in a damn Fortwo, I got a ride. I don't care what car ya'll take as long as them nigga's know they going with ya'll." They think the shit funny but I'm dead ass serious about them nigga's going.

"Jas, I can't believe you was about to pass up letting me soar in this damn car. I thought we were better than that." I look over at Dena, her eyes are closed and she's laid back and loving it.

"Shit, I forgot about this." Dena is looking down at her phone texting somebody as I pull up to the stop light.

"I need to go down to the O'Fallon Place and sign the paperwork for the movers to deliver mama stuff to her new place." I look over at Dena like she's crazy.

"Well let me hurry up and get back to the house so you can do that."

"Jas, it will only take a couple hours. We will be in and out I promise. Come on Jas, it will take a couple hours for you to take me out there and for me to make it back down there. Please Jas." Dang, I know Tristan will be upset if I go down that way but she's right.

I turn off leaving Aaron and Roman at the light and speed off towards the highway. We pull up in O'Fallon Place with all eyes on us and my phone starts going crazy. Dena jumps out and walks over towards the movers. I get out and make my way over to see how much longer we will be.

"Dena, why is Mrs. Terry moving back into the Cochran?"

"Girl this is all mama knows, she feels like if she moved out in Earth City to her house she'll be leaving her family behind. You know she's had that house out their longer than you've been alive. Trust, she ain't going nowhere out the hood." I just don't get why she would want to be around all the foolishness that goes on down this way. They tore down the old Cochran to only rebuild it and let all the same knuckleheads back in. My phones ringing so much, I go back to the car so that I can charge it.

"Hey baby, how's your day going?"

"Don't give me that Jasmine. Baby why them nigga's say you ditched them at the light." I can't help but laugh at Tristan.

"I love you so so much. How long are you going to be? I have something I want to try out on you." Jasmine slick as hell, she has me laughing and picking up my speed to get to her ass.

"Hold on baby let me help Dena with this bo—" Just my luck, I dropped my phone trying to get out the car too fast and didn't unplug it from the charger. I stoop down to gather the pieces and notice the darn screen is shattered.

"So I guess my man still wit' yo' ass huh?" I stand up and look behind me and see none other, Stephanie.

"I'm sorry, do I know you?" She laughs but all her teeth are practically black. She's wearing pajama pants twice her size with dirty house shoes. Her hair is all over like she just rolled out of bed.

"Bitch please, you know who da fuck I am. Anyway, since you stole my man da least you can do is let me hold five dollars 'til I see yo' ass again." She moved closer and pulled a ran over stroller from behind the end of my car that I didn't notice was there.

When I looked in I knew it was Fred, I can't help but smile at his handsome face. Then I want to pull every rotten tooth out of her mouth, shove them in a bag and beat her to death with it. She deserves a slow painful death. Then I hear a cry and move closer and see a newborn behind him. I have tears race to my eyes seeing just how grubby they both are.

"Hi Fred, I've missed you so much little man. Stephanie, can I pick him up?" I was squatting down in front of Fred and looked up, Stephanie pulled them both away, I stood to my feet.

"Now you know my name? Bitch please. You gon' give me da twenty dollars or what?"

"Stephanie, what's the babies name? Is she yours?"

"Naw bitch, I'm 'round dis mufucka stealin' kids fo' da hell of it. Would you hurry up and give me da damn forty dollars so I can take dem to my mama? She waiting on me to get back so she can go to da store and I need da money so she can get dem some pampers." She went from five to forty and still talking to me like I'm her enemy.

"Stephanie, how much will it take for me to take them? I mean for good?" Her eyes saw gold when I asked her that, she was excited, rocking back and forth like a child.

"Ten thousand!" At that moment I wanted to tie her to a pole and find the smallest pebbles I could and stone her until she died.

"I'll tell you what, you sign over your rights and agree to have your tubes tied at my expense and I'll give you twenty thousand." She looked like she won the biggest bingo jackpot ever heard of.

"You'z a dumb bitch, you know dat right. You know damn well Cargo not gon' give you no twenty thousand. But if you want all that it's gon' cost yo' ass twenty two. Cash!" I looked behind her as Aaron and Roman pulled up jumping out the truck coming towards us.

"I don't need his money I have my own. I'll give you my number and you

221

call me when you're re——" Some guys were coming over calling Stephanie, she looked like she was about to run for her life.

"Damn bitch, I told yo' ass to hurry up. Give me a——" The guys were now behind Stephanie. Roman's pulling me behind him and Aaron's on the side of her.

"Bitch, where da fuck is my money?" the taller guy said to her.

"I told you I waz waitin' on dis ho to bring it down herrre." They all laughed. The taller guy didn't, he stepped forward out the group and Aaron looked like he was about to snap. The guy took notice and kept his distance.

"You know damn well dis bit——"

"I don't know why the fuck you would let her ass take you for two grand when you know damn well she can't pay the tab." I moved from behind Roman because Tristan came out of nowhere. When I looked around I noticed we really had all eyes on us, there was about eight cars with guys all standing around.

"Cargo, I don't have any beef wit' you but dis bitch using yo' name to get shit and dodging when it's time to pay," the taller guy said but he didn't sound as confident as he did before.

"Go holla at Bobo Cortez, tell yo' boys to go on about dey day, this shit not worth it." Tristan looked back at me and Roman, he didn't say anything but Roman opened the door for me and put me in the car.

Dena was already inside looking out the window like she didn't know why we were here. When I looked back they had moved out of my way so I backed out. Before I made it out the parking lot I saw Stephanie getting into Tristan's car and I feel like I'm going to throw up.

"I'm sorry Jas I di—"

"Shhhhhh!" I turned up Jazmine Sullivan, 'Bust Your Windows' remix with Trey Songz and drove the couple blocks to Mrs. Terry's new place.

She lived in a new townhouse right behind the Center. Dena jumped out to open the door for the movers and went inside; I guess to get them started. I need to clear my head, I was so freaking close to getting Fred for good and Tristan sends me away while he takes care of Stephanie. They were so dirty and sick looking, I can't forgive myself for leaving without getting them. His hair was all over his head and the tail tail signs of abuse were branded into his little legs.

When I look up I'm almost to the riverfront, I guess my mind took over and guided me to a comfort zone. I figured I'll keep going and take a moment to myself and call Roman to pick me up. The entire time I sat out looking into the river I couldn't think of anything else besides Fred and that newborn. I let my tears fall until they were all out.

"Bitch, where is my money at?" I jumped at the familiar voice and looked behind me. It was Queen Ruby, I feel a hard wack come across the back of my left ear and neck sending me to the ground.

"I told yo' ass it was Esta. Stupid bitch thought she was just gon' run off, check her pockets. Hurry up bitch before da police come." I can feel them going in my pockets but I can't move, I'm seeing spots as I fade in and out.

19 ANGER

"Miss, can you hear me?" I'm struggling to open my eyes and when I do I can see a nurse standing in front of me then a doctor walking into the room. I ask them where I am and they tell me the hospital.

"What's your name Miss?" Dr. Hannah, a tall white man who looked like Frasier asked me so I told him.

"You've been here for two days unconscious. Do you have any family or relatives we can call?" Two freaking days, what the heck does he mean I've been here for two gosh darn days?

"I need a phone. Give me a phone to call my husband." I try and sit up but the lights go out again and I feel my body no longer.

"Jasmine, baby wake up. Come on baby wake up for me." I can hear Tristan talking but I can't open my eyes. My parents are waving at me while I ride around on the carousel in Magic Kingdom.

"Mr. Hornet, your wife was beaten severely, her ankle is broken and she may have some hearing loss in her left ear. We'll need to do more testing to determine that. It's all in the report; however, she was six weeks pregnant and the fetus didn't survive. I'm sorry for your loss Sir." I can't hear shit but *ringing in my damn ears after hearing what he said.*

Shit, is hearing loss contagious? I feel like I den lost my damn hearing with all the ringing in my fucking ears. All I can do is yell at the top of my lungs. I wanna fuck somebody up, hell I wanna fuck the world up for taking my first born.

I'm pacing so hard into my thoughts that I turned and slammed right into someone. When I focused on the here and now I was being guided to an empty room, it was Ghost. She put her arms around my neck and I caved in like a baby almost taking us both down to the floor. We didn't say a word to each other. I don't know how long I was going but something told me to pull my shit together. I jumped to my feet and went back in the room with Jasmine. I need her to get up and tell me what happened.

"Jasmine, I need you to wake up baby." I kiss all over her battered face and thought back on how many times I saw her like this. Then it hit me like an asteroid to the chest.

"THAT BITCH!" I'm on my way out the door when I hear my baby call for me stopping me in my tracks.

"I'm sorry Tristan I...I."

"Jasmine, damn I'm glad to hear your voice." I sat next to her trying to stop her from crying. The doctor and nurse came in and checked over her.

"Mrs. Hornet, welcome back. I have som——"

"Hold up Doc, let me speak with you outside for a moment." Tristan kissed me and walked out with Dr. Hannah closing the door.

"I would rather tell her when we get home." I start to walk away when he stops me.

"Mr. Hornet, I don't think that will be a great idea. Your wife's blood pressure is unstable and with this type of news she may go into shock. That runs the risk of her falling unconscious, she could possibly fall into a comatose state. It's best to give her the news here where we can monitor her and treat her if that's the case."

"GOT DAMN!" I can hear Tristan yell from outside the room, after a couple minutes they both come back in. Tristan kisses me and I can see the tears break from his eyes as he leans into my ear.

"Baby, I'm so fuckin sorry this shit happened to you. Please forgive me for this and be strong." I don't know why he's saying this, he kissed all over the side of my face and ear as Dr. Hannah started talking.

I didn't hear a word after six weeks pregnant, I reached down and held my stomach. Then all I could do was scream when he said those three words sending me into the pits of Hatis. The next morning we were scheduled to leave out of the hospital. Tristan looked down at his phone and draped a blanket over the top of me. He kissed my lips before he pulled it all the way down and there was a knock at the door.

"Mr. Hornet, I'm Detective Sledge, this is my partner Detective Elkins. We need to ask your wife a few questions and get a statement about the incident that took place."

"I don't have a statement and I don't remember anything, you can contact my lawyer, Dr. Hannah has her information. Please excuse us so we can be on our way." I can see Tristan walk back behind my wheel chair and start towards the door. The two detectives didn't budge to allow us to pass.

"Please Mrs. Hornet, we're here to help find who did this to you, we're

not the enemy. Mr. Hornet, may we have a moment to speak wi—"
Detective Elkins said.

"GET THE FUCK OUT MY WAY BITCH!" I looked down in shock
hearing Jasmine go off on her the way she did.

"Ma'am pl—"

"GET ME THE FUCK OUT OF HERE, NOW!" Jasmine screamed, I don't
know what the hell's going on but I snap out of it and had her in the car
before she really let loose.

She wouldn't let me take the sheet off of her and it's tearing my heart
apart thinking back on when I found her. The shit seemed like it was
happening all over again. I carried her to the room and she asked me to
leave. I didn't want to go but she started yelling and cussing me out so I did.

As soon as I heard Tristan close the door I pulled the sheet from over me
and crawled to the door to lock it. I grabbed my laptop from the desk and
started my bath water. I'm heartbroken and need to get the fuck out to clear
my head.

After I cleaned up I was dressed and sliding down the steps trying not to
be seen. I saw the cab pull up as I climbed out the window and managed to
limp my way inside. I was seated on the train leaving out of Jefferson City in
no time. I don't give a damn where I go I need this more than anything.

"Jasmine baby, can I come in?" She didn't say anything so I tried again
with no answer. I tried to give her some space, it was almost ten, she had
been in there since two and I'm getting in to see her. I took her food upstairs
and knocked, not getting an answer I jimmied the door and went in anyway.
I looked around and didn't see her anywhere, I'm baffled and pissed.

When I looked in the bathroom I see her laptop on the counter so I searched it. I feel my world end when I see that she was looking at flights and different places to go. I jumped on the phone taking the laptop to track where she was headed. After a couple hours of searching with no luck I knew I needed to make the call and I'm not going to wait any longer.

"Bateador, I need you man." Hearing the words come out my mouth had me holding back the pain in my voice while the tears streamed down my face.

"Chill out youngin', I know this shit is hard but I got you covered. It's two of my best on the train with her and I need you to pull it together. Get to the airport they waitin' to take you out to Minot so you can meet up with her."

"Thanks big dog, I owe you my life for this shit."

"We family nigga, stop playin' and get yo' ass to the airport and get my lil sis back. Cargo, sorry for your loss bro. When you get up with her come out to yo' house, she may need to be around family right now."

When I arrived in Minot station, I waited as everyone got off the train before I limped my way off. It's hard just seeing how far I have to go in order to get another ticket at the counter. I sat down on the bench and cried for what seemed like hours. The sun was about to come up when I finally had the strength to stand up and get another ticket. A guy held the door open for me as I limped my way in the doors towards the counter.

"Please let me help you Ms," an older heavy white man said to me.

"I'm fine I ju—" My body was lifted off the ground. I looked up and Tristan's holding me in his arms with tears in his eyes. I feel horrible for what I'm doing to him and dropped my head into my hands not wanting to look him in the face.

"Do you know this man? I'll get security," the man said as he walked away calling for security. Tristan kissed my hair as he moved towards the exit.

"Hold it right there!" I looked around, Tristan was still walking like he didn't hear the black guard say a word. The three guards came over as Tristan opened the door.

"I'm fine thank you." He closed the door, they turned around walking back inside, he pulled off. We rode to the airport in silence, he pulled up, turned off the car and looked over at me.

"Jasmine, who did this to you?" She looked out the window and said nothing. After a while she opened the door pulling herself out the car. I walked around to help her.

"Is this really what you want baby? Do you really want to leave me?"

"I need sometime a—"

"Away from me? Is that what you're about to let come out your mouth? Jasmine, it's me baby, Tristan. Please baby don't do this to me. Let me take you to your place on Koro, I can stay outside if you want." Jasmine looks down letting out a long sigh as tears drop from her eyes.

"Let's go Tristan, if that will make you happy." He backs up and when I look at him his face is wet and he looks so hurt.

"I want to make you happy baby. Tell me what I can do to make you happy Jasmine."

"I don't fucking know Tristan, damn! Just give me a break, I just lost my got damn baby two days ago and I told yo' ass already I needed some space. Shit, I practically abandoned yo' thick headed ass and you still in my damn face. Just move Tristan and let's get this shit over with!" She pushes me in the chest but I don't budge and she screams out for me to move. I pick her up and carry her onto the plane as she cries in my arms.

After we arrived I told him I didn't want him around me and to get another ride. I closed the door and told the driver to pull off, he helped me inside and I fell on the couch crying my heart out. A second turned out to be a week that I spent sitting on the couch crying. I only got up to use the restroom. I didn't shower, eat and rarely drank anything.

My hair's a mess and my mind's even worse. I know Tristan's around, every time I wake up there's a letter and some gift from him. I don't bother reading them, I toss it all in the trash whenever I see something from him. As I walked back out the bathroom back to my spot I went to lie back down and I noticed someone sitting across from me.

"Leave me the fuck alone, I'm not up for your shit today." I meant every word I said. She can laugh all the fuck she wants but she's not pregnant and about to catch a beat down.

"You better watch who the hell you talkin' to." I had enough, somebody's getting their ass whooped and it's not going to be me today. I got up off the couch ignoring the boot on my left foot and the pain.

"Say something else bitch." She stood up with a grin on her face. As soon as her mouth looked like it was about to open I went to smack the shit out her ass. She grabbed my arm pulling it around my back holding me in place.

"Yo' dumb ass should've waited until yo' ankle was better before you stepped to me." She laughing like she has the upper hand. I broke free and sent a right kick to her but she managed to step away as I stumbled to catch my balance.

"This ain't what you want lil girl, but if it is bring that ass out back." She skipped her ass out the side door and I'm hot on her tail. When we made it out I walked over and sent two to her face and an elbow to her stomach. This crazy ass laughing telling me to do better before she shut it down. I tightened the straps on the boot and said fuck it.

"Bring it on bitch!" We moved around and when I see my shot, I took it. I didn't know she could fight but that only made me more furious. She didn't hold back though, she was landing some shit mostly to my sides trying to break me down. I wasn't having it, I tried to snap her fucking neck but she broke free sending me to my knees with an elbow to my stomach.

I rolled away with her coming forward kicking my forearms like she wanted to send my head across the yard. I grabbed her leg pulling it forward sending a right fist straight to her pussy. She dropped down giving me time to hit her a couple more times in the face.

"Bitch you crazy," she said laughing. Then she turned up the heat and it felt like she had bricks in her hands when they touched my face. I recovered but she kicked me in the chest sending me crashing to my back. She's on top of me, I'm too weak to get her off.

"Told you dummy you didn't want none of this. Now listen up, you're not the only one going through this shit. Your fucking husband is losing his mind over you and I don't like what the fuck I see. He lost his first child too. The least you can do is spend some time with Cargo. I don't give a fuck if ya'll don't say shit and sit there.

Let him come in with you and be close to yo' dumb ass because that's all he wants. I'm tired of him peepin' in the fuckin' windows mopping around here like a dead man. Just so you know bitch, you ever come at me again, I'll kill yo' stupid ass!" She laughed and got off of me. I grabbed her hair and punched her in the face. She whipped around me and had me in the sleeper. I'm seeing spots and hearing her fucked up laugh.

"I like you Jasmine, but I'll snap yo' neck." I see a figure that's running towards us.

"T, let her the fuck go! What the fuck you doing over here T? Didn't I tell yo' ass to leave her the hell alone," I hear Pandillero say as he walked over picking me up. I told him to leave me alone as I cried again.

"Cargo, get over here for yo' wife!" He snapped his phone shut and walked back to Treasure, she was laughing like she's insane.

"Deangelo, don't give me no shit about this. I told her and she brought her ass out here swinging on me. Go 'head—" She stopped talking. He pulled her up into his arms and kissed her like I'm not sitting here. She wrapped her legs around his waist as I stood up to my feet.

"Thanks Treasure, I needed that." She laughed and said no problem, Pandillero looked at me like I was crazy. I turned around feeling better running right into Tristan.

20 DIVINE ORDER

"What's going on?" I see Jasmine and Treasure, look like they had been going at it. Jasmine put her arms around my neck, I pick her up and carried her away not caring what happened. When we made it upstairs, I sat her on the bed and ran her some water. She asked me to stay and get in with her and I'm too happy to do it.

"I'm sorry baby." I pulled away from Tristan and turned around sitting on his lap.

"You comfortable?" She said yes but she sho' don't look it. Her leg is on the edge of the tub so her cast won't get wet. I told her I was sorry again and she kissed me.

"It's not your fault baby. I'm sorry for treating you the way I have been. I'm scared that my life is cursed and no matter how much good happens to me there will always be something horrible to follow." Tristan kissed me like he was trying to suck out my feelings and replace them with his love.

"Don't think like that because it's not true. You still love me?" She moved and I felt her slid down on me. I'm trying my best not to jump up from the tightness of her walls.

"I never stopped loving you Tristan, I think I stopped loving myself and couldn't be around you seeing how much you loved me." I don't know if he heard me or not, his eyes are slammed shut like he's in pain.

I swirled my hips and he held my waist still grinding in and out of me slowly. When he found my spot it was like his penis was jumping, knocking on it causing me to burst into a thousand pieces. He stood up to his feet and carried me to the bed flipping me over onto my knees while he was still inside of me.

"Now we about to fuck all night, 'til this shit get right!"

"I'd rather have some lazy love, just so you know." My shit gettin' harder just hearing the words come out her mouth.

"I love you baby. Tell me you'll never do this shit again." She moaning and I'm beating the pussy up only slowing to get my answer.

"Tristan...don..don't stop...Please don't stop." He's pumping in and out of me fast and hard while playing with my pearl at the same time.

"SHHHH...FUUU...answer me Jasmine!" I have her lifted in the air still banging her back out.

"I..I..promise..I   won't..won't...mmmmm...dothisshitagain."   I'm depleted, we collapse down to the bed riding simultaneous waves together. I feel like eight hours has past and I'm still nuttin.

"Damn I missed you baby, I told you forever even after death so don't do this shit again Jasmine." He pops my behind pulling me into him more.

"Don't move Tristan, stay right there and let me sleep." I kissed her on the neck and moved anyway. My dick still hard, I put her on top of me and eased my way back in as she held on under my shoulders burying her head into my chest.

Tristan's hard on is bringing me out of my sleep making me rock up and down on him. I pulled myself up with my eyes still closed bracing my hands on his chest helping me ride him. He wrapped his hands around my thighs bringing his knees up and pumped into me at a furious pace. The sound of my butt smacking against him as my breast bounced up and down was so arousing. I grabbed them holding them close as a flood came breaking out of me. Tristan yelled out with a few more thrust and I can feel the hot liquid fill my insides.

"You awake now baby?" I giggled not knowing how he didn't know that I was awake.

"Of course I'm awake Tristan." I laughed and rolled her on her back.

"That's the fourth time we den' had sex since you got on me after we got out the tub." She looked at me like I was lying to her, I told her again and she laughed hard.

"Told you I wanted that lazy love. You have me craving it so bad I don't want to go anywhere, I hope you feel the same."

"You betta know I do, now come on here so I can get yo' freaky ass cleaned up, you need to eat. You've lost a lot of weight and I need you healthy baby." After we cleaned up and got dressed we headed to the restaurant to eat.

I feel like a new man with my wife back on my arm smiling up at me. The next morning we sat down to eat breakfast and it was just like old times. She was on my lap as we ate talking shit about what we wanted to do to each other.

"What's good ya'll?" I laughed and sat Jasmine in the chair walking over to greet Treasure.

"I don't know if I should be pissed with you are happy right about now." I hugged her as she laughed, hugged me then pushed me away walking towards Jasmine. Jasmine stood up and they looked each other down then laughed and hugged one another. Before I could make it over Bateador came in followed by Jack and Hammer.

"Let's go Treasure!" Bateador said without even looking at me walking towards the two of them.

"Corey, I'm grown! Shouldn't you be in the meeting with Deangelo? You put one finger on me and I'm breakin' that mufucka!" We all laughed but Bateador looked pissed.

"Don't start no shit with me today Treasure, I'll drag yo' little ass out of here with the quickness," Bateador said walking up on her. I walked over to him.

"Come on Bateador, it's all good." He didn't look at me he kept his eyes on Treasure.

"My bad Cargo. How you doing Jasmine?" he said all that shit still looking at Treasure as she stared him right back down. Jasmine stepped in front of him and hugged him, he looked down at her and smiled.

"I'm fine Bateador. Thanks for asking. I'm not upset with Treasure and I don't think she's upset with me. I guess sometimes a good fight can clear your head up." She turned and hugged Treasure thanking her as they both laughed. Bateador looked at me then back at them and asked me to step outside with him so I did.

"Cargo, I'm sending Dr. Mapenzi over here, I think yo' girl just as crazy as Treasure and Sammy." I thought I would shit myself laughing so hard at what this nigga said. He was serious as a mufucka looking at me like I was looney.

"Bateador, she already has a shrink, you already know that." He pacing back and forth.

"I'm serious Cargo, this dude specialize in what's going on with them. Just let him rap with her for a minute and hear him out. If he say she good then so be it. Do this for me Cargo, you said you owed me and I'm collecting." I laughed again.

"That's fucked up nigga. You claim we were good already." He laughed with me.

"Damn nigga, I had to try and use something. Just do this shit as a favor for me. Give the nigga an hour." I told him cool and we went back inside, they were sitting down talking. Treasure was eating some fruit.

"Let's go Treasure," Bateador said pulling her around in her chair.

"Go 'head, touch me Corey. Try me if you want to." I'm stunned at the new Treasure, this girl's the truth, she not backing down for shit.

"T, get yo' ass up!" Pandillero said coming from behind me. She was doubled over laughing hard.

"What's up Cargo." I spoke back waiting to see what she would say to him.

"Hey Jasmine." He hugged her. Treasure was still laughing in her own world. He kneeled down in front of her and whispered something in her ear. Her head shot up and her laughing stopped.

"I dare you. First you wanted me up, now you want me back in the damn bed. I'm grown, I can do what I want to do. Corey, I can't believe you called him on me. I was ready to take you up on yo' promise to me." Pandillero looked back at Bateador, he looked behind me towards the door.

Next thing I know in runs Shay, Frick and Frat I look back and Unk, Aunt, and Gran were being lead in by Ms. Jackson and Mrs. Kilberg pushed in a stroller with Pam, Alejandro and Kathy inside. Sammy came down the hall pushing a stroller with her newborn son Corey and Treasure's newborn son DJ.

"Sammy, didn't I tell you not to leave out the house?" Bateador said walking over to Sammy.

"What? Man I'm grown, miss me with all that!" We all fell out laughing, Bateador picked Sammy up taking her back outside.

"So what's up T, we doing this now?" Pandillero picked up Peppermint placing her on Treasure lap then picked up Ali.

"What do you mean husband? I'm doing whatever you want me to do, you know that." I don't know what the fuck happened, I had to move closer to get a good look at Treasure.

I took one look at her then back at Pandillero, he cracking up laughing now. The shits unreal, her eyes were brown not yellow like they were before the kids came in. I looked at Jasmine then at Treasure back to Pandillero and took off out the door for Bateador.

"Look nigga, get that mufucka over here not now but right fuckin' now!" This nigga laughing hard at me. I was so fucking serious my ass started pacing.

"Naw, you straight remember. She already got a shrink, I can fly Dr. Cooper out when she's available."

"Bateador, stop fuckin' around with me and get that nigga ova' here man." They both started to laugh at me.

"Cargo, calm down. Jasmine is nothing like Treasure and damn sure not me. Trust me, I know that. But White's already here, see, he's pulling up," Sammy said, I turned around and then looked back at them. I see this supposed to be doctor step out a black and red Maybach 57S Coupe that's bumping Tupac's "Hit 'Em Up".

"Stop playing!" They both laughed again. I walked back to the door and called for Pandillero to step outside for a second. When he came out I looked at the nigga then looked at the nigga coming up the steps and busted a gut laughing my damn self.

"What the fuck is going on? You nigga's are something else." We all were laughing.

"Hello, I'm Dr. Mapenzi, you must be Mr. Warren." I shook the nigga hand still laughing at the shit like I was nuts.

"What's good man, you can call me Cargo. My wife inside, give me a minute and I'll bring her out."

"Hold up Cargo, we leaving out. Come by tonight for dinner we all can chill out before ya'll take off," Pandillero said.

"How you know we leaving?" They laughed and started packing kids up, Jasmine didn't want to let Sammy pull the babies away. She had tears in her eyes when Sammy told her to come by later to see them. I walked her to the couch and helped them out the door before going back inside with her.

"Hey baby, hear me out for one second. There's a Dr. Mapenzi out front wanting to speak with you for a minute. If you're not up to it then it's fine, I'll send him away." She didn't respond. I kissed her and she held me closer to her.

"You alright with this?" She nodded her head and kissed me again. I jumped up and told him to come in. Jasmine looked over and slowly stood up.

"Damn!" Jasmine said, I don't know whether I should be mad, jealous, embarrassed, or amused with how she reacted to him.

"Tristan, he look just like, like, but darker and slimmer, but like, umm, umm." I couldn't get the words out my mouth.

This man's drop dead beautiful without a doubt. His skin's dark chocolate and glowing like he's an angel that has his own sun. His lips look so soft, full and kissable. His smile is bright and cold from the chill of those diamonds on his canines and bottom outer incisors. He didn't dress like a doctor, he dressed more like a thug with Timberland boots on his feet. They weren't even laced up, he had a vibe coming from him that was unstoppable; like a hustler.

"Hi. It's nice to meet you Mrs. Warren, I'm Dr. Mapenzi. Lately I've been told on numerous occasions that I look like Mr. Joseph. Believe it or not, we're related and get this, Mr. Taylor is his half-brother right. Well Mr. Taylor has a strong resemblance to my half-brother Abdalla." I looked at Tristan, he was looking at me like I was about to get beat down for staring at the doctor.

"Hello Dr. Joseph, I mean...well...okay. I need to speak with my husband please." Tristan's laughing like he found something funny. I pulled him by the arm up to the bedroom closing the door.

"Tristan, you know that man looks just like Pandillero right?" Jasmine's limping back and forth, I pulled her into my arms laughing at her crazy ass.

"What's up Ma'? You feeling them nigga's like that? You ain't ever reacted like that to yo' husband. Here this nigga come and you can't think straight." She was laughing hard now.

"I'm sorry baby, I love you to death and they don't have anything on you but that shit is spooky!" Tristan bit down on my lip stopping me from talking.

"I don't like the new you with the cursing baby. Can we get back to the funny curses you used to say?" I laugh and shake my head because I don't know what has come over me lately.

"I'm sorry baby, you won't hear another profanity come from these lips, I promise."

"Can we get back in there so you can talk with him?" She raised her eyebrow like she wanted to know if I was serious.

"Of course, but did you see how Treasure's eyes changed colors and she seemed like another person?" Now it was my turn to look at her wondering if she was serious.

I took her ass right on back down the steps because to hell with Treasure, Jasmine's my only concern. She sat down and I asked if she wanted me to stay and she said yeah. I told her I'd be in the back but she wanted me by her side so I said to hell with it. One hour lead to two followed by three before the two of them were finished. Dr. Mapenzi thanked her for *her time and stood to leave out.*

"Hold it one second Dr. Mapenzi." I was not about to let his tale walk up out of here that fast.

"Yes Mrs. Warren, is there anything else I can do for you?" This nigga smiling in her damn face like he know what she's about to say.

"I want to know your opinion on what's wrong with me." I looked at Jasmine then at him, he grinnin' and shit like that's exactly what he wanted her to say.

"Nothing." He tried to turn and walk away but I moved right on in front of him stopping him again asking for him to explain.

"Mrs. Warren, I don't have to tell you what you already know."

"Well tell me because I want to know what she already know and apparently you have the answer, so tell me." Tristan stood on the side of us as Dr. Mapenzi laughed and asked me if I wanted Tristan to know. I didn't know what he was talking about. Tristan sat there the entire time, he heard everything that was said. I told him to tell it.

"Okay, Mrs. Warren, you're suffering from the horrific loss of your baby and of your family. Your trying to come to terms with the fact that your grandmother should be treated as a stranger on the street. Not to mention an enemy. It's a hard thing for you to do, that's why you've reacted the way you have, mainly with the language. It's your way of trying to hold on to your grandmother because that's how she spoke to you all those years.

Even though you didn't say it, the fact that your grandmother and her boyfriend killed your child is making you doubt the love you feel for your husband. As far as I can see, your husband loves you and will stick by you not letting you continue down that path.

As far as you go Cargo, she's nothing like Mrs. Joseph, she's not even close to Mrs. Taylor. In time she will be the woman you married and not the woman you've seen over this time and defiantly not the woman you met." He walked out leaving us there staring off into space.

I turned and looked at Jasmine as a smile slowly spread across her face. The next thing I know she was all over me and we were going at it. By the time we finally came up for air we were an hour late and my phone was going crazy. We made it over just as everyone was about to sit down and eat dinner. They all laughed as we came in and we had a good time chillin' out like nothing happened. Jasmine spent some time with all the kids and we were on the first thing smoking back home.

21 ATTRACTION

It's been almost two months since we've been back, Jasmines been doing her thing staying busy. Her first foster home she planned on finding an older married couple, upgrading their home, and that was supposed to be it. That was basically the jist of it with her checking in on them to make sure everything was on the up and up. Now her entire outlook has changed. With the families help around the table, she's been working hard on making it come to life.

Ma' Earlean wouldn't back down on gifting her twenty acres of her land to build homes on. Treasure was able to get a deal together to purchase the surrounding eighty acres. Jasmine gave me hell about buying it for her but I wasn't having it any other way. She's also included a school, counselors and security around the clock. Tony put a rush on the build out so she has three houses already complete. I head over to her office in the green top and instantly I'm heated when I see Steph sitting in her office.

"Damn bitch, how you gon' set me up like dis?" I walk over to this slime bucket ready to put her damn lights out.

"So what, you gon' hit me nigga?" Jasmine walks over and I hold my *hand out at her.*

"I'm gon' tell yo' silly ass one last time to watch yo' fuckin' mouth when you talk to my wife!" Tristan looks like he's on fire with Stephanie, I tried to defuse the situation but he's not trying to hear anything.

"I ain't gotta watch shit! Fuck dat bi—" I jumped up from the side of my desk and walked over trying to get his hand from around her neck.

"Tristan, baby please let her go. For me baby let her go." Shit I hate this trick so fucking much. I'm trying to find some reason not to catch up with her ass later on and kill her. I let the ho go as she falls to the floor.

"I'm sendin' you to jail nigga! If dis bitch don't pay me my money I'm sendin' yo' black ass to jail." I laughed at her ass and sat down watchin' Jasmine help the trick up on the sofa. I pulled out my phone while she was still cussing and tellin' me what she was telling the police.

"Casper, you remember that pigeon dat was on my shoulder until it dropped the seed and flew away?" I walked over to Tristan trying to take his phone but he moved me back.

"Well it's back sayin' all kinds of crazy shit about caging me up and I think a guest appearance is needed."

"Shit, I got a seed in the microwave now and it'll be ready in another eight minutes. But for you, I can run the club for a couple of weeks tops. I gotta clear that with my old dude though, you know how silly he acts." I laugh hard at the thought of Ghost answering to anybody, I guess times sure have changed.

"It's cool, I'll see you in a few." Tristan hangs up his phone and I'm ready to smack the grin off his face. I turn and look at Stephanie and she looks like she's seen a ghost for real.

"Cargo I'm sorry, I won't talk shit to her nomo, I won't say shit! Call her back. Don't do dis to me Cargo, I'm sorry damn!" Stephanie is on her knees begging him to call her back.

"Tristan, get out!" I looked at Jasmine like she lost her damn mind telling me to get out.

"Go 'head wit' dat baby, you heard all the shit she flappin' on about." Jasmine walks over to me, I pull her in my arms and kiss the hell out of her before she can say anything. When I'm done she looks like her ass is dizzy.

"Stephanie, do you still want to proceed with this or what?" She rolls her eyes at me and sits back on the couch.

"Tell him to call her back and I need ten more because he called." I can hear Tristan laughing behind me.

"I'll call her myself and *he'll* give you fifteen more. When you go downstairs Mykell will be waiting for you to take you over to Pandora's Box. They'll go over your options and you can decide what you want to do. Don't forget our agreement though because Mykell will stay with you the entire time. Once the procedure is done and your given the all clear you can stop by here to pick up your payment." Stephanie tells me whatever and storms out of my office.

"What's all that about Jasmine?" She brushed past me grabbing up her things.

"You love me?" I walked behind her pulling her against me.

"You betta know it!" Jasmine laughed, we walked to the elevator as I bit on her neck.

"I sure can't tell. You run in and go straight to your ex like I wasn't even in the room." Tristan's sucking on my neck, I know I'll have a huge mark left behind.

"Fuck dat' girl Jasmine. I didn't know what the hell she was up to and I damn sure was not about to let her pop off at the mouth with you. You still haven't told me what all that was about." I help her in and jump in pulling off. I look over and she's tying her hair in the back into a knot like it's a ribbon or something.

"Why you do that to your hair all the time? Don't it get damaged or break from being tied up like that?"

"I don't think so. Dena hasn't said anything about it being damaged. It's thick enough for me to tie it so I do. You're not that worried about my hair being damaged when you're pulling on it."

"Hell, it's long enough so why not Rapunzle?" We both laugh, Tristan reaches over and tugs on my hair.

"So let big daddy know what the deal is." Jasmine reaches over as I cruise down the highway heading home, she's smiling biting on her lip. I'm watching her unzip my pants wondering what the hell she's about to do.

"Lift up a little and pay attention before we get into an accident." I do what she say's and pull into the right lane. I'm in straight shock as she leans over stroking my dick. The second she blows on my head I'm looking for somewhere to pull the fuck ova'. She wrapped her lips around my shit and I'm fighting to keep my eyes on the road. I put the pedal to the floor and got off the highway, I found a gas station and pulled on the side where I can see in all directions.

I hit up Aaron and Roman to head our way so I can enjoy what she's doing to me. I look down at her head moving up and down as she slurped and sucked me like she's starving. My chair started to move back, Jasmine smiled looking up at me with her mouth still sucking me in. I see Aaron and Roman pull up and take post as my eyes close, Jasmine's all hands, mouth and head bobbing.

"SHHHHHITTT!" The feel of her throat squeezing my head is making my damn toes numb. I'm rocking up holding her head long stroking her throat as she slobs down me. I can feel her swallow and I'm done dealing.

"I'm cumin' baby. Shit, I'm about to cum!" Jasmine gulped her juices up again swallowed and gave me nothing but short throat shots. I'm reaching for anything to hold on to so I won't rip her head off, my load shot straight down her throat.

"I love the hell out you Jasmine." I look up at Tristan and he's sweating like he's been working out. He pulled my face to his and kissed me trying to pull me on top of him. I wouldn't let him, I'm trying to get him covered back up.

"I'm really tired, can we go home now?" I pecked him on the lips and his mouth formed an O.

"So my wife denying me my pussy?" Jasmine laughs and unbuckles her seat belt.

"I'll never deny you baby, I just wanted you to recognize that I'm your wife." He laughs as I move over, he moved me to where I was sitting on his lap like I was about to drive.

"Is that right?" He pulled me down hard ramming inside me as I moaned louder than what I thought I would.

"Talk that shit now Jasmine!" I'm waxing her ass, she quiet as hell I told her to speak up.

"Ooookay. I get it daddy. Mmmmmm freak don't stop. Right there make it, make it, yes like that, make it jummmmmp." I'm trying my best to stop from continuously slamming into the horn.

Tristan's moving hard and fast pounding up into me like it's no one's business. I can feel all ten inches of him deep inside of me then almost nothing at all. I don't know how he's able to move so fast with so little space. He's moving like a jack hammer, I'm dripping by the time he relinquished his release. I fall back into his chest trying to snatch as much air up that I can.

"I can't move so somehow you need to drive with me here." I laughed, after a minute I moved the seat up pulling off still inside of her. When we made it home she knocked out not helping me one bit. I put her in the bed, jumped in the shower and was out the door to make my rounds.

My first stop is the Olive Garden in Maplewood, I pulled up right in time. I walk over to see just the two people I was meaning to catch before they left.

"What's good Trina, it's funny seeing you here." She looks at me then drops her head.

"What the fuck you doin' here youngin' and how the fuck you know my wife?" I look at Pig Brown like he stupid if he can't tell by the look on her face.

"Hey Stanley, long time no see. Stanley, this is my husband Ronald."

"That didn't answer my question Trina, how the fuck do you know this nigga?"

"Calm down Ronald, he's a personal trainer at my gym." I can't help but chuckle, dis' nigga don't believe a word she said.

"Yeah Ronald, I've been whipping that body of hers in shape for what two-three years?" I can see this nigga ball his fist up, he about to lose his mind right in front of me.

"What the fuck you want lil nigga, I thought yo' ass didn't know how to speak English?" I laugh in his bitch ass face.

"Shit, I saw my star pupil and she was always head strong so I came over to holla at her for a minute." This nigga slams his fist down on the car and look at Trina who's smiling in a nigga face.

"Get the fuck in the car Trina!" She waved and got inside.

"You know you should at least open the door for the lady, maybe she wouldn't have spent so much time with me training her." He walk up on me pulling his chain out from under his shirt.

"Put yo' hands up bitch and turn the fuck around." I laugh and look at the nigga like he crazy. He pulls out his strap and yell for me to follow his orders.

"What the fuck is going on here?" His punk ass mug the shit out of me.

"Mr. Pierce, please step back inside the restaurant until my back up arrives. I believe this is the fugitive Stanley that we've been searching for." City laughs and tells him to put down his weapon but he doesn't budge.

"Officer, you know damn well he's not a fucking fugitive and you damn sure don't have backup on the way. Now get that fucking weapon out of his face." He puts it back on his side and snatches the door open to his car.

"Please believe I'll do everything in my power to have your ass for what you pulled out here tonight," City said to him as he slammed the door and I winked at Trina walking off with City.

"Damn Cargo, what if I would've been late? That nigga would've killed yo' ass out there." We sit down at the bar.

"Come on man, you saw how close that nigga was. I could've taken his shit and beat the bricks off that nigga if I needed to."

"Let me guess, he was one of the nigga's that Jasmine called me about." I shook my head yeah as we laughed.

"I saw you looking at the lady, you not doing Jasmine in are you?" I laugh as we get our drinks.

"Hell naw! I love my wife nigga, I wouldn't do shit like that to her. That was his wife, I used to get at her on a regular for a couple years nigga. When wifey told me we were together she dumped my phone in a glass of water and I ain't hollad at Trina since." We both laugh again.

"Damn, she did yo' ass like that?" I nod at him.

"On a serious note Cargo, I'm sorry for you loss man. I can't wait to see the new you when ya'll have some shorties running around. I can already see that ring then slowed yo' ass down like a mother." We laugh more.

"Thanks man. I can't wait either, I'm trying my damndest to make it happen everyday. I never realized how much I wanted to be a father until that shit happened. Jasmine got a nigga going crazy."

"Speaking of crazy. Treasure told me what went down with her and Jasmine. Her silly ass told me Jasmine was about to take my spot as her best friend. Then she call me back and say she changed her mind because she's not fit for the role." We laughing but I'm thanking my lucky stars that Jasmine don't meet the requirements.

"And you Cargo, I can't believe you let yo' damn wife speak to that fake ass Mapenzi. Next thing you know yo' ass gon' let Safari and Blitz play around in her ass. I know she already using their office here, Pandora's Box." I'm laughing so loud people looking over at me.

"Negro please. Dem nigga's can try. And hell yeah I let her see Mapenzi, I damn near begged for her to holla at his ass. After watching Treasure and Bateador thinking Jasmine was like that. Shit'd, nigga I'd do it again." We were really rolling.

"You talking about me nigga, what about yo' fiancé, Sharon, you letting them nigga's play in her ass."

"Hell yeah! I'm waitin' on that nigga Safari to gon' take her off my hands. What the fuck you thinking?" We dying.

"City, how long you gon' wait around for Treasure? I mean why propose to the girl knowin' damn well you sticking around waitin' on Treasure?" He took a gulp and sat back.

"Man I love Treasure so fucking hard the shit at times makes me physically sick. I mean in a 'as long as she's happy' type of way, not no 'break up a happy home' type shit. When she was happy I was happy and I fell for Sharon. Then soon as all that shit went down, I was miserable and Sharon was making it worse. I know she love that nigga, shit she's loved him before I met her ass. Now I can't tell if she's happy or not and the shit fuckin' with me." He run his hands down his face and take another drink I look over at him.

"Anyway, hopefully it won't be too much longer and I'll find out what's up with Treasure. When I do, then I can go from there. I'm not sticking around waiting on her though, Sharon's on borrowed time as is. I've had my eye in the field for a minute and keeping company around when needed. I just don't want to start shit and get pulled back. But I'm ready to start a family that I can go home to everyday and watch them succeed. Hell, all Treasure kids are mine, I don't give a fuck how that nigga Pandillero feel about the shit."

"I hear you man, but back to Mapenzi, I didn't know that nigga looked just like Pandillero ass. That shit had me wiggin' out looking at the two of them up close."

"I told Pandillero he crazy as fuck bringing that nigga around her like that. It's like he's trying to push her to see how far she'll go before she snap on him again. I hate that I can't be there with her all the time."

"So you think she'll go at them again if she's pushed too far?"

"Man, she had been doing so well I didn't think she would do the shit she did. But that's the thing with her, it don't always go like you think. I tried to tell him but he so stuck on me loving her that he don't want to listen to me."

"Thanks for everything bruh, on errthang."

"Yo' ass can thank me by stop making me worry so much about seeing yo' file come across my desk or seeing yo' ass in a box."

"I don't know what you talkin' 'bout." We both laugh.

"I'm going to see lil sis tomorrow after I get off. She gon' be at the green top or home? I plan on getting her something so what she want?"

"Green top if she have her way but I told you what I was on so her ass gon' be at home with me. Jasmine so used to not having anything that she won't let anyone give her shit. She'll be happy with a book or candle from Deal's and cherish it like it cost a mil. She already had me downsize something serious. We down to three cars, the house and my loft at the club. I got her a Bently she only drove once and of course the houses on the island.

You know she tried to give it back but Bateador refused, then she tried to play him and use it to get me a ring. This nigga say he played along and before she got out he told her the house was still hers. Say she looked like she was about to cry begging him to keep it.

Like I said, she don't want shit and if it's expensive she really won't accept it and if she do it'll sit without her touching it. I have to get on her ass all the time about keeping her ring on. She been walking around all this time without it but I plan on using Gorilla glue on her ass tonight!" We kicked back and chilled for a minute then rolled out as the place closed.

22 REFLECTION

Istopped by my spot out in the county to see what was poppin' before I headed to the crib. The place was packed of course, I kicked it in the back for a minute then went to my office. I see Bobo come in and I already know what this nigga on so I wrap up what I'm doing waitin' on him.

"What's up Cargo, I thought yo' ass would be hiding out here wit' these county nigga's tonight."

"You know what it is man, gotta get this money, you should get yo' ass in on some of this legal shit." He laugh and sit down.

"Man, I'm tryin' to make a run for you. I been trying to make that real money like yo' ass been doin' all these years."

"Nigga please, only run you can make for me is downstairs unloading liquor or food off the trucks when they pull in. If you need a job man you know I got you at anyone of the clubs. Shit, I'd even let yo' ass figure out what you want to do as long as you don't bring no street shit in my place." I get up, go around the desk and pull a chair up close to the nigga.

"Come on Cargo, you know da..." I hit the power on for the radio and let 'Snitch,' by Wayne tell the nigga the truth about his self.

255

"I leav..." I watch the nigga sweat just muggin' his ass all the way 'til the song end.

"I gotta run man, holla at me if you serious on getting' yo' life together homie and you get tired of running all that dope and shit in the streets. You gon' fuck around and get a Rico charge for heading all that shit up like that nigga." I laugh and damn near throw his ass head first out the door. I watch the nigga run his scary ass out my club.

"Damn nigga, what's the deal wit' Bobo ass? I tried to rap wit' the nigga he take off like I'm chasin' his ass or something."

"I don't know man, that nigga silly. I'm out though so I'll holla at you later Big Hen." We dab off and I laugh my ass right out the door.

When I make it to my car I feel some hot shit hit me twice in my back slamming me into the door. I turn around blasting, I can see Big Hen and a couple other nigga's from the club bussin'. The truck pull off with the back and both side windows blown out. Big Hen run over ask me if I'm alright, I look at the nigga like he crazy for askin' me the shit.

"Hell naw nigga, I just took two fuckin' shotty rounds to the back, feel like my fuckin' ribs broke." I sit up as five o pull up followed by medics and the fire truck.

"Hey it's me again, I was wondering when you would be home. This the fifth time I've called you tonight and you still haven't called me back. I miss you baby, come home." I hang up and fall back into the bed wondering where in the heavens Tristan can be. He freak me to sleep then leave me without a word staying away all day and now the sun is coming up.

I'm about to show him just how it feels to worry, I know he was going insane worried about me on Koro, he's about to be reminded. I get up and get dressed making sure I'm breathtaking by the time I'm finished. I'm glad Dena taught me how to do my own make up. Looking in the mirror at myself has me wondering if it's really me.

It's eight in the damn morning before I make it to the house. I know Jasmine must be going crazy seeing I left out of here Friday and now it's Monday. I tried to get my ass out the hospital but they had a nigga so doped up I slept the days away. Good thing I was wearing my vest because my ass wouldn't be able to walk away after taking two to the back.

I see Jasmine coming around the corner wearing a light blue and white striped strapless dress. She has on tall teal colored wedged heels that show her rose painted toes. Her hair is pulled into a pony tail high on her head and she's wearing long teal wooden circle earrings that get smaller towards the bottom. She has the same style chain around her waist and a jean jacket on. I'm standing as she walks past like she doesn't see me, I go into the kitchen behind her. She grabs some things out the fridge putting it all in her bag grabbing her blue and white striped purse coming towards me.

"Hey Tristan." I pecked him on the cheek and kept it moving right to the door. I can feel him looking at me and I don't care to look back at him. I want to smack him upside the head but I thought against it knowing I'd never do that. When I felt him coming I picked up and almost ran to my car jumping in.

I was kind of surprised that he didn't catch me, it looked like he was having a hard time moving as I think back. It doesn't matter, whatever it is I hope he had fun doing it with whoever he did it with. I pull up at my office and go straight up to Nova's place, she said I can use it anytime I wanted. Hours pass with me sitting working away on my laptop trying to drown out Tristan's nonsense.

"What the hell you doin' hiding out here?" I look up and see Rider, I look away trying not to be so distracted with how gorgeous this man is. I've seen a few of his games on TV, he plays for the Bulls and is as cocky as can be. Not to mention flirtatious as all out.

"Hello to you to Rider, I'm working if it's okay with you. Nova said I can use her place if I wanted, she gave me a key. I didn't have to break in and I don't plan on stealing anything." He sits across from me laughing as I continue doing what I'm doing.

"What's up Jazzy J. I didn't say all that, I was just surprised to see yo' sexy ass up here that's all. This the last place I thought you would be with all that has happened." I look up at him not knowing what or why he would say that. I was about to ask when there was a knock at the door. I can hear who he's speaking with and stand to meet them.

"What's up Jasmine, what you doing here with Rider simple ass?" He's looking at me like I was doing something inappropriate with Rider before he walked in.

"Nigga please, I just walked in, she was here before me. Stop starting shit nigga, you know damn well I know better than that shit," Rider said to him then said he was leaving.

"Hello Bateador, I'm feeling some kind of way with what you just said. I hope you don't think that I would violate my marriage with another man." He laughs and walks closer to me.

"Naw, I know you wouldn't and I already knew that Rider had just come in here. I'm feeling pissed off at you right now though so I had to give you a hard time." I can feel my face scrunch up at him.

"What did I do to make you upset with me?"

"Yo' ass has Cargo lookin' for you again. I thought all this runnin' off shit was over and done with, yo' ass did ask the man to marry you."

"I'm not runnin' off Bateador, I'm working. If Tristan was looking for me all he had to do was call me or come to my office, he knows where I am. I can't say that about him though." I sit right back down and start working again not letting him get me upset.

"So that's why you hiding out up here? You upset that he didn't call or is it that he was away for a few hours?" I looked at him like he kicked me.

"A few hours? You're funny. Either way, call or not, away or not, he needs to be reminded how it feels when the shoe is on the other foot." He's laughing at me.

"Women are something else. Jasmine, let's go!" I look at him again wondering why he would think I took orders from him.

"Come on Jasmine, I told Cargo I would send you to him if he sat his ass down for a few and recovered." I was on my feet.

"What's wrong with Tristan? Why did you say that? Rider said something about all that's going on before you came in. I just saw Tristan, he looked fine but I have a feeling that's not the case. Are you here as his lawyer or what Bateador?" He laughed, told me to calm down and go home. I was out the door trying to get back and see what exactly was going on with Tristan.

I know wifey upset wit' a nigga and I was tempted to go up to Nova spot and bring her ass home with me. If Bateador didn't stop me, I know she probably would've kicked my ass for the shit I pulled on her. My body wore the hell out, even the sleep at the hospital couldn't help me rest like I needed to. I need my wife and I wasn't leaving her ass down there. She lucky his ass stopped me because she was coming home whether she wanted to or not.

I ran in the house kicking off my heels at the door along with all the stuff in my hands and my jacket. I ran up the steps looking for Tristan to find out what was going on with him. He wasn't in the room but I heard him in the tub so I went in without even knocking. I took one look at him and I couldn't hold my tears from rolling down my face.

His clothes were on the floor with a brace and his back was to me with his head under the shower. I stepped out of my clothes and opened the door getting in behind him. He didn't move, I leaned in and kissed the gigantic bruises that covered his entire back. He was purple and even a gentle kiss caused him to wince. I washed him then myself and we laid in the bed together, he was in my arms nuzzled into my chest.

"I love you Jasmine."

"I love you too baby." He kissed my chest and was out cold holding me close not willing to let me move. After a few hours I turned on the muted TV while he slept. The sun was long gone when I finished making him dinner, I took it up to him and woke him up so he could eat. I wasn't hungry, I was too worried to eat. I planned on watching him until he told me what was going on with him.

When he finished I helped him up to the bathroom and took his plate back down while he finished up. I made it back in and he was back in the bed waiting for me to get in with him. After he pulled me close again he was back asleep. I couldn't believe he hadn't said two words to me. I watched the TV all night waiting on him to get up but he didn't. I tried to make him breakfast, he asked me where I was going and he wouldn't let me go anywhere except to the bathroom.

Late afternoon, I still hadn't slept a wink, he was about to get up and tell me something. I eased out of his arms and kissed all over his neck down his chest as he rolled over to his back. His body is heating up as low groans come from his chest. His shaft is getting harder right in front of my eyes. I licked from his sack all the way up to the tip of him. His hands held on to my out stretched arms as I pinch on his nipples slightly.

He's slippery and shinning as I ease him into my mouth sucking him back. His hands tightened above my elbows, I tongued him down as if we were kissing. I pulled my hand loose holding his manhood while I shoved it in the back of my mouth. It's so good I want to swallow him whole, I'm trying my best to make it happen. He's grinding slowly into my mouth, I can feel him in my throat. I reach back up using both hands to pull on his flesh.

His grinds pick up almost thrusting himself into my stomach, I pull my nails down his chest pushing him into his release. I lick him clean and make my way back up to him. He pulls me on top of him as he sank deep down into my womb. I don't want to hurt him so I brace myself on my toes as I slowly bounce up and down on him.

Tristan's eyes never opened but I know he's awake, his throaty groans and breathing excited me. I pull myself up a little and turn around facing his feet twisting my hips around and around. The slow meld of our bodies is sending me in and out of my own self destructions. Tristan tried to sit up, I gently push him back down and continue my slow ride. When he couldn't take it any longer he sat up and cupped his hands around my shoulders. He's pumping into me like a mad man.

My body is shaking and I'm screaming at the top of my lungs. He blasted his life force in me at the exact moment I felt my body contract and break free. I fell forward as he feel back, I don't want to move I'm exhausted. Tristan didn't let me stay there long, he guided me forward and started our dance all over from the back.

Sleeping with Jasmine had me feeling right but waking up to a head job had me energized to the max. I know she's tired so I let her sleep and warmed us up some food. I woke her up to eat and we jumped in the shower together going at it. I had forgotten all about the shit that went down and really don't give a fuck. I know she wants answers, I just don't want her to be all worried about a nigga. Plus I have a lot of shit to do and don't need her wanting me to stay put. She walked in and sat on the floor looking over at me. I laugh and ease down beside her.

"You missed me huh?" I see Tristan has jokes.

"Of course I missed you. You've had me all worried and I don't need it right now. I'm in no condition to be worried about anything." 'What?' I looked at Jasmine then down and laid her on her back kissing all over her stomach.

"What you trying to say baby? You telling me you're pregnant?" I can't focus on him with the way he's sucking my hips licking his way down to my kitty. I close my eyes and block him out just wanting to feel him devour my insides.

*   *   *

When my eyes opened Tristan's buried in my chest asleep. We were covered with a blanket resting on pillows and still on the floor. My eyes were drawn to the TV, a breaking news story had come on and I didn't see the remote.

I saw a picture of Stephanie come on the screen and the captions read she was dead and set on fire in an abandoned building. I jumped up for my phone, I know Tristan has been here for the last four days. He still hasn't told me what happened to him over the weekend when he was missing. If the kids weren't safe in their new home I would've probably kicked him in his back waking him up. I sat down beside him just looking at him trying to see if the man I married would break his promise to me.

"Tristan, wake up." I called for him a couple times before he finally opened his eyes and pulled me back in his arms.

"I'm up baby. Just give me a second and I can get us off this floor into the bed." I pull away knowing he doesn't need to be lifting his self let alone lifting me up. I help him up off the floor and he pulls me down on top of him in the bed.

"What's up beautiful. I love yo' ass to death you know that right?" I kiss her and she pulls away, I know it's time to come clean.

"What happened Tristan?" I'm not about to let him distract me.

"I was shot twice in the back but I had my vest on so I'm good and happy to be holding my pregnant wife in my arms." Jasmine looked surprised at what I said.

"Shot?" I felt like my heart exploded and my stomach drop all at once, I'm in tears like I lost him. All this time I've been thinking he was playing around in the streets, not once was I thinking that he would or could be shot. I jump up off the bed running to the bathroom but it's too late. I barfed all over the floor and cried even more because I'm humiliated.

"Crap!" I got out the bed to help Jasmine, she crying and still hurling all the way into the bathroom. I grab one of her hair ties and pull her hair up in the back. When she was finished I pick her up ignoring her pleas for me to not hurt myself. I took her into the guest bedroom, ran her some water, put her into the tub and called for Janine to clean the room up.

23 GRATITUDE

"I'm glad one of us can keep our promises." Tristan's laughing sitting beside the tub rubbing on my stomach.

"Jasmine, baby I'm sorry about having you worry about me I put all my stuff in the car and Big Hen took it to the spot. I couldn't call and I had to play the role until I was able to get out of there."

"Couldn't call? All you had to do was pick up the phone Tristan. I thought you didn't play any roles here?"

"Baby I don't have any records here or anywhere in the states for that matter. Like I said Jasmine, I couldn't call."

"That's not true. You came to the hospital with me." He's really getting a kick out of this.

"You only told them yo' first name before you passed out on them again. When you did we were able to find you. I thought you told me you did yo' homework on all the businesses we have?" I can see the light bulb above her head come on, I tried to steal a kiss but she moved away.

"My mouth feels yucky." Tristan laughed and held my head still and kissed me anyway.

"You're nasty you know that right?" We both laugh I grab her tooth brush and shit with a cup for her.

"Thanks that's much better, I'm Listeren clean now."

"So you ready to tell me if you're pregnant or not?"

"Did you kill her?" I had to scratch my head on hearing that come out her mouth and ask who.

"Tristan tell me the truth, did you kill her or did you have someone else do it after you promised me you would leave her alone. And usually when people are asked a question like that they answer no not who. We'll talk about that later." He's laughing like I'm playing around with him.

"I figure we're talking about Steph and last I heard she was already proof of the walking dead. So no, I didn't have anything to do with her or her drug habit. If she is dead, I'm not surprised seeing how far gon' she was the last time I saw her in your office."

"She's dead Tristan, I saw it on the news that's why I woke you up. You sound like you don't even care."

"I don't, I'm actually pissed that I couldn't do her ass in myself after we took her kids in to the doctor. Thinking back, I need to be asking you if you knocked her ass off." I couldn't help but giggle at the thought of killing her myself. Fred's arm had been broken in two different places and he needed ORIF surgery because he went so long untreated. Yolanda, her five month old daughter weighed four pounds two ounces and she was addicted to herion.

"As much as I wanted to baby, I didn't, as long as she didn't have any more kids I was happy to pay her. Back to you, who shot you, why and how did they out fox you?"

"Go 'head and finish up while I get the door."

"You can let Ms. Janine get the door Tristan, come get in here with me, you're looking really dirty right now." He chuckles knowing he has to tell me as I stand letting the water out stepping into the shower with him pressed behind me.

"Remember I told you I was fucking around with three married women?"

"Baby, I'm starting to doubt your choices in women right about now. One of them shot you? If so you won't have to ask me if I killed her because I'm telling you now that I am if that's what happened." He's still laughing, I'm not playing around with him about that one bit.

"You know you finna ride daddy dick now talking like that." I picked her up kissing her jaw across to her ear down her neck and back up.

"Sit down Tristan, I'll ride, you sit down and tell me." Didn't make me any difference. I've been eating up this I'm hurt bit for a minute now. I felt better when she came home and fed a nigga after I slept anyway.

"Friday I met up with City because I found out that the punk ass pig that rolled up on us that night would be there. One of the chicks I was messing with is his wife come to find out. He pulled his strap out on me and City stopped his ass and told him he would see to it that he paid up for trying to set me up. When I left the club, I was on my way home and the nigga shot me in the back but the security was on it so he took off."

Jasmine throwing the pussy like a mufucka, I'm tryin' my best to hang in there. Her ass is a professional rider now, I guess reading all those books on different positions has been helping her out. She thinks I don't know, but when I walked in on her and Dena on the computer I saw that she was looking the shit up. I ain't mad at her for it, I'm tempted to suggest a couple flicks for her ass to watch.

"So how did you know it was him." I'm beat after we got out the shower but I still want to know.

"She went to the club, Big Hen told me she kept asking if I was alright because her husband said he killed me." I tried to rush Jasmine to finish getting dressed, we've been up here for almost an hour already.

"I'm ready Tristan but hold up for a second. What are you going to do, you can't go after him, he's a police officer."

"Fuck dat nigga baby, come on." I don't know why he's in such a hurry.

I know he doesn't think we're about to go anywhere, it's almost ten at night. When we make it downstairs, City and Sharon are sitting in the living room. They stand when we head in and we all say our hellos. City hugs me again and kisses my cheek causing me to blush and look away from Sharon.

"Man, would you keep yo' hands on yo' own woman and leave my wife alone." I hear Sharon mumble something inaudible that makes City let out a short humph and smirk smiling back at me.

"I'm sorry for your loss baby girl. You know I would've found a way to make it to your wedding but I guess my invite was loss in the mail."

"City, why you have to lie all the time? Don't make me blast you out while you trying to get her to put me in the dog house." We all laugh except for Sharon, she sits back on the couch with a sour look on her face.

"Anyway congrats, I'll be at the reception whenever you put it together.

Here, this is my gift to you." I look over at Tristan, he sits down in the chair as City grabs a bag off the table pulling a folder out of it.

"Come here baby, have a seat. City, you pull anything out that bag that has her cry we going outside nigga." We all laugh again.

"Sorry about that too Jasmine, I didn't mean any harm." He pecked my cheek again and sat down next to Sharon. I sat on Tristan's lap as I opened the folder reading what was inside.

"Thanks for this City, the kids will most defiantly enjoy learning how to protect themselves. Right now I only have newborns so this is way too generous of you."

"Before you say thanks but no thanks. I already sent all the details over to your office so just look it over. When your fully up and running you can use it then. I have a gift for you and it's not expensive so don't worry. Cargo, I'm pretty sure she'll cry if I give her this so if you don't want me to I won't."

"I'm sure I can handle just about anything right now City as long as it's not expensive like you said." City smiles and hands me the bag, I pull out the photo album and sit it on my lap.

"Thanks City, I'll make sure to put as many photos in it that I can." I started to get up and hug him but he started laughing.

"I can get you another one then because that one is already filled. You're not a very good receiver of gifts you know, you're supposed to at least look inside." I pull her into my arms knowing full well the only thing City could've already had inside the book. She opened it up and looked back at me I can see the tears already coating her eyes. She closed the book back and stood up walking towards him as he stood up. She hugged him so long I had to pull her ass off him, he thought the shit was funny.

"Thanks so much City, I really appreciate it. I can't look at it now because I don't want to cry anymore tonight." I kissed City cheek again and went to clean my face.

We sat and talked for a while, Sharon was mostly quiet. City asked Tristan to step outside with him, I really didn't have anything to say to Sharon. Something about her said she couldn't be trusted if she wasn't right in front of you. I'm guessing her encounter with Meka has closed her mouth a little. I hated that I was judging her but the only conversation with her had something to do with money.

She always swanks about how much this and that cost like that was all she worried or cared about. Each time that I've seen her she's asked how much everything I was wearing cost. When I told her that I shopped at Target you would have thought I smacked her. She was on my case saying Tristan should be getting me this and that and she had the nerve to write down some stores for me. I made a note of how she took one look at my ring and looked at Tristan like she was hungry. City noticed it to, I didn't ask but he looked at me and started laughing, he mouthed 'don't trip' to me.

"So who did this to you?"

"Straight to the point huh City?"

"Hell yeah, I wanna know who almost took my lil brother out so the nigga can get a cell for his ass." I laughed at him and told him I didn't know.

"I knew that's what you would say. Good thing I had a call from my guy at the precinct. He said a Trina Brown came in claiming her husband Officer Ronald Brown killed her lover Stanley. This just so happened to be the same nigga that had a gun to yo' ass right before and I do recall him calling you Stanley." We laugh and I stick to I don't know what he's talking 'bout.

"It's all good, he on lock down until the investigation is over and I'm making it my business that he's held accountable for what he did."

"Do you man, I'ma' do me. Can you please get yo' girl out my damn house man? I don't need any more drama from Jasmine and yo' girl keep lookin' at a nigga like she about to fuck me in front of ya'll."

"I already saw that youngin' I'm so tired of her ass it don't make any fuckin' since. It's all good though, she a done deal as soon as I drop her ass off. I'm headed out in a minute anyway to talk to Treasure." We go back in and we walk them out. I made sure I held Jasmine in my arms after I dabbed City off. Sharon silly ass tried to hug a nigga but I played the shit off pulling wifey in front of me.

"City can do so much better than Sharon." I chuckled and watched Jasmine cross the room.

"Did you know what he was giving me?" I shook my head no as she picked up the folder and called me over. I laid back on the couch as she rested back on my chest holding the folder open so we both could see.

"What do you think, I mean I know I said the school should be a home instead of some institution type building but now."

"It can still be a home just leave enough room to expand when you need to." I pulled the folder out of her hands and picked up the photo album.

"I would love to see my wife's parents and what she looked like truly happy." I turned around and looked at him, he leaned in and kissed me then pulled away.

"You gon' show yo' husband or what?"

"I thought I was showing my husband." Tristan smiled so hard I thought his face would split in half, it was my turn to bite his lip and get a taste.

"Thanks, I needed that but I still want to see unless you don't want to show me." She tried to turn over but I had my hands full with ass and it took me a minute to let her move.

Her mother was tall but not taller than her father, he looked close to six four. She had short curly hair and Jasmine looked just like her. Her mother was so St. Louis though. She was slugged up with two gold teeth on her fronts and if I'm not mistaken, looked like she had a tongue ring. She had an eyebrow ring above her left eye and a tattoo on her right wrist like a bracelet with Jasmine written on it.

Her father had a dark taper fade but he didn't look like the type to wear one. He was Italian, Jasmine had peridot colored eyes just like his. The more I looked at the nigga the faster I wanted her to turn the page so I can get a closer view of him. She stopped on a single photo of him and I found myself sitting up and pulling the book from her hands. Next thing I know I'm on my feet heading outside so she couldn't hear me on the phone. He picked up on the first ring and I only had one thing to ask his ass.

"Tell me I'm not related to my wife nigga!"

The next morning Tristan was acting weird. I know it has something to do with my father, I didn't think anything of it. We were sleeping in the same bed at night but like old times. I was doing all the sleeping, he wouldn't let me hold him so he could sleep. A couple weeks had past and I started to worry because he was keeping his distance.

He'd forgotten all about wanting to know if I was pregnant or not. I honestly didn't know, my monthly was missing that was all I knew and was afraid to find out for sure without him. The more I thought about how he was acting the more it irked me that maybe I should be concerned. I called up City and asked him for a favor, reluctantly he agreed and I made him promise not to tell Tristan.

I told Tristan that I would be working late, he didn't seem to really be bothered by it. After a twenty minute flight, I arrived at Taylorville Correctional Center and was taken to a room for attorney's to speak with their clients. City had given me everything I needed to get in the minimum security prison. I was told he was in housing unit three in a drug and alcohol recovery program. This was hard to believe seeing he has been behind bars for the past twelve years. I figured he should've dried out by now.

Standing in that cold room caused my head to spin, I feel like I'm trapped with a musty odor strangling me. I thought the smell in Africa was something to get use to but the smell in here is something I never want to get accustomed to. When I heard the door I turned around wanting to run out of there. The guard told me he would be down in a few more minutes and my heart tried to make a run for it.

I calmed myself down taking short cleansing breathes thru my handkerchief that I pulled out when the smell first pierced my nose. I hear the door reopen. I didn't turn, they told me to let them know when I was finished. I nodded my head in agreement.

"Who da fuck is you? You damn sho' ain't my lawyer so what da fuck do you want?" he said to me not even taking one look at my face seeing I still had my back to him.

"If you here to give a nigga some pussy you need to hurry da fuck up!" Really? The way he said that I can only assume that this is not his first time in here to have sex.

I turn around slowly and took a step forward. Harper Campbell is short, round and he looks remarkably like the black guy from 'The Voice'. He stared at me for what seemed like forever as I stared at him. His body tensed up and he started to turn pale, his lips started to quiver.

"Bitch, you supposed to be dead!" he mumbled and blinked faster and faster trying to figure out how. Something inside of me was getting a kick out of seeing the sweat form on his brows. I stalked forward pulling the chair out slowly and taking a seat in front of him.

"Dis a dream, I know it is Shawna, get da fuck out my head bitch. Get da fuck out my head!" He started banging his head against the steal table. I giggled at his silly attempt to make me disappear. He looked up knowing this was all too real.

"You're an idiot if you think this is a dream." I smirked at him and he looked like he wanted to end my life right there.

"Who da fuck is you?"

"You know who I am."

"I know you ain't Shawna, you look like her but you don't have gold's, and you missing her tats, and yo' ey——" He blinked a few times staring into my eyes then he started to laugh.

"Damn, I should've known. What da fuck yo' ass want?" This is supposed to be my family? This sick monster is supposed to be my uncle, the brother to my mother. He was supposed to lookout for her and protect her, yet he killed her and talks to me like I'm nothing.

"I want to know why." I leaned back in my chair and waited as he laughed in my face like I was a piece of dirt.

"Why not? Man get da fuck outta here bitch!"

"She was your baby sister, your only sister. What did she do to you to make you kill her and hate me so much after all these years?"

"Dat bitch ain't eva been shit, you herrre me? If it wasn't fo' dat trick ass ho—" He stopped talking and just stared at me. Then I saw something in his eyes that flipped my stomach upside down.

"Yo' stupid ass really wanna know? Shit'd, how bad you wanna know?" I didn't respond, he was licking his dry lips. I could see his forearm moving and I can hear the handcuffs sliding along the metal chair.

"Come get on nis' dick and I'll tell you bitch."

"You do know you're supposed to be my mother's brother right?"

"Bitch, get up and get on nis' dick! Yo' ass ain't shit to me and neither was dat slut."

"I wouldn't waist my spit on you." He slammed his fist on the edge of the table, I giggled at his attempt to intimidate me.

"Bitch think yo' ass tough huh? We'll see ho. Trust and believe me when I tell yo' ass dat." He started calling for the guards to come get him.

"You take after your mother you know that?" I stood to my feet and laughed right out the door. Everything within me really wanted to see him beg for his life only to take it from him. I kept going ignoring him cursing me and behaving like an arse.

24 HARMONY

After I handled Bobo snake ass I walked in the house looking for Jasmine. It's three in the morning, she said she would be working late but it don't look like she's been here. I know I'm hella late and she probably doin' the shit on purpose, but fuck all dat'. She should've been here waitin' on a nigga. I called her phone a couple times with no answer. Then she text me back wit' some I love you we should do lunch. I'm hot! I called her ass back and it went to voicemail on the first ring. She turned her phone off.

"Baby I'm trying here, I really am. But whAT THE FUCK YOU MEAN DO LUNCH? GET THE FUCK HOME NOW JASMINE, DON'T FU——" Got damn it, I was cut off and I'm livid. I snatch up my keys and tracked her ass down.

Pissed me off even more when I realized where she at. I'ma fuck her and nis' nigga up when I get there, I know it for a fact. I pulled up and damn near kicked the door in. She answered the door and I almost knocked her over going inside callin' his ass looking around for him.

When I made it downstairs she was sitting in the basement with all kinds of boxes spilled out on the floor. I asked her where he was, she said he wasn't there but I'm not buying it. I called his ass and was waiting to hear his phone ring close by but I didn't. When he picked up I yelled clean into his ear.

"FACE ME LIKE A MAN NIGGA!" He laughing and shit but I can't hear him in the house. I listened harder and heard all kinds of shit in the background telling me he wasn't here for real.

"I guess you calling because Jasmine is at my spot right now huh? Well I'm not there and damn sure not after her, you my bruh and I wouldn't do some dirty shit like that to you." Sounded like he was about to go on but someone pulled the phone away.

"Don't start no shit Cargo! Ethan is not after Jasmine and yo' silly ass already know that for a fact. Stop being a pussy and tell yo' fuckin' wife the truth nigga. Then she won't be running around trying to figure the shit out." Treasure hung up on me.

I felt like shit for stepping to City the way I did. I know damn well he wouldn't do what I claimed he did. I turned around and looked at my wife reading papers in her hand. I walked over to her and pulled them away from her. I pulled her up on my lap and we looked in each other's eyes. It was now or never.

"Monroe "Mack" Campbell, that's your fathers real name right?"

"Yes, can I explain first?" I climbed off of Tristan and headed to the kitchen. I was intending on getting something to drink but I also wanted to be close to a knife just in case I followed thru with cutting his throat. I made a cup of tea and sat at the table across from him and told him to go ahead.

"I was nine years old when Mack was indicted. When his lawyer took me to see him he was smiling like shit was cool and he would be released soon. We rapped about a bunch of shit on the business side like I told you already. Then he told me that his case was really about to fall apart because they had to get another prosecuting attorney.

I didn't think anything of it until we were looking at your parents. Something about your father was stuck in my head, he reminded me of someone. I was thinking back trying to figure out why he looked so familiar to me. I called Bateador to see why I couldn't shake your father face from my head.

I asked him if we were related meaning if I had something to do with your parents being killed. See I was young but I was in control. Mack needed a lot of nigga's handled so I had to reach out and let nigga's touch them mufuckas and quick. It was so many on the roster I didn't even trip off the names and didn't give a fuck to know the details. I know if anybody knew it was Bateador 'cause dem nigga's know all kinds of shit.

He tell me we not related but yo' pops was the same prosecuting attorney my dad was speaking on all those years ago. Bateador told me how yo' uncles worked for my pops and they were in major debit to him. He used the money against them and planted a seed in them to get the money. My father didn't give a fuck about the money, he knew they would kill yo' parents, that's what he wanted in return. I'm sorry baby, I didn't know about any of this shit." She let out a long sigh and looked me in the eyes again.

"So you didn't have anything to do with this Tristan? Please don't lie to me or hold back the truth." He stood up and walked around the table pulling a chair out then lifted me onto his lap so I was straddling him.

"What was the date exactly? I mean what time on that day did I lie to you baby? I seriously don't remember when I started lying to you about anything, let alone holding back." I kissed her neck and felt her give in.

"I was nine baby, I didn't catch my first body 'til I was eleven and it was the guard that killed my pops. I finished off the rest of them over the years. After that, those are the only six bodies I count." I knew he was serious, the situation just had me confused and feeling angry. I just didn't know who I should be angry with.

"You don't trust me do you Tristan?" He looked at me like I was crazy.

"I trust you wit' my life Jasmine, I know I came over here fucked up but damn. You hit me wit' some bullshit text and you over here in the wee hours of the morning. You spittin' about trust when trust should've brought yo' ass home last night."

"Yeah, so you could avoid me like you've been doing since you saw my father's picture? I trust you and I knew that you wouldn't tell me unless I forced you. I came here because I knew sending you that text would bring you over here." He started laughing and shaking his head.

"You played daddy huh? Hell yeah I'm coming fo' yo' ass if you not at home waitin' on a nigga. Where the ring yo' husband put on yo' finger and keep tellin' you not to take off?" She moved her arms around my neck.

"I love you husband and I trust you." I suck on Tristan's neck while he laughs holding my rump.

"Jasmine, you haven't worn yo' ring and it's been almost three months. Which one is it? You don't want to be married or you don't want anyone to know you married?"

"I am married but my ring is so expensive it should be locked in a vault. I've been debating on putting it in a safety deposit box at the bank. I can get a fake one just like it and wear that."

"No the fuck you not! Jasmine, don't take my ring off again, I'm tired of telling you the same thing. Naw, don't 'but Tristan' me! Keep my damn ring on yo' finger, I'm the one debating on getting it permanently attached on yo' ass. Keep it up and that's just what I'm gon' do." I put her ring back on as she laughs and gives me a kiss.

I took Jasmine to breakfast, called City up, set that shit right and made one stop before taking her home. We both were all teeth and gums when we made it in the door. I couldn't wait to get upstairs and lick her ass down from head to toe front to back. Every nerve ending in my body was on fire and alert, the energy between us was some shit I'd never experienced before.

The next morning I pulled out all the stops, she couldn't tell me shit, we shopped all muthafucking day. A couple days later Ma' Earlean was sitting in my living room when we returned home. I knew she was upset the moment we made eye contact.

"Monfs ago I'z had a dream of da sixth room on da chird table sat da secondz wickerz basket all grey wit' one rooster. Den dat rooster moved and a chicken wuz next to it, dat chicken moved and I'z seez mez a egg. Fo' six weeks I'z see'z da egg and like dat' it wuz broken inchu pieces only da shell left. I cried tear'z I'z didn't know'z I'z had in'z me.

Den out da' blue a little ova a monf later another egg wuz back on dat table and it'z been dar eva' since. Almost tree in a half monfs now and here I'z sit pissed off at the two'z of ya'!"

I didn't understand a word of what she's saying. I looked at Tristan, he was smiling trying to hold back his laughter. I walked over to hug her and speak but she held her hand up at me stopping me.

"Childz you betta spit the piece of hay out cha mouf before you'z think about comin' any closer." Her face is twisted and I know she's serious. Tristan walked over and kneeled down in front of her.

"Ma' Earlean, I'm sorry but things have been crazy lately. You're right, we did lose our first baby and we officially found out three days ago we're eleven weeks pregnant. So don't be upset, we had to make sure. I was planning on visiting you tomorrow." Ma' Earlean stood to her feet and I followed, she wacked me upside the head then smiled hugging Jasmine.

She turned back to me and hugged me tight. We spoke for a while then Clancy, her security, took her back home. We cleaned up, ate dinner and were in the nursery getting everything set up. Jasmine wanted me to explain what Ma' Earlean said.

"She old school baby, the rooms are her children she had eleven, the sixth room is Ma' Bells. Ma' Bell had five kids, the third table in Ma' Bells room is Grandma Lorraine. Lorraine had four wicker baskets, meaning her children. The grey one was my father's because he's dead, he only had one child which is me. So the rooster is me and the chicken is you. You can figure the rest out from there right." Jasmine turned and looked at me like I was crazy for understanding all that she said. I laughed and got down putting my head on her stomach kissing her until she laughed.

"She knew all that from a dream, that's unbelievable."

"Ma' always been like that, I told you she ol' school, she be on errbody in the family when they having a baby." We finished up and she worked my ass over wit' her lazy love that she always talking about. Shit was going smooth, we let errbody know the good news and I couldn't have been happier.

I turned over the throne to my nigga's and told them to work it how they want. I sold the clubs, mainly because I didn't want to be connected to anything. Jasmine was in her sixth month when I got the call that would be the end to my murkin' season for good. I was more than ready to handle my business but I knew gettin' her to understand would be hard.

I wined and dined her ass for two days trying to prepare her for what I was about to tell her. When we made it to the house I was ready to get it over with. Plus I had a flight in four hours so I had to get it done.

"I need to talk to you." I knew this was coming, I walked over and sat beside Tristan on the bed really not wanting to look at him. He moved around so that I was in front of him holding my chin so I could look at him.

"I have to make a run, it'll take two weeks and I'll be back here worshiping the ground you walk on like usual." I couldn't help it, he made me smile.

"Do what you have to do Tristan and get back here in one piece so I can love you like the king you are."

"Now dats what the fuck I'm talkin' 'bout!" I laid my baby back and loved her ass into a coma like sleep. I was in the air and could still smell her aroma on my lips the entire flight.

When I awoke the next morning I knew immediately that Tristan was gone. It was like the house was naturally darker and all the joy was sucked right out of it. I tried to ignore it as I did the usual getting ready to head into work. The entire day seemed to drag along second by second as slow as possible.

I heard a tap at the door and looked over it was Roman, I looked at my watch and it was midnight. The entire day had swept right past me without me knowing. I packed up my things without either of us saying a word as he walked me to my car following me home.

Two days had passed in the same fashion, I thought it would get easier but it was only getting worse. I don't think I was experiencing morning sickness it was more like Tristan withdrawals. It seemed like the three days he was away caused my body to get rounder faster. Dena came down to help me pass the time, she was aware that this would be hard for me. I appreciated the fact that she flew in from New York when I told her Tristan was away.

"Cargo is going to freak when he see's yo' hair like this, I'm telling you now he is going to lose his mind."

"You don't think I should've went shorter? I mean I never realized just how fast my hair grew, it's still past my shoulders." I turned in the mirror, my hairs full of deep curls but instead of my natural brown color, my hair was auburn.

This was the first time I had ever had a color in my hair. I wasn't about to do it because I didn't want the chemicals harming the baby. Dena of course never used any in my hair, she says I don't have the type of hair for them. The stuff she mixed smelled like Koolaid and when I asked she laughed so hard I thought she'd never stop. I was the one laughing after she finished and told me that it actually was.

She spent the following five days with me and we hung out like old times, laughing, watching movies and having a good time. Before she left she said she'd be back in a couple days but I couldn't keep pulling her from doing what she needed to do. I told her I would be fine and I would call her every day to prove it. I didn't have a problem calling her at all, it was Tristan I didn't want to call. I still worried that I would jinx him and something bad would happen if I distracted him with a phone call.

I had to get my mind off the subject so I went out to check on things at Serenity. The name I called the mini post like neighborhood that I was working hard to establish. My plans for becoming a lawyer have slowly dwindled. Something about taking the time to study instead of helping needing children didn't sit right with me. I wanted to give it my all and make sure that the parents I found would be who they said they were and not what they wanted anyone to think. Things were picking up and moving at a fast past.

I couldn't have imagined all the resources that Sammy, Treasure or any of my extended family have. The thought of calling them extended family for some reason bothered me. They felt more like family than anything I could've ever imagined one would feel like. It wasn't like I spoke with them on a daily, but we did speak at least once or twice a month. Even then I can feel the honesty in their hearts that they truly care for me. It's nothing like I experienced with those two.

I met up with Damon, he's one of the Eight Hundred. He has a deep smoky voice and of course he's extremely attractive and has a great head on his shoulders. Not to mention a sexy smile, I need to focus. I don't know what it is, Tristan being away, my hormones, or not being able to get my daily lazy love. I keep reminding myself of the conversation with Dena about those Red Hot Ripplets and can't help but laugh.

"What's up Beautiful?" His voice always makes me blush, we hugged and he kissed my cheek making me shake my head.

"Hey Damon, how are things going?" He smiled at me and hugged me again.

"Don't hey Damon me. How are you doing? I know Cargo silly ass gon' and by the look on yo' face it's bothering you. We family so tell me what's up and if it's anything I can do to make it right."

"Of course it's bothering me Damon. I miss him and worry about him every second of the day. I don't want to talk about it though and unless he's in that folder somehow I don't think you can make it right." We both laugh and he walks me into the house to show me all the work that has taken place. It looked like any other normal gated community, two blocks were complete. Four houses on both sides of the streets and the backyards were fenced off for the next block of four homes and so on.

When I finish I'll have twenty homes in the next two years. The homes closer to the entry housed security, medical, fire, and a store. Anyone on the outside looking in wouldn't know it just looking at them. Inside of them it's setup just like the real thing though and fully equipped. Each block has a school at the bottom of the cul-de-sac equipped to handle the children based off their grade and learning style.

Damon took me to look at the neighborhood Center rightfully named,

Terry's Hands. She was thrilled when I asked her to run the place just like she had done all those years in the Cochran. There was still a ton of work that needed to be done but I can see it all coming together. The building's three storey's, the bottom housed the gymnasium, main offices, locker room, equipment room and storage area. Second floor was filled with computers, a library, and dance area. The upstairs is fairly open with a kitchen in the rear and two rooms one had a boxing ring.

By the time I left there I'm exhausted, all the walking around really kicked my tush. When I made it home all I wanted to do was sleep so I did just that. I woke up to Ms. Janine telling me I needed to eat and I had company. I looked over at the clock and it was two in the afternoon, I slept over eighteen hours and still feel like I need more. I dragged myself out of my warm spot in bed and cleaned up.

When I made it down I was happy to see Shameka and Prime. The closer I walked towards them the harder it was to hold back my tears. I was wishing Tristan was like Prime. He wasn't into all the craziness and I desired that from Tristan. They both held me waiting on me to finish. I thought I would never stop, I needed my husband to hold me. I needed him to make me feel better.

"You getting big sis." I laughed and wiped the last of my tears away at the thought of Prime saying I was big.

"I thought it was all in my head, I am getting big and fast, I can't believe it myself."

"What do you think about coming to stay with us until Cargo comes back?" I thought I didn't hear Shameka correctly but I knew that I did.

"Thanks bu..."

"No buts', she was asking but I'm not taking rejection, you coming with us. I know you not answering Cargo's calls and you're not making any. He won't be coming here, he's picking you up from our place. Your bags are in the car and our ride is waiting." I had to laugh, seems like all the men in this family thinks they can tell you what to do and when to do it.

"I have work here Prime, I can't just leave so thanks but no thanks."

"Please Jasmine. I need to know that you're alright, I've been worried about you like crazy." Shameka had me laughing she was on her knees in front of me like she really had to beg me to go.

"Get up crazy I'll go, Tristan will be back in four days. I guess I can go hang out with you until then." She bounced up and hugged me.

25 GLUTTONY

"The package is with El Muerte in Manzanillo, you'll be on yo' own for a minute which I know you can handle. If you get the chance to get on the package before we get there then fine, if not, don't force it."

"It ain't shit I got you. All I need you to do is make sure my wife straigh..."

"Come on Cargo don't do that shit. We all coming home on this here. If this is too mu..."

"Get that shit out of here! I'm out, I'll see ya'll when ya'll land." I jump back on the plane and leave Bateador in Koro heading to Manzanillo to take care of this last problem. This nigga El Muerte was going to get dealt with for once and for all. He thinks he's pulling a slick one with the body double shit but he's about to be in for a rude awakening.

When I touch down it's not hard for me to blend in, it's not the first time being down here and I already have the layout. Took me four days to get the layout of his compound and another three to get their schedules. I needed to find a way inside, after two days of thinking, the only thing I could come up with was pussy. Pussy was the only thing going in unchecked, this is one of those times when I really needed Ghost with me. She never gave the pussy up but she could sho' nuff us it to get in and out of anywhere she wanted.

I stayed close but changed my lookout several times a day just in case. Two days before the meet there was a big party thrown for El Muerte by his men. It was the closes I had been to the real nigga since I had been staking him out. I sat off to the side in the cut listening in for any information I could.

These nigga's were smart, they didn't discuss business, all they really talked about was Diablo. Talkin' shit about how they would make the darkies pay. I found myself chuckle, these nigga's really need to look in a mirror, they all dark as fuck. Damn sure darker then the nigga's they trying to get at.

I left there feeling good, my ear hustlin' and patience paid off. They were so fuckin' lifted by the end of the night, I don't think they cared what the fuck they discussed. I found out that in a few hours the security would be down to two men out of the fifteen they kept around. They would be out for around two hours to check out several spots for the meet. The day of the meet, El Muerte would stay behind and send in his double to do the transaction. He would have at least ten men with him while they took care of his business.

The package was scheduled to leave out four hours before they were to leave. They planned on taking it to some shit hole town near San Mateo Tepopula, and getting rid of it. It made me wonder more about what the package was that they would just get rid of it like that. Then again it wasn't my job to worry about what was inside, my job was to make sure it didn't get out of my sight and turn it over. They didn't plan on giving it up, they were amped about getting justice served for Diablo.

I only had a couple hours, I would've called Bateador and Pandillero but I know they're already in route. I made it back to the hole in the floor I was staying in and grabbed all that I needed. I made it back to the compound and waited until the trucks rolled out giving them a couple minutes to get away. The place is covered with cameras which is another reason I needed a couple minutes. I used my phone to loop dem bitches giving me time to get in unannounced. Once I was in I had to let it run making sure to loop individual cameras as I made myself acquainted.

I know the package will be leaving soon so I figured I'll check the bays and garages. The only thing Bateador told me was I'd know it when I see it. Go figure. It's dark but I can still see using my night vision goggles so I'm still winning. I checked all three bays and I'm standing in the fourth garage looking at a camouflaged tarp draped across something.

The closer I walk to it the more I don't want for this thing to be the package. Everything inside of me said it's exactly what the fuck I'm looking for. I move the tarp and drop my head shaking it slowly with disappointment. I want to scream at the sight of the treasure box with DAX inside of it. I try to open it and it came right open, I guess the contents are no longer inside.

When I open it enough, I jump back because it felt like I have on those 4D glasses from Disney World. That Cryptkeeper lookin' ass nigga seemed to jump right up at me. I know the story behind this nigga, if you wanna know check out, *Lifelong Love: When you know better, you do better,* by Taz

Will. He look pissed, and dis' nigga still has hair on his fucking skull. I've seen death before but never the dead and this shits giving me the chills. All in all I would've never thought this was his life after death.

The garage door sprang to life and I'm stuck looking stupid. I close the lid, fixed the tarp, and hid in the only place I could. Under dis' stiff ass mufucka. The guards pulled in and stood around lolly gagging about how they would kill the darkies and whopty whoo. My mind drifted but not far to how in the hell I'm going to get out of this shit.

I thought about making a call and was heated even more that my battery is about to give out. I turned it all the way off and listened back in on what they were saying. I know one thing, they're in for tonight and they have no plans of leaving where they stand until the sun comes up.

The thought of my phone being off made me smile. What are the chances that Jasmine's trying to call me right about now? It made me feel antsy to get the fuck back to her and my baby as soon as this shits over. I let the images of my wife's beautiful face consume my thoughts.

The smile on her face, the way she talked in her sleep, and the way she looked embarrassed when she climaxed has me feeling better. I can't wait to rub her stomach, the shit's insane how drawn I am to it. Her tight abs being pulled to comfort my child has my dick hard, I don't even know why.

The nigga's had me there all fucking day, some would walk up as the others left. I was cool with the new crew, they were dropping can after can but stayed right outside the door. It gave me enough room to snatch one up and piss. It took everything in me not to jump up, tell dem nigga's to not mind me and walk pass them nigga's to do it.

I had to check myself a couple times because I could've sworn the Cryptkeeper was talking to me. Dis nigga kept laughin' and shit sayin' I should've stayed my ass at home. I stopped myself from tellin' him I was there for his ass so he needed to shut the fuck up. My mind is defiantly playin' tricks on me.

Right on time the nigga's were loading up, it gave me just enough time to roll from under the table undetected and slip on the other side of the garage. They're so busy talking, they didn't see that they had a visitor under one of the trucks. I wasn't sure just who it was because I had two guards coming towards me and had to duck down. After they loaded the package they pulled off and their visitor was gone. I don't have time to look for whoever it was, I have to take care of something else.

I checked out the rooms one by one making sure I wasn't surprised by someone coming behind me. Took me about a minute just to clear the bottom half of the house. Before I can make it up the steps two guards are coming down towards me. I only have two pistols on me and they both have some good shit that I want.

It was easy to overpower 'em because they weren't expecting for me to be here. I pulled them into a closet in the kitchen and took me a quick lunch break. A nigga stomach in his back and it ain't like I'm hurting anybody by eating the shit. Hell, they all will be dead in a few so I might as well get my energy up so I can make dat shit happen.

With two down I have at least eight more to go plus El Muerte. I'm looking forward to gettin' at his ass for the bullshit he pulled. I'm feeling fucked up because all the rooms I check are empty, I'm down to the last four.

I don't know where the fuck his security can be. With two rooms left, I look around and found dem nigga's. They piled up in the closet like the ones I put in the kitchen closet.

The last room I open the door slow, on the floor close to the door laid one guard. I move around the corner where I know El Muerte will be waiting. I fall back against the wall when I look in on what's going on. I see his head get dropped into a bag then the bags being tossed in the air. Next thing I know it hit hard against the right side of my head from being kicked with precision to me.

"SCORE!" she yelled covered in blood. Her bloody hands are in the air, she's making cheering noises while coming fast towards me. I don't know what to say or do. She look down annoyed at her phone then pushed her ear piece.

"Damn Sammy I said I would be there...Fuck you to nigga I told yo' ass I would be there on time...Shut. Da. Fuck. Up!" She ended the call coming closer picking up the bag again.

"You know yo' ass fired right?" I look at her just like I should, like she crazy.

"You can't fire somebody that quit you fucking nut case." She laughed a laugh that made me want to cover my ears, the shits horrible to hear. She looks at the bag then picks it up holding it in between the two of us.

"Yo' bitch ass hear this shit he spittin'? I do his fucking job while he take a nap on duty and he mad because I fired him. What part of the game is that? Huh nigga, speak up. You know what, you'z a bitch made nigga you know that? I mean, who the fuck kidnaps a fucking corps huh? Who does that? When I see yo' punk ass in hell I'ma fuck you up again, you hear me? What's wrong bitch, you don't hear me talkin' to you?" I looked on wondering how long she goin' hold a conversation wit' dis' nigga head. She slung it across her shoulder and was going to the hall. I grab her wrist stopping her.

"You gettin' out of here." She pull away, toss the bag in the air, kick it again down the hall.

Next thing I know one of the three guards coming towards us is hit smack dead in the chest with the bag. BOOM! BOOM! BOOM! She pull out a fifty caliber pistol and let loose on dem nigga's forcing me to fall back into the room. I don't know how the fuck she held that bitch down in her little ass hands but she looked comfortable. Then I realize the thunder she let loose fosho sounded the alarm letting nes nigga's know we're here.

When the firing stop I look out, all three of them are done. I don't know where she went but I can hear more nigga's coming up the steps. I run out the room down the hall where I thought she went. They see me and open up as I let a couple off so I can clear the corner.

Now that I know fosho the nigga dead I can get the fuck up out of here with ease. I can't leave Treasure here to make it out on her own no matter how crazy her ass is. I gotta give it to her, she's a bad bitch! No wonder dat' nigga wife'd her ass up. I don't think I can deal with that much crazy though, she fine a fuck but all that goes out the window after I just saw how she get down. As I make my way around a series of corners, I can hear kids crying. Then that laugh made me move faster.

I open the door and Treasure is standing there laughin' in the damn kids faces. I can't hear what she's saying but they crying like hell. She picked the oldest boy up by his hair and let him go. I didn't realize I was holding my breath until she did. Then I look at her do the same with another two, I don't understand what the fuck she doin'. Then I can't help but notice the three she let go aren't moving.

Bloods pooling around them, I look closer, she cutting their fucking throats. I yell out as a guard came in the door about to kill her ass, I have to stop him. I pull his arm down kick the back of his knee and snap his neck. I look back at Treasure she killed three more of the kids and cradling an infant in her arms. I can't believe she killed six children and has the nerve to be treating the infant like one of her own. Another nigga came into the door, I don't have time to fight, I put a hole in his temple.

When I turned, I see her slam the baby into the wall then stomp down on its head and it splattered errwhere. Dis fool laughing when she look at the expression on my face. I walk towards her but another guard came in, I did him the same way. I checked to see if anymore were coming and hear seven shots back to back. I look back in, she's coming towards me leaving out the room. I look at the kids, she put holes in all dey heads including one in the heart of the infant. I turn back around she gone.

I went back to looking for her and was spotted in the living room. One of the nigga's was saying that Thomas said they needed to get back to the compound. He was pissed that Thomas didn't tell them sooner and said they would deal with him when it was all over. I check to see how many rounds I have left and just like I thought, I'm out.

I duck behind the couch, I can hear them coming towards me I look around and know I'm trapped. I turn on my phone before they get too close. It went straight to voicemail like I figured it would, something in me needed her to pickup though.

"Jasmine baby I'm sorry, I love you." I hang up and call straight thru to the server to leave a message for Pandillero, before it goes out.

"Treasure and Sammy, all of them are here! Drag set us up!" I hate that I have to do it like that, fuckin' message will take about ten, fifteen minutes before he get it. It may even take longer in this fucked up country.

I drop the phone as three figures come into the room with their AK's pointed at me. I'm hoping one of these Mexican nigga's come close enough so I can get my hands on a burner. The nigga in the middle muggin' hard. Fuck it, if it's my time I'm not gon' make it easy for these bitches. A noise comes from the hall and they all look over.

I rush the nigga closes to me and all hell breaks loose again. I can feel the heat come over my body, we all seem to drop to the floor together. Treasure coo coo ass had a damn stripped Ultimax 100 Mk.3 with the fucking drum on it spraying these nigga's. She spitting a hundred fucking rounds like it's nothing with a slick ass grin on her face.

When I look over I see Treasure again, look like she's talking to someone. Then I chuckle because she was just talking to a fucking head in a bag. I can see her mouth moving but I can't hear what she saying. My eyes fall closed, I can't even force 'em to stay open no matter how hard I try.

26 FREE WILL

"What's up sis? I know you don't think you about to sit out here all night."

"Yes Prime, I am about to sit out here all night until my husband brings his tush up that driveway." He's laughing like I'm playing.

"You know how mad he'll be with me if I let you sit out here waiting on him to pull up? Come on Ma', work with me. When he get here he has a key and the code to get in so stop worrying."

"I can't help but worry Prime, I need to see him and I can't sleep knowing he'll be pulling up here any moment."

"I see you got it bad sis. I can't wait until Shameka have my first so I can see how bad she have it." We both laugh.

"I think she already has it bad Prime so don't worry."

"Look who talking. The queen of worrying telling me not to worry, now that's something."

"Tell me something Prime." He looks over at me wondering what I want to know.

"How did you meet Tristan?"

"He was born." We both laugh and I tell him to tell me everything.

"Cargo never told you about our mothers?"

"A little. He said they grew up together in the Cochran then May went to school and his mother Lisa couldn't afford to go. He said she worked as a stripper that's when she started dating his father. She had seen him a few times in the Cochran but she didn't want anything to do with him. When he saw her in the club he took her out of there and they stayed by each other's side from there. He said when May found out who Lisa was dating she begged her not to fall for him. That's pretty much it."

"Yeah well, when May graduated she moved back to St. Louis and Lisa worked for her at her interior design company. When Tristan was born I was two and we were raised pretty much together. From what Cap and Flight told me, Lisa was in the house when they came to arrest Mack. They bombed the hell outta the house with tear gas and all kinds of shit.

After they cuffed her they left her and it took from what they say, a half hour before they go back to question her. She didn't respond so they put her in the patty wagon. A hour later they go to take her into the jail, she wouldn't get up so they carried her in. One of the female guards noticed she wasn't breathing and called for the doctor.

They found out she was dead. Cap said she was dead when they handcuffed her based off the medical reports. Mack was fucked up about it and his lawyers had it to where he didn't have to turn his self in. A year pass, Tristan was nine and it was the day after his moms death that they arrested Mack.

May wanted Tristan to live with us but Mack wasn't having it, he said

Tristan needed to be in the hood. May knew what Mack really wanted from Tristan and she knew there was no way to stop him. Cap and Flight were twenty five when Cargo went to live in the Cochran. May knew what was up with them and she blamed herself for letting it happen.

Anyway, they looked out for the both of us and the shit was driving us insane. A year or so later Mack was beaten to death by the guards who claimed he was resisting arrest. Flight said it's bull because Mack had the shit on lock and in all actuality Mack's charges were going to be dropped the next day. The state's case was weak and falling apart by the seconds. Plus they had no physical evidence on him.

Everything they had on him was hearsay and those nigga's were dropping like flies or backing out of testifying. Cap said it was a hit and that's why those guards did that shit to Mack. They were on payroll to protect Mack so whoever paid them off had to have long money. Still to this day they don't know who could've paid those guards off.

After that we were pretty much prisoners because of all the protection around us so that brought us closer. The bigger my brothers became the further away they wanted me plus Cargo was on his own shit. Cargo never said it but he didn't want me around and I knew why. We stayed close still but that's it." We talked about a ton of things and before I knew it the sun was up.

I was sick with worry, no word from Tristan and I was so tempted to call and find out what was going on. My phone for Tristan was back home so I figured now was the time to at least check my messages to hear what he had to say. My in box was full, everyday Tristan called and left a few messages telling me he loved me and he would be home soon. I cried so hard I couldn't hear the other messages, I wanted him to tell me his self.

Three days had past and I told Prime I was going home no matter what he said. I was furious and sitting around watching how happy Shameka and Prime were together only made it worse. I tried to block everything out of my mind thinking maybe he just needed a little more time. A week had past and still no word and I felt it in my heart that something was terribly wrong. I went back thru my messages to the ones I didn't delete.

The last message had me in the car driving like a maniac over to Ma' Earlean. I ran in without even knocking looking for her to tell me what was going on. When I didn't find her in the house I called Mrs. Terry to find out where Ma' Earlean could be but I didn't get an answer. I tried everyone and all I could do was leave a message for someone to call me. I tried Treasure and Sammy with the same results. I called Bateador and Pandillero and the lines were no longer in service. I can't believe this is happening to me, I tried City and even he didn't return any of my calls.

The next day I'm rocking in the middle of the bed when there's a knock on the door. I didn't bother looking over because I know it's not Tristan so I don't care. May came in and held me while I cried, I know she has bad news that no one else wants to tell me.

"Jasmine baby, I know this is a hard time for you. Everyone is over at Ma' Earlean house and I told them I would bring you over."

"Just tell me May please. I don't want to go anywhere so just tell me so I can figure out how I'm going to deal with him being dead."

"No baby, I don't know where Tristan is, it's Ma' Earlean, she passed away in her sleep." I don't know how to feel about the news, on one hand I'm happy that Tristan's not dead and on the other I lost my great great grandmother.

When we made it to the house it was filled with sad faces which only made me feel worse. Two days later the funeral was jammed packed and there's no sign of Tristan. I don't know if he knows and that's why he's not here or what's the deal. I asked everyone I could if they've heard anything from anyone and still nothing. I was nine months along when I was admitted into the hospital because of the depression I found myself in. I was hating everyone and refused to let any of them come near me or contact me.

The only company I have is Dr. Kevin Sullivan, he's twenty six years old and about to transfer to Wisconsin. Dr. Sullivan checks on me even when he's not on call, most times he'll just sit in the room with me. I don't want to be bothered but he won't take no for an answer. When I had my first contraction he was supposed to be off but was right there with me. The pain was excruciating, I'm giving birth to my first child and my husband is nowhere to be found.

When the family came to meet the baby I didn't let them come near us. I turned everyone around and demanded that I be released. They tried to keep me there but I wasn't having it, I called up my lawyer and they had no option but let us go. Dr. Sullivan begged me not to leave. He followed me to the house wanting to know where I was headed. I didn't have the time or energy to fight with him so I told him. Once I did he said he'd be in touch, I really didn't care. I jumped on a private flight with my baby in tow and didn't look back.

I arrived in Hawaii and checked into a hotel with my son Tristan Warren, I left everything behind. I don't have a phone, clothes or a place to live, it don't bother me a bit. I do have my ring which I contemplated throwing in the ocean. It didn't take me long to find a small house to call my own, I cared for my son day and night trying to keep my mind off his dad. After taking Prince in for his checkup I was shocked to see who was standing at my door.

"What are you doing here?"

"I came to check on you and lil man there. It took me a while to find you." He helped me with Prince into the house, we sat down after I put Prince in his bed.

"Why'd you run Jazzy J?"

"Why stay there? There's nothing left in St. Louis for me to stay. Why are you here in Kaunakakai?"

"I told you that already. I can assume that this is your new home and you don't plan on going back."

"Don't assume, know I don't plan on going back." He chuckled, we talked for a long time before he left.

The next morning I opened the door and smiled from ear to ear. It set in on me just how attractive Dr. Sullivan is. He's light skinned, probably six one maybe one hundred eighty or ninety pounds. He looks young and dressed like he's a model.

Kevin told me he was staying at the hotel not far from me and would be sticking around for a week. By the week's end we had spent many hours together. When he left he wanted me to promise to stay in touch. I didn't know how I should feel about it but I promised with no real plans about keeping it.

A year had past and I had no clue of where or what happened to Tristan. My heart was saying to give him more time and my mind was saying to hate him for leaving me. Prince is getting bigger every day and he's a spitting image of his father. He has my eyes and he's tan, not as dark as Tristan and not lighter than me.

He's walking, talking and can sign like a pro, a fast learner to say the least. I've grown accustomed to speaking with Dr. Sullivan over the phone at least once a week. He came to see me twice during the time I stayed in Oahu and each time he made my life seem a little better.

On Prince birthday he flew out to spend the day with us and I couldn't believe he would take the time out to do it. Before he left he asked me if I would consider moving to Wisconsin with him. I turned him down reminding him that I'm still married. He didn't give me a hard time about it and I know he's a little broken about it but he respects my decision. Three months later when I returned home he was right at my door with a smile on his face.

"What's going on with you? You didn't say you would be coming over to see me when we spoke last month." He laughed and pecked my cheek helping us inside.

"I moved." I looked at him and asked him to come again.

"I moved here to be close to you and little man so you have a new neighbor that you actually know." He started to laugh causing me to laugh. Kevin purchased the home across the street from mine and I didn't even know it.

I still don't know how to feel about it but something inside of me wants me to let it go. Times passing and my hormones are kicking my tale every time I'm with Kevin. I tell myself everyday that I waited eighteen years to have sex and these thirty four months are nothing. Two years and ten months have passed since the last time I saw Tristan and he made love to me. Kevin and I shared a kiss a few times but something was missing stopping me from going any further.

Kevin and I have somehow grown closer even without a physical connection. He loves Prince deeply and I can see it in his eyes when he's around. He was there when Prince was born so I know he's genuine with his feelings. I didn't allow Prince to call him anything that he should have called Tristan.

I don't want Prince to think that Kevin's his father and it's hard to stop that from happening. Kevin's the only man that Prince knows, he's seeing him on a daily basis pretty much. I talked to Kevin about it and he said he understood and helped me by reminding Prince to call him Kev. I thought it was funny hearing Prince call him that and was happy that Kevin was so understanding.

Kevin and Prince were at the beach, it was his day off from the hospital and he hadn't seen Prince for two days. I was heading home from my meeting with a case worker. I'm feeling like I need to get back to work. All this time has passed and not once did I check in on Serenity or feel the need to do so.

I have a strong team back home that I'm confident will keep working hard. When I arrived at home I jumped in the shower and was going to make dinner before Prince and Kevin came back. The moment I turned into the kitchen I thought I saw a ghost sitting there waiting on me.

"Do you know who I am?"

"Of course. I'm wondering why you're here White." He smiled and hugged me.

"I'm here to see how you're doing."

"Why? All this time has passed, why now? You think I'm crazy or what?" He thought it was funny, I walked to the refrigerator to gather all I needed to cook.

"No, not at all. I'm here to see how you handle what's coming in the door in a few." I turned and looked at him holding my breath wondering what was coming in the door and what a few meant to him. He told me to breathe and take a seat but I couldn't do either one of them. When the door opened I saw spots and the room started to spin faster than ever. The last thing I saw was diamond teeth and soft kissable lips over me.

ALSO AVAILABLE
PRE-ORDER

Lifelong Love; When you know better, you do better in stores now.

Just Another Day; Cochran Affair available August 27, 2013. Chapters available Kindle Edition on Amazon.

Cargo's Flower; Universal Laws and Sins available September 15, 2013. Chapters available Kindle Edition on Amazon.

Be the first to review books by Taz Will by sending email to keepitfunkypublishing@yahoo.com, subject: Review for details.

ABOUT THE AUTHOR

Born and raised in St. Louis, MO. She spent her younger years living in the infamous Cochran Garden Housing Projects. She decided to put her stories on paper after many years of thinking about just how much life has changed since those exciting days in the Cochran.

She wrote her first novel, Lifelong Love: When you know better, you do better and took a long memorable stroll down memory lane. With the help of an over the top imagination she's been busy putting together her next piece of work. Please enjoy Just Another Day: Cochran Affair, the second book of this series which is set to release August 27, 2013. Also checkout Cargo's Flower; Universal Laws and Sins, chapters on Kindle in Amazon. Be on the lookout for the complete book set to release September 15, 2013. You can preorder both books now.

www.ingramcontent.com/pod-product-compliance
Lightning Source LLC
Chambersburg PA
CBHW032147190626
46814CB00005BA/1874